THE GLASS PASS

A NOVEL

THE GLENBERRY CHRONICLES
BOOK 1

LEE CAREY

SOME KID PUBLISHING

1

It was the day before, in Mid-June.

The Village of Berry

IT WAS ONLY MID-MAY, so they had been lucky to get the bumper crop of picture-perfect strawberries that now filled the kitchen, in various stages of the mini production line. Taking a moment to survey their progress, Inez felt a flutter of apprehension. She still couldn't believe her niece had managed to talk her into this daft project, but Katie was so thrilled about the whole thing, that she kept her qualms to herself. Katie was taking her part in the process very seriously and was closely examining a strawberry to decide if it should be the whole fruit in the centre of a tart, or if it was big enough to be cut into halves for the surround. There was a quiet contentment in their labours, and Inez returned to arranging the sorted berries atop the creme patisserie filled pastries, then brushing them with a glossy glaze, and stowing them in neat lines in the containers Katie had brought down on the bus.

It was a mystery to Inez how Katie had managed the stages of her journey prior to landing at the bus terminus in the neighbouring village of Kilmour, where Inez met her a couple of days prior. Hugging her tightly, she cradled Katie's head and her long auburn locks for a second just to breath her in, as she had done when she was a little girl, and she would wrap her in a towel and smell her freshly washed hair after bath-time. Standing back, she surveyed the enormous piece of luggage lying beside them on the pavement and said, 'What's with the leather trunk, pet? I feel like you should be getting off a steam train like the wee evacuees who were sent down here from Glasgow in the war.'

'It's full of amazing outfit options that I picked out for you with the wardrobe department,' Katie replied. 'We're going to have so much fun trying them all on for your TV debut. I can't wait!'

They seemed to have filled in their time just fine, enjoying each other's company as they always did, so the fashion show was going to take place tonight after all the strawberry tarts were safely and perfectly stowed. Inez was secretly looking forward to it but for now was relishing just being in her cozy cottage kitchen with Katie. Neither said it, but being there together and the quiet industry at hand, held nostalgic memories of Inez's mother, Vic. When she arrived, Katie had smiled as she picked up the antique butter ball, which for some reason had a picture of a Clydesdale horse on it, where one would really expect a Friesian cow if anything, and savoured the familiar aroma of the kitchen. She could almost capture a similar smell in a particular high-end bakery up in Glasgow, but it was merely whatever is the olfactory equivalent of a fleeting glimpse. Coming back here into the cottage in Berry, where she used to spend her summer holidays, was a fully immersive sensory experience, with the warm, buttery, floury smell top of the list.

'Hello Marshmallow Kitchen,' she had said contentedly, 'it's good to be back.'

GROWING UP, Inez and her sister had been embarrassed by their mother's pink Willow Pattern china dinner set, which was proudly displayed in an even older baker's cabinet. It was literally from a different century and seemed so fussy and bright when all their friends had up-to-date simple designs in the beiges and browns of the seventies.

Living in London in the early eighties, Inez and her best friend Andy were invited to the champagne opening of a trendy concept home store. They were wooed by the famous owner – Andy more so than Inez, who ended up dating him for several months. He caught Inez lingering over a minimalist cream-coloured pottery set which had caught her eye. Known for his extravagant gestures, he told Inez he'd have the whole set sent to her as a gift. As she demurred, he insisted, and eventually a compromise was reached whereby he would send half a set to her mother. Vic couldn't believe that Inez mixed in circles where such things happened and insisted on sending a thank you card. She carefully placed the simple cream pottery among her busily patterned china, and along with the lengthy thank you note, she sent a photo of her new array.

When Inez heard about this, she cringed slightly, wondering what the designer would think of anyone not making his coveted wares the sole focus of attention. However, the next time she visited the store he rushed to greet her and take her over to a newly arranged corner which featured a designer's-eye version of her mum's vignette, with the plain cream crockery now displayed alongside a patterned version of the set. Vic was thrilled to receive a copy of his glossy catalogue featuring his copycat display.

Many years later, when Inez returned from London to care for her mother following a particularly hard-to-hear treatment update, her frustration at the unfairness of it all left her sleepless. As her mum slept soundly, thank God, she worked through the night painting the dull pine kitchen cabinets off-white, and the baker's cabinet pink. The freshen-up was worth her labours in the morning, as her mum's face brightened, and she said with a quiet smile, 'I love it. I feel like I'm inside a bag of marshmallows. You must send a picture to that designer Andy used to go out with – he'd probably copy us again.'

'Do you ever miss living in London?' Katie asked randomly. She couldn't hear enough of Inez's stories – about Gran, about the two sisters growing up in Berry – but her favourite ones were the ones that happened in the capital city.

'No, not really. I mean I go and visit Andy and Billy a lot. And on the rare occasion that *** is at his Islington house we see him too. I have the best of both worlds – my quiet life up here and then I go and live it up with my old pals whenever I feel like it.'

'Can I come with you sometime?' Katie asked.

'Of course you can! They'd all love that,' Inez replied, and they fell into a contented silence again.

In the final stages of their endeavours, Inez handed Katie a misshapen strawberry tart which, conveniently, had not been deemed worthy of tomorrow's adventure and said, 'Right, this is for you, and then we'd best get cleaned up and get this fashion show done.'

'Won't that mean we're one short?' Katie asked.

'Seventy-two strawberry tarts was a ridiculous amount in the first place. No one is going to count them and ask us why there are only seventy-one are they?' Inez replied. Katie hadn't waited for the answer to the question anyway and was a bite in already making appreciative noises.

The roads around Glenberry
She, Charles Aznavour

Alec had been avoiding the family all afternoon. When he ran out of unnecessary errands, he just drove around, lost in thought, oblivious to the bright greens and yellows of spring around him as his old car wound around the gorse hedgerows and through pine forests. He had no music playing, which was highly unusual, but he knew the roads so well there was a kind of rhythmic lull of the twists and turns and rises and falls of his aimless routes. Someday he'd get around to buying a new car – his sisters' little sporty numbers must be much more fun to drive these roads in.

Two of his three younger sisters were home just now, and Alec's role was to listen to their dramas of the moment – work, social-life, love-life, or all of the above – and offer wise counsel or good-natured ribbing as appropriate. They treated the saying that blonds have more fun as more of an edict. Until recently Alec's life had seemed much more straightforward than theirs – which wasn't to say it was dull – far from it. As a music historian, he had created a cache of lectures which found him in high demand as a visiting professor at universities all over the world. One series intertwined historical events with the music they had spawned, while another demonstrated how this generation's music would not have existed without the prior's, or the prior's, or the several priors' before. The lectures, of course, included excerpts of the music he referenced, and he could hone the ones with more popular content to make them relevant and bespoke in order appeal to high-end corporate retreats for the odd junket too. All this suited his gregarious personality and desire to experience and travel as much as he could, forging his own path, before the time came to take over the family business.

Between jaunts, he appreciated the grounding that he felt being back home at Glenberry. From deciphering landmarks of Scotland on the last leg of his flight in, to being greeted at the airport by his mum and/or dad and caught up on the goings-on of the business on the journey home, to nights with his lifelong friends at the Gillie's Rest, the local pub, it all felt like home. His friends were irreverent, with no deference to his professional standing or anything else, and after a quick round up on who'd got engaged/married/had babies, they'd mostly reminisce and laugh about all their antics over the years. The main downside to single life for Alec was that he had to constantly fend off his mother's and sisters' attempts to set him up with women they thought could be *the one*, efforts which ramped up with every birthday. His mum had wasted no time in campaigning for him to meet the latest person she had in mind as soon as he landed – an impressive go-getter type, who ran her own business and had masterminded some new events hosted by the estate, including the recent, very successful, 10k run. Unfortunately for his mother's matchmaking ambitions though, events had quickly taken over and Alec's romantic status changed. Not that he could tell her that.

Alec reached for his phone deciding he'd play one song after all. Not *the* song, just *a* song. As his car filled with the inimitable longing tones of France's own Frank Sinatra, Charles Aznavour, singing *She*, he indulged himself with a two-and-a-half-minute reverie of the best of what tomorrow would bring.

The narrow road reached a tight bend, which he could either take to keep going, or make a sharp left onto a single-track road. Conceding to himself that he'd have to go back at some point, he took the sharp left. The road stretched ahead for half a mile, flat, straight and purposeful, with only one destination ahead. On either side the trees towered so high that the sun had already fallen behind them. From those ancient Scots pines above, a testament to the efforts of many generations, to the potholes below which he knew had been on his father's to-do list for several months, everywhere were reminders of the noblesse oblige that had kept his family shackled here for centuries.

Alec wondered how the family would react if instead of avoiding them he strode into the kitchen in the middle of dinner (he had no reason to think tonight would be a dining room occasion) and told them the truth. If he interrupted the meal that his sisters no doubt put together over a glass of wine or three, and said he had news. If after kissing his mother hello on the cheek, in answer to her question, *Alec, darling, can I get you plate?* he instead asked for their attention. He imagined a stunned silence as he delivered his soliloquy: *I've fallen in love. Deeply in love. I've never felt like this before, but it's the real thing so I don't want you to talk me out of what I'm about to tell you.* He'd take a deep breath and brace himself before going on to the shocking part. *She's married, but a few weeks ago we set a date for her to leave her husband, and that date is tomorrow. I'll be picking her up in Cormully first thing in the morning. I'd ask that you please keep this to yourselves because her husband is not a good guy, to put it politely, so we'd like a head start, before he realises she's gone.*

But of course, Alec wasn't going to put his family through that worry, so he'd bluff it through dinner and go to bed early. The narrow road ended at two grand pillars swamped by rhododendrons and Alec heard the familiar sound of gravel beneath his tires which meant he was home. The grand edifice of Glenberry Castle loomed above him in the afternoon light.

Cormully Village

The stealthy packing was going smoothly – after all she had been mentally packing for as long as she had been dreaming of this escape, which was months now, but she daren't have started a second before she had to. She moved about her bedroom, quickly but quietly in the fading daylight, not wanting to switch on a lamp for fear of attracting unwanted attention. If she got caught there would be tears, tantrums and, she shuddered at the thought, much worse. Any hesitation she had at leaving in the morning was stamped out by remembering conversations with a couple of friends she'd told, who had been in similar positions with their husbands.

Snippets of those counsels became her internal pep-talk if her nerve wavered.

When I was at that stage I just had to get away, no questions asked. You owe it to yourself. Do it! If I text you that morning and you're still home, I'm coming to get you myself.

I'm envious. I could only dream of what you're about to do. I'd never be brave enough right now, but can you do me a favour? Do this for me too. You're living for both of us. Maybe someday it'll be me, but for now, please tell me I can imagine you that morning, getting in the car and being whisked away.

Her mind wandered to him, the other person she had to do this for, and she imagined looking up into his soulful blue eyes and letting him know, *I made it, I'm here. I'm all yours, right here, right now.*

Tomorrow could be the greatest day of their lives. She smiled and hummed a tune ever so quietly. There was no point in being heard rubbing salt into the wound. Zipping up her bag, a rush of excitement hit her. The plans were all in place – she'd be picked up first thing in the morning and they'd be on their way.

The Village of Kilmour

Fraser Bam, Member of the Scottish Parliament, was on his knees in front of an office toilet, hoping for some relief from the crippling nausea he'd had all afternoon. Tomorrow was supposed to be a triumph. He would take a major step forward in establishing himself as a committed and influential player in these parts, and step out of the shadow of his predecessor – the revered, nay, hallowed, Les Mitchell. Oona, the fiancée he worshipped, and his mum of course, would beam with pride. Perhaps he'd even manage to impress Oona's father. Last, but maybe not least if he was being completely honest, he would meet, greet and show off the first in a long line of dignitaries he hoped to attract to his little dominion with his grand plan for the future of Mid-June. His current sorry state was a far cry from his vision.

Giving up, he put his hands on the toilet seat and used it as a brace to ease himself off the mosaic tiled floor. Realising what he'd done, he looked at his palms in disgust then down at the knees of his trousers and didn't know where to start. He left the cubicle and decided to dust down his knees with the back of his hands and then washed his hands thoroughly. Looking in the mirror he wished he could muster an inspiring self pep-talk, but in its absence, he slouched back to his small shabby office. The constituents who were gradually coming around to him and took the opportunity to raise issues with him during his surgery hours, often made comments along the lines of *they might have given it a lick of paint before you moved in* or *jeez, this old desk must have been here for even longer than Les Mitchell was.* Fraser had worked so hard to get here though, that he was proud of his little office no matter that its decor didn't even warrant the word 'decor'.

Officially, Fraser was the second-youngest serving MSP, but the youngest ran for office on a dare and represented a constituency inhabited mostly by sheep, so Fraser didn't count her. And he'd been elected twice already, in fairly quick succession –once in the by-election held upon Les Mitchell's retirement last year and just a couple of weeks ago in the main 2016 Scottish Parliament elections. On his campaign trail he had answered as many questions around the subject of his age and inexperience as he had listened to heated opinions on a massive and to-date ill-fated civil engineering project known as 'The Big Belt', and quiet laments that the long-serving pillar of community Les Mitchell was retiring. He patiently smiled and nodded every time those doorstep chats ended with a handshake and the caution, 'You have big shoes to fill here in Mid-June son.' Fraser wished he had a pound for every resident who had claimed to have been in the Gillie's Rest pub the night a local wag coined the name 'Mid-June' for the area.

The story went that there was a new policeman moving to the area from Glasgow. The chat over sipped pints was how bored he was likely to be in this uneventful part of Scotland – *I hope he's no expecting to be solving mysteries like Midsomer Murders – he'll be sorely disappointed.* According to legend, the jokester didn't miss a beat: *Mid-Summer? Maer like Mid-June!* Everybody recognised the old Billy Connolly joke that Scotland doesn't have a summer, just two seasons – winter and June, and self-congratulatory laugh went up, the collective sharp wit they prided themselves in proven once again.

Fraser had to admit it was impressive that a quip in a pub a couple of decades ago had been comprehensively adopted and stood the test of time. Even in BBC coverage of election night, his name on the screen when he was interviewed appeared as *Fraser Bam, MSP for Kilmour and Berry Valley (known as Mid-June)*.

The office seemed even smaller now with its corners in darkness, with just a small lamp and his monitor illuminating his desk and the space around it. Fraser hit Refresh on his email inbox. Nothing. He went back to the sent folder and read his last email for the umpteenth time since sending, never mind the dozens of times he checked it prior to finally hitting send.

Dear Mr Wyllie,

Profound apologies for the delay in this email thanking you for your extremely generous offer to underwrite the cost of gym equipment at the Mid-June Youth Training Ground. As you know, the new pitch and adjoining changing facilities and fitness room have been a huge boon to the community – there has been a boost to morale and an increase in camaraderie in the younger members of our community. I will be delighted to announce your donation when I meet with our principal donor tomorrow, and I thank you for the funds you already forwarded which I will also pass on as appropriate tomorrow.
My sincere thanks again, and I hope my tardiness is no indication of a lack of gratitude. I look forwarded to keeping you abreast of developments and working together.

Yours sincerely,

Fraser Bam
MSP, Kilmour and Berry Valley

It was a good email, Fraser thought. A way out of this mess for both of them. The email made it seem like there was nothing illicit at all about the two cheques Fraser had taken from Wyllie, but instead they had been given and received with the intention of the funds being passed on to the local youth football team. Would Wyllie see the wisdom in this exit plan though? If not, Fraser desperately hoped the email was at least an insurance policy for himself.

He hit Refresh again. Nothing again. He supposed he

should go home, and looked around for his work phone so that he could continue the fraught Inbox-Refresh vigil at home. In his pocket, his personal phone pinged, a different sound than usually accompanied a text. Pulling it out, there was a message via an app he seldom used. He opened it.

Wyllie: *I see what you're trying to do, you slimy little fuck. It won't fly – you already trousered that first cheque remember? You're just not getting how this works. You and your VIP better be careful on the roads tomorrow. The Glass Pass is notorious for accidents after all.*

Fraser put the phone down on his desk and stared at it for a moment before a new wave of nausea sent him to the bathroom once again.

2

Glenberry Castle
Danny's Song, Anne Murray

This surely wasn't the traditional image of a knight in shining armour. Sure, Alec was in his room in the castle he'd grown up in, which had medieval origins and even a suit of armour in the grand hallway, but his nervous pacing, then briefly sitting and biting his nails, then urgently standing up to pace again, wasn't exuding the suave confidence of a knight about to rescue the love of his life.

The die had been cast upon their very first meeting, a few weeks before Christmas. Thinking back, he smiled wryly to himself remembering saying his goodbyes, leaving the pub and saying out loud to the cold night air, the heat of his breath forming short, staccato bursts of cloud, '*Shite. Just bloody, bloody shite.*'

. . .

It was the first night after coming home from several months abroad that he was able to extricate himself from the family and finally leave the castle grounds to head to the Gillie's Rest to meet some friends. Gemma had started working behind the bar while he'd been away and Ravi introduced Alec proudly, with his arm around his shoulder. 'You've heard all about Alec Douglas-Lauder, future 25th Laird of Glenberry Castle and Estate, my oldest and best friend in the world? Well, here he is, finally back from his latest travels!'

Alec offered his hand, but Gemma got up on her tiptoes and stretched across the bar, saying, 'A handshake? Come here and give me a hug! It's so nice to finally meet you, though I feel like I know you already.' After an awkward embrace due to the obstacles of the bar in between and their height difference, they pulled back and she looked into his eyes and smiled and said warmly, 'Welcome home Alec.' Her smile mesmerised him for a split second. It was a sweet smile, not overly confident but not self-conscious either, just open and curious. Throughout the evening her interested questions and the way she held eye-contact while she listened intently to his travel stories, while his friends made pantomime yawning noises and gestures in the background, drew him in further.

So along with *Shite. Just bloody, bloody shite*, he told himself, *Don't do it man, don't fall for her. She's taken. She's with someone else. On no account are you going to let yourself fall for her.*

The first time they were alone together couldn't have gone worse for this steely determination. In the calm before the storm of all the Christmas nights out ahead, he planned a quiet catch up with Ravi at the Gillie's Rest. Shortly after Alec got there Ravi sent his apologies that he was caught up in something at work and would be late. 'Oh good,' Gemma said, 'the pub's nice and quiet too, it'll give us a chance to bond. Let's see – let's start with your job, it sounds so interesting.' One of the things Alec enjoyed most about his job was that humans love music – most people have at least one song or album or artist which speaks to their very soul and people enjoyed arguing its case to Alec when they found out what he did. He'd come to think that he could tell a lot about someone from what that piece of music was. They chatted about his US tour and Gemma asked which of his lectures was the biggest hit. The answer was one which hinged on the music of Anne Murray, and how she bridged the gap between country and pop music, and which artists she influenced and paved the way for. Murray's beautiful vocals never failed to move Alec's audiences. It helped too that she had been his grandmother's favourite, and her voice still brought back memories of her apartments within Glenberry Castle. Usually it took people a while to place who Anne Murray was, but Gemma gasped as soon as Alec mentioned her name. It turned out that Alec had unknowingly jumped straight to the part where he finds out someone's visceral piece of music, because for Gemma it was an Anne Murray song. Alec was always fascinated to hear people's reasons why, but watching Gemma tell her story of a song by an artist that held a special place in his heart too, was particularly special.

Gemma grew up as the only child of a single mum (she didn't mention when or why her dad left, but Alec gathered it had almost always just been the two of them). Gemma was a latch-key kid in a neighbourhood her mum was saving hard to get them out of and she made Gemma promise she'd go straight home from school every day and not kick around the tower block courtyard getting up to no good like some of the other kids. After her homework was finished, she spent her time going through her mum's record collection, some of which had been passed down from her own parents. She laughed to Alec that she was the only twelve-year-old whose tastes in music covered everything from Fats Domino to the Four Tops to Miles Davis. One day her mum came home to find her in tears listening to Anne Murray's *You Needed Me.* Gemma couldn't express why she was crying, but her mum simply squeezed her tight and said she got it – music sometimes overwhelms you – it's why she kept hold of all her records and record player even though they were old-fashioned and they could use the space in their tiny flat.

'Wow – that's your song? That's a cracker – a heartbreaker, but a cracker,' Alec said.

'No, no, that's not my song,' Gemma corrected, enjoying keeping Alec hanging on by a thread, and now this last-minute twist in her tale. 'Mum made us listen to Danny's Song next – is that in your lecture?'

'Of course,' Alec confirmed with a nod and a smile.

'So here's what to picture when you play Danny's Song the next time and you're talking about Anne Murray's legacy. A mother and daughter, each other's whole worlds, holding hands, swaying to the music in a tiny, badly decorated living room singing that song to each other.' Gemma added to the picture she was painting by singing three lines of the chorus. Alec said nothing, he couldn't. 'Ha! I gotcha didn't I? Got you a little emotional there! What were the chances of that? That we have such a connection through your favourite lecture and my *Desert Island Disc*. I think that counts as exceptional bonding this early in our relationship!' Gemma laughed. 'Let me play it actually.' She turned to look for her phone as Alec composed himself.

When Ravi arrived, he gave Alec a bro-hug and said, 'Oh no! What's this playing? This can't be a Gillie's playlist.'

'It's Anne Murray, you philistine,' Gemma answered from behind the bar, already pouring Ravi's pint. 'I got your bestie here all choked up telling him how much I love her.'

'Who? Never heard of her. Oh Gemma, you didn't get him started on music did you? First you indulge him about his world travels now you're talking to him about music? Don't get involved. I love him, but he's the man that if you're playing a cover, he'll literally lecture you on why the original is so much better, or if you're playing the original there's an obscure cover he prefers. You have been warned.' Ravi clinked glasses with Alec and gestured towards a seat in the corner. 'Excuse us Gemma, we have top secret things to talk about that only best friends can share.'

As the Christmas season kicked in, Alec attempted being stand-offish. He tried to make excuses not to join festivities, so he wouldn't find himself in a noisy celebration standing close, towering over her, having to lean in even closer to hear what she was saying. When she told a story, if he struggled to hear it fully, he'd pull back and watch her face, filling in the gaps by her expression, her eyes searching his for his reaction. If was a funny story she'd touch his arm gently as if to stabilise herself and throw her head back laughing. An absurd anecdote about some Mid-June denizen would make her squeeze his arm, wide-eyed, in solidarity at what a weird little place in the world they lived.

In this way, Alec came to know every muscle in Gemma's face, every fleck in her iris, falling in love in plain sight, against his will. Unknowingly and mercilessly, she wangled her way further into his heart, deeper into his being, until he accepted that though the time and circumstances were disastrous, he loved her. 'So shoot me,' he'd say to the advice he could hear in his head which knew it was fighting a losing battle against his heart.

Whenever Alec took part in whatever the latest trendy personality test was, the results always showed strong protective traits in his nature, so it was inevitable that he'd feel protective towards Gemma – it was how his love manifested itself. The difference in their size – his *big teddy bear* stature, as one sister called him, to her petiteness - meant he instinctively physically shielded her when they were together, sheltering her from the wind if he walked her to her car, or from stumbling drunks as she collected glasses in the bar.

Alec sensed a fragility in her eyes from the start, even before he began to learn more about her bastard of a husband. She didn't tend to talk about him much, but Ravi had heard some of the stories and filled Alec in. It hadn't taken long before he got to lay eyes on the husband – John. He was often in the pub and rumour had it that was the only reason he had agreed to let Gemma take a job there was because he was there regularly enough that he could keep an eye on her, and presumably any customers foolish enough to flirt with her.

When he was in, brooding over his pint in the corner, Gemma was a different person. She'd still be smiling and polite and would even still have a laugh with Alec's gang of friends, but there was a distinct wariness about her and her eyes would dart over to his corner, trying to read his mood and detect if something had pissed him off. By his menacing appearance, and with Ravi filling in some gaps about his possessiveness and how controlling he was, Alec quickly despised him. He struggled to understand how on earth the relationship had come about. Knowing she'd grown up without a father figure it would have been easy to explain it away with a sweeping *daddy issues* assumption, but along the way Ravi had learned more of the story and John had been altogether calculating and fraudulent from the start.

Gemma met John when she was working in a pub in Glasgow. After university, she set her sights on the hospitality industry, and she set them high. The pub was one in a highly successful chain founded by a brother and sister team, who were now well-known throughout Scotland, not just within the industry – one sub-headline in the business section declaring: *Everything they touch turns to gold.* Each property they owned was very different –they seemed to be able to succeed in everything from running cavernous rowdy Friday-night destinations to intimate restaurants with twelve week waiting lists for their coveted tables. Gemma wanted to soak up everything she could learn from them so as a starting point applied for the position as bar manager in one of the mid-sized venues. John frequented the bar when he was up in Glasgow for business – *whatever the hell that meant* – and got to know the lulls when Gemma wouldn't have an excuse to not chat with him. He charmed her ambitions out of her and said he'd known right away that she was more than '*just a barmaid.*' On trying to make sense of things Ravi agreed with Alec that he couldn't fathom how a date had ever come about, but unfortunately it had and when John then took Gemma to Mid-June, she was charmed by it too. John painted a picture of investing in the boutique hotel and bar she dreamed of and assured her that tourism was going to explode in Mid-June once The Big Belt was finished. She believed her visions were now shared visions of their future.

And yet she had to get special dispensation from him to even work at The Gillie's, Alec had pointed out to Ravi – *I don't know what to tell you Alec – he's the Bernie Madoff of Gemma's hopes and dreams. I'm just as offended by it all as you.*

Gemma's mum was heartbroken when they eloped suddenly – *of course John had suggested that, why leave time for anyone in her life to give her cautions or counsel?* - and for a long time now she'd only meet Gemma halfway, just the other side of the Glass Pass, not wanting to lay eyes on John at all.

When John was out of town on business, as he was intermittently, Gemma was visibly happier. She'd be relaxed at her shifts at the pub and hang out with the gang when she wasn't working, and they'd all just pretend her husband didn't exist. Alec couldn't forget it though and it killed him.

Then one night Gemma looked drawn and her mood seemed off throughout her shift. At closing time Alec and Ravi were as usual the last two stragglers and when Ravi weaved his way for one last toilet trip before the walk home, Alec stopped

Gemma on her final clearing up rounds to ask if she was OK. She shook her head slowly and her eyes welled up as Alec searched them. It was worse than ever. John's behaviour had become erratic in the last couple of weeks and he'd rant and make oblique references to there being too many people pissing him off lately, and if they only knew about the contents of his gun locker. Every day she was growing more fearful for her safety and what he was capable of. Alec's protective instinct was overwhelming, and his heart hurt as she alluded to unpleasant domestics.

'Gemma. My God. Please. Let's make a plan. Ravi's not in a state to hear all this tonight, but I'll tell him in the morning that we need to set a date. We've got to get you out of there.'

3

The Village of Berry

Katie had rosy cheeks, maybe from the fire, but more likely from the red wine. As Inez was changing in the other room she called through, 'When they make your life story into a movie, this will be the fun clothes montage, like Julia Roberts in *Pretty Woman*! *You work on commission, right? Big Mistake. Big. Huge!*' She pointed at an invisible shop assistant as she quoted the film. 'Ooh, we should watch that later!'

Inez stepped into the living room, looking uncomfortable in a brown and black print dress, which she thought was perhaps leopard inspired, but it was hard to tell. It was a little too short for her taste these days, and the wrap detail across her not insubstantial boobs was definitely not going to work for her. In fact, she thought in this outfit, at her age, it would be called a bosom.

'See! Julia Roberts. You have exactly the same hair too,'

Katie said. She often admired Inez's hair, and hoped her own auburn locks would be as shiny and lush as Inez's when she reached her fifties. 'I think that's gorgeous and wish I could talk you into it, but I can tell by your face I've got no chance. Wow Inez, your boobs! Your legs! What a bod!'

'Aye right Katie. OK, let's wind this up. What are we thinking here? I need a glass of wine and to start catching you up there, Miss Rosy Cheeks.'

'Och leave me alone, I'm on a wee holiday. Right, so since your face is tripping you in the dress, let's think. Hmmm, I liked you in the shirt and wide-legged trousers. Pockets are good. Particularly for your first time on TV. They make you look relaxed, natural.'

'First time? Only time, Miss. Don't you be getting carried away here.'

'It's funny to think that it's your first time on TV, actually. Changed times – nowadays they'd have had you on the morning shows by Monday. And you never know – maybe you'll be so good they'll want you on a regular segment,' she smiled taking a large sip from her glass. 'Anyway, back to business – so it's a shirt and trousers option we think. Navy or black? I'm leaning towards the navy.'

'Well, your Gran always said she liked me and your mum in navy with our colouring. Guess that includes you now too, our little clone.'

'Lucky me! Navy it is then. Gran is still in charge, even though she's not here anymore. Right, go and get your pjs on and I'll get you a glass of wine.'

They drank and chatted, lying on an overstuffed couch each. As often happened, Katie didn't want the cozy evening with her aunt to end and as it hit the hour when they should have been thinking about bed she said, 'Tell me a London story before we go up. You were so glamorous. I loved when you came home – I couldn't get to sleep the night before and would wait by the window for Dad to drive you back from the station.'

'We do not have time for that young lady.' But Inez couldn't resist one lovely memory of a very young Katie. 'When you were wee, you'd ask me if I'd really seen the Peter Pan clock.'

'I know. That's because when we watched Peter Pan, and they were flying over the London skyline, Mum would say *that's where Aunty Inez lives.*'

Inez smiled. 'I remember I brought you back that cheap Big Ben souvenir. It sat on your windowsill for years.'

Katie mused. 'If it was a clear night, I would leave the curtains open and I'd look up at it with the moon behind it. At first, I'd imagine I was Wendy, flying over it with Peter Pan. But then when I was a little older, I'd pretend I was you, gorgeous Aunt Inez, flicking my hair around, imagining I was coming back from some fabulous night out.'

'Aww, you were just so cute,' Inez said, on her feet and clearing up snack bowls and wrappers, trying to indicate to Katie that it really was time for bed.

'I was in awe of you,' Katie continued, ignoring the activity around her. 'You were my beautiful idol. I'd walk on my tiptoes pretending I was wearing high heels and walking arm-in-arm with Andy, talking about all the famous people we'd just been with. Or I'd get a jacket and sling it over my shoulder as I strolled along past my windowsill Big Ben, because I knew that in London it's sometimes warm enough to have no jacket on at night. I must have heard you say that once and I was fascinated. What an exotic place London must be that it even had different weather.'

'We have a long road trip tomorrow and we can reminisce to your heart's content, but I really think we should be getting to bed.'

But Katie kept talking, wanting to get one last part of the story in, 'Then of course, if ever Uncle *** was on the TV it was particularly exciting for me knowing that you were his friend. Dad would rib Mum about it. He'd say, '*You're really trying to tell me that your sister Inez is the only woman who has ever crossed that man's path and been able to resist him?*'

Inez stopped her busy-ness and put her hand on her hip. 'Your dad knew as well as your mum did that there was never anything between *** and me. He just enjoyed teasing us both about it. We were just good friends. Always have been, always will be.'

'You're no fun – I need Andy here.'

'Why? Because he's prone to embellishment?'

'Something like that!'

'At the beginning he was quite disappointed we were only platonic friends. If *** had swung both ways as we said in the old days, Andy would have jumped at the chance.'

Katie laughed and said, 'Yes, he has mentioned that once or twice.' With some effort she slung her legs off the sofa from her reclined position. 'Well, I guess you're right, we both should get some beauty sleep. Big day tomorrow!'

4

Glenberry Castle
The Power of Love, Frankie Goes to Hollywood

Sitting on the bed, in a rare extended moment of still for this evening, Alec looked at the screen saver on his phone, which was there under the pretence of it being a picture of all his old school friends. They were celebrating this past New Year together, probably sometime around the 8th of January since in Mid-June, like the rest of Scotland, New Year's celebrations extend to well into the month. They had been in the Gillie's Rest of course and Alec was centre of the picture, his left arm extending behind the shoulders of the people on that side. Gemma had been doing the rounds collecting glasses when the merry photo shoot began, when someone shouted to her, 'Gemma, jump in! Get in the photo!' Alec had extended his right arm around her shoulder to draw her in. The camera caught them before they all posed for the next picture, which caught Alec and Gemma looking right at each other laughing, as she half-resisted being dragged in. They looked for all the world like they'd been a couple for years, her perhaps the new wife being cajoled lovingly into a group picture by a proud doting husband.

It wasn't unusual for Alec to be staring at the picture. One of his sisters had noticed it once, and said simply, but knowingly, 'She's very pretty.' Alec had said nothing.

He sighed and was on his feet again, deciding to pace the hallway around the grand staircase for a change of scene. It was lined with ancestral portraits, and he stopped at one of one of his predecessors on a horse. What number of Laird would this be? 18th? 20th? Who knew? Not Alec. He sighed and fixed the ancestor's gaze. 'You know what?' he muttered, 'I'm blaming you for this!'

Alec's father, Sandy, was the current and 24th Laird of Glenberry, and Alec as his eldest son, was the future 25th Laird. As a young boy it was a story-book adventure to live in a castle with a tower and secret spiral staircases to explore, vast swathes of rhododendrons for building dens and a small loch to row on and swim in. As a university student the illustrious history of the family and his future title proved to be an excellent chat-up line. Now however, he was under increasing pressure from his father to step back from his current career and become more involved in the running of the estate, and he could feel the weight of succession starting to press down on his shoulders.

The estate had passed to Alec's father in the 1970s, when he was only twenty years old. The 23rd Laird, Alec's grandfather – Alexander – had enjoyed the spoils of previous generations with little thought of the future ones. Until he was almost fifty, he technically lived out of an apartment in London, but mostly travelled the world, living lavishly, hardly visiting Glenberry. Its care was left in the hands of the estate manager, Iain Watson, who, in order to keep the 23rd Laird in the manner to which he had become accustomed, had to gradually shutter up parts of the castle to save on running costs, which also made it easier to ignore the extensive capital maintenance required. The acreage of land that was properly tended similarly shrunk, and acres of the estate were left for nature to take care of, leaving formerly manicured gardens tangled and overgrown, and once carefully forested woods with rotting fallen trees and ruinous moss-covered stone walls.

Watson made sure he understood the family tree from roots to branches to twigs, as it looked less and less likely Alexander was going to produce an heir. However, Alexander, in his late forties, surprised him with a telegram saying that he was coming home with a new American bride Mimi, who, to Watson's surprise, was a mere ten years his junior. (He had previously noted that the Laird got older, but his girlfriends did not.) They had tied the knot in a registry office in London. Watson doubted that Alexander had the nous to take the route of so many of the landed gentry in the prior century who sought to marry into new American money to support their crumbling estates, but hoped that it might have happened by happy accident. Alas this was far from the case and not only did Mimi bring no riches to the table, she herself was disappointed by the lack of riches already on the table when she first came to Glenberry. She had expected luxury and found things dusty, threadbare and with no mod cons.

At first Watson figured Mimi to be somewhat of a social climber, but she was truly in love with Alexander, and it was proper that the estate had its Laird back living there. She was so sweet and bubbly that it didn't take her long to win him over. To his eternal relief, the couple fell pregnant within a year, and better late than never, a sense of duty emerged in Alexander, and he engaged Watson in catching him up on estate business.

While in nesting mode Mimi worked with Watson to decide

which rooms in the castle could be brought up to date. Watson was resistant, but acknowledged that a new kitchen and bathroom were practical since Mimi would mostly be keeping house herself and one of the sculleries was plenty big enough to become a modern new kitchen, leaving the main kitchen intact. A sunflower yellow Formica fitted kitchen, as well as a bubble-gum pink bathroom suite with black and white tile were duly installed, and Watson thought it appropriate that she had brought a touch of sunny USA to old Glenberry Castle. They adopted an oak-lined room - probably originally the Laird's private study – as the living room, because it faced south, and Mimi established it as being the brightest room at that end of the castle. She found the short Scottish daylight hours very hard in winter and craved as much light as possible. Unfortunately, even with the large south-facing windows, the living room still felt dark, and Watson arrived one morning to find her, six months pregnant, in overalls and headscarf, rolling white emulsion paint onto the gothic oak panelling. He was horrified, but she had made enough progress that the damage was done, and so he halted work only to insist that she go and take a bath in her new pink tub and relax, while he called some local tradesman to come and finish the job.

Mimi lived in her bright sequestered rooms in the castle after she was widowed and until she passed away. Alec and his sisters loved their grandmother's sunny yellow kitchen and exotic baked goods, recipes imported from America, such as brownies and snickerdoodles. Over treats and hot chocolate, her advice to *ask for forgiveness not permission*, was always accompanied by the story of getting up very early one morning when she was pregnant, to make sure she could whitewash enough of her living room that Watson would have no choice but to concede when he came in for his shift that morning.

. . .

ALEC FELT sorry that his father, Sandy, had fallen heir at such a young age when the excesses of Alexander's life caught up with him and he passed away only in his sixties. Sandy hadn't even completed his degree at Glasgow University.

However, fate decided to make it up to him one day in spring in the early eighties.

As big an encumbrance as the Glenberry Estate itself, was Sandy's earnest sense of belonging to the place, a slight embarrassment that his father hadn't given the role its due and a strong need to put that to rights. An avid historian, he learned with increasing pride what an essential part of life in this part of the world Glenberry had been – a key employer through the ages, a centre of community traditions and celebrations, as well as an innovator in lots of things from labour law to horticulture.

Sandy spent his first few months as Laird literally following in his father's footsteps as he walked the estate with Watson, which took some time now as the faithful employee was slowing down. They compared Watson's lifetime memories with Sandy's knowledge of times gone by, gleaned from library ledgers, records and drawings. They discussed what was the bare minimum needing done in each corner, compared to what they would do if their budget was endless. They mused which grandiose legacies of historic Lairds they would honour and restore – unequivocally the nearly two-hundred-year-old ornamental gardens, laid by the 18th Laird who had been inspired by a trip to Tuscany, should remain and be returned to the height of their splendour. At the opposite end of the taste spectrum, that Laird's self-aggrandising son had commissioned a twice life-size statue of himself to place on a manmade island in the middle of the loch. The manmade island had never transpired, and the giant statue lay unceremoniously beside the boatshed, entwined in weeds in Spring and covered in fallen leaves in Autumn. Even if they struck gold or oil somewhere on the estate, Sandy and Watson were in agreement that the budget would not extend to the overdue fulfilment of the supercilious 19th Laird's wishes.

They agreed that more people visiting the estate could only be better for its future, not worse, and Sandy reached out to a former professor of his, to offer an informal and rudimentary tour to him and some history students, and perhaps pick his brain on how to best position Glenberry as a destination on the Historic Scotland map. The professor jumped at the chance for an intimate tour of the castle and some of the legendary artefacts it contained. There was obligatory evidence that Mary Queen of Scots had slept there, which any castle worth its salt had, but far more interestingly, Sandy had found a manifesto signed by the residing Laird and his estate manager in the mid eighteenth century, laying out their responsibilities towards their employees. The document contained details like minimum pay requirements and the working conditions those people could expect to receive. As such, this document would predate the Scottish renaissance and beg the question: Had the figures deemed pioneers such as those at New Lanark truly been cutting edge, or had they copied models already in existence in outlying areas which had never hit the history books. Perhaps the advancement of employee rights had simply been the Zeitgeist among the more socially-minded landed gentry and entrepreneurs of the time.

One of the small party who travelled down to Glenberry was Susan Bailey, a masters student of history and architecture. It was love at first sight for Susan. As the mini-bus rattled along the single track road her excitement grew and as soon as it entered the gates and she caught her first glimpse of the historic building with its rolling lawn and avenue of trees, she was in awe of the place. She scanned it, guessing at its metamorphoses through the centuries. The tower to the far right of the building was original structure, dating to somewhere between the twelfth and fourteenth centuries. The main front edifice was in Gothic style, symmetrical around a grand entrance, with castellations and twenty-foot windows and she surmised it dated to the beginning of the 19th century. Susan's trained eye picked out that the wing on the left was probably a Victorian addition, when bigger was better and perhaps the family entertained more, so they added sculleries and cold storage with simpler bedrooms on top for increased staff levels. She tingled with anticipation.

Susan peppered Sandy with questions as soon as, or perhaps before, it was polite to do so. He was flattered by her genuine interest and was just as quickly attracted to her intellect as her pretty blond looks and cool aesthetic. He couldn't resist Susan's fascination for the evolution of the castle and Mimi's apartments were a key stop in the personal tour he gave her, while the professor and his other students immersed themselves in what the library had to offer. Upon meeting Susan, Mimi was smitten and went to work with some not-so-subtle matchmaking.

The following Spring, there was small wedding at the castle, and Glenberry Castle and Estate was blessed with dream team of the 24th Laird and his savvy, hard-working wife, who had a joint calling to serve the estate, turn its fortunes around and raise its standing to where she thought it deserved to be. Alec's memories of his parents included one morning when they were dressed in their finery to greet Prince Charles, who had requested a tour of the restored gardens, and later the same afternoon they were in overalls and up to their elbows in oil as they repaired the ride-on lawnmower. His admiration for them was boundless and part of his trepidation of taking tenure as the 25th Laird was the pressure of following in their footsteps.

. . .

Alec shook his head at the portrait of his ancestor. *Damn you all and your passed-down sense of duty and doing the right thing. Damn Noblesse Oblige.* Even if he hadn't fallen in love with Gemma, he'd still have felt compelled to help her get out of her increasingly dangerous situation. He looked back to the New Year's picture. But he had fallen for her. Hook, line and sinker, and there was no going back now.

He swung his legs into bed and pulled the bed covers over his head, hoping for sleep.

5

Cormully

Fraser drove home, gripping the steering wheel and trying to take deep breaths, hoping the oxygen would clarify something in his head, help him come up with his next move. He had already called Oona from the office explaining that he had a dodgy tummy, which wasn't in fact a lie, so she probably shouldn't bother coming over tonight. She was sweet and understanding as ever, and told him he was probably just nervous about tomorrow. Little did she know.

When he got home, he paced back and forth past his personal phone which was lying on the couch. When he realised it had got dark without his noticing, he turned on the lamps. He happened to glance out the window. In his small cul-de-sac of eight new-build houses, two of his neighbours had not got around to buying curtains yet and he could see right into their living rooms in the front and through to their kitchen/dining area at the back. Not wanting his neighbours to witness his manic pacing and temple-rubbing, he closed his own curtains, which Oona had chosen and directed the hanging thereof. They pretended that the reason she wasn't moving in was because her dad was old-fashioned, but Fraser knew she was prolonging it because she was worried about her father missing her, rattling around in the big house on his own. His non-exec roles as a semi-retired luminary in the West of Scotland business community kept him occupied but not busy.

Fraser picked up the phone and took its place on the couch, holding it in his lap. He had not yet replied to Wyllie's message, because responding via the same App from his personal phone would mean he had no deniability of any dealings with Wyllie that were outside the above-board between local businessman, as Wyllie purported to be, and politician.

Reading the message yet again, he sadly had not become inured to its menace.

Wyllie: *I see what you're trying to do you, slimy little fuck. It won't fly – you already trousered that first cheque remember? You're just not getting how this works. You and your VIP better be careful on the roads tomorrow. The Glass Pass is notorious for accidents after all.*

Fraser sighed heavily and shook his head. The Glass Pass and The Big Belt project had dominated most of his time in office so far, but this was a new level of trouble even for that debacle.

The Glass Pass was a precarious stretch of road which wound around the short but steep and imposing mountain range that separated Mid-June from the rest of Scotland to the north. No one knew how many decades ago its name had been coined, but everyone knew that like the name Mid-June itself, there was a wisecrack type of history to it. Visitors often assumed that the Glass Pass was so-named due to the sheer rocky cliffs below the east edge of the road, but Glass Pass was in fact short for Hourglass Pass. The twisting narrow road funnelled several busy roads from the north, into a larger number of small rural roads to the south, which serviced the collection of villages and farms that formed Mid-June. From the populous top half of the hourglass, roads fanned in, bringing supplies year-round and tourists in the summer, mainly from West Central Scotland, and both were then distributed across the rolling acres of Mid-June. It was to all intents and purposes the only road in and out of Mid-June - technically there was an easterly route, but it was torturously slow and circuitous, with long single track stretches of road, so it was hardly ever even remembered to be an option.

The northerly half of the hourglass and beyond was generally referred to as 'Up-By' by the residents of Mid-June. There was a rhythm of life involved in going Up-By. People with children at university would take them Up-By in loaded cars in September and bring them home even more laden in June; in the days before the supermarkets delivered to Mid-June, it was common to go Up-By a few times a year to do a Big Shop; if someone had been unwell, they may be required to go Up-By for further tests, or if the tests confirmed the worst, treatment.

The Glass Pass had been maintained in piecemeal over the years, always just-and-no-more hitting the needs of current usage and traffic, never with an eye on the future. The accompanying roadworks for the patchy repairs were a legendary pain in everyone's rear ends for their duration. Despised by locals and tourists alike, it was slow going at best, but the topography and tight nature of the road meant any minor incident caused major delays which would ruin your day venturing Up-By, or the first day of your holiday if you were coming south.

Due to its infamy in the country, it had made headline news when funding was granted to build a completely new road at the foot of the hills. An ambitious engineering project, The Big Belt, as the new road was known (if not officially named, but as usual that was another story) was effectively a system of bridges spanning the marshy valley bottom. Unfortunately, it was beset with technical problems from the outset, and the amounts of money being poured in were so great it was discussed from Holyrood to Westminster, from tabloids to BBC News, and from the Gillie's Rest in Mid-June to pubs in Glasgow.

The Big Belt plan was supposed to spare everyone the pain of more remedial roadworks, since the project was completely separate from the existing road which could remain open until the new road was completed. But the Glass Pass gods had other ideas and there was a significant landslide during the winter, which, along with the subsequent shoring up, had rendered the Glass Pass a single-track road for a sinuous stretch of more than half a mile. There were temporary traffic lights at each end, one hundred meters before the road became single lane, and once the school holidays came along and there was generally more migration between each side of the hourglass, long lines of frustrated carloads were expected at both sides.

Fraser had to hit the ground running on all matters Big Belt. As the new MSP, he took Les Mitchell's place on the extensive team managing the project and was invited to their regular meetings, which was where he first met Wyllie. Fraser hadn't figured out Wyllie's role exactly, but Wyllie certainly had in-depth knowledge of both the new and old routes. When Fraser's personal dealings with him took the turn they did, he wasn't sure who to turn to ask exactly why Wyllie was so in-with-the-bricks on The Big Belt. He wondered if anyone else was wary of his scruples or, indeed, as Fraser had recently figured out, knew he had none.

Fraser now thought about what it was likely that Wyllie

knew about tomorrow's plans. It was common knowledge in Mid-June that there was a secret special guest coming to visit the new football ground and some of the boys and girls who play there, even though people hadn't RSVP-ed in the numbers Fraser had hoped. They were probably drastically underestimating how special the special guest was, but on the day he anticipated that phones would be drawn quickly, word spreading fast, and everyone who had been too busy to attend his ribbon cutting would arrive in droves. The kids would probably be confused by the hullabaloo, but you can't impress all of the people all of the time. This was just the first step in Fraser's quest to raise the profile of Mid-June and attract funding into many more worthy projects.

The finer details of the plan for the day had been kept on a need-to-know basis. Oona of course counted as need-to-know and even then, he made her refer to the surprise guest as 'Blah Blah' for fear of someone overhearing his name.

The original plan had been that Fraser would travel north and meet Blah Blah at a country house a couple of miles on the other side of the Glass Pass. Just yesterday though, the plan was changed as the guest had secured his own driver and would meet Fraser at his office, before heading to the Mid-June Youth Ground. So ironically, if the Glass Pass was indeed the intended stage for Wyllie's nefarious plans, Fraser was safe. It was Blah Blah, a veritable national treasure, plus his driver and anyone else traveling the Glass Pass who were the ones at risk. Fraser had to have the Glass Pass shut down. He pictured the lead in to the Glass Pass as it looked just now – all the new signage and the infuriating temporary lights. His thoughts lingered on the traffic lights, and he willed a plan of action to come to him. When it did, he found a pen and paper and jotted down a few key points in a kind of rough script. Resisting the temptation to pick up the phone immediately, he went to the kitchen to get himself a glass of water, then came back to look at the script afresh and think through what he was about to do. Lie to a police officer, that was what he was about to do. But he couldn't think of anything else for it. Surely where lives were at stake, this counted as a white lie. He took a deep breath and dialled Inspector Beattie's number.

6

Baldowie Village

Sergeant Tom Armstrong picked up the phone to his friend and colleague, Inspector Kenny Beattie, who apologised for calling him so late, but explained there was a change in tomorrow's shift – he should head to the Glass Pass to cover the traffic lights there, which may be malfunctioning.

'Eh?' Tom asked. '*May* be malfunctioning? How they hell can we not tell whether they're working or not?' He shouldn't complain, he thought – he'd been called too many times to the old, perhaps ancient, road for accidents or near misses, so preventative measures should be a relief. This whole structural blight on life in Mid-June had gone on too long though, and such things seemed to make Tom weary nowadays. He did not hide his consternation now to Beattie.

Beattie continued. 'We're sending a team up as soon as we

can, but it'll be easier and safer to wait for daylight. It's particularly important that they don't fail tomorrow.'

'It's important they don't fail any day!' Tom was flabbergasted. 'So does failing mean that we have both ends of the Pass sitting at red or, God forbid, both at green so cars are driving towards each other on a single track road with blind corners?'

'Well, ahem,' Beattie had hoped he wouldn't ask. 'We're not sure.'

'What? Tell me you're kidding.'

'The thing is, things are bad enough with the whole Big Belt fiasco, that there's a concern this will make the papers again. I've had pressure from Fraser Bam to man the lights tomorrow especially.'

Tom flinched at both the names 'Big Belt' and 'Fraser Bam'.

THE BIG BELT was the name coined by witty locals for the new road. If the old shape of the road system was an hourglass figure, the new one had a thicker middle, so needed a bigger belt. Tom continued to be a little disappointed that the name had stuck. Officially there was supposed to be a naming competition, a local version of how they named the Queensferry Crossing road bridge, where suggested names would be narrowed down by a panel, which included Tom's late wife Ann, in recognition of her many years of service as a primary school teacher. The shortlist would then be voted upon by all the tributary villages. When Tom bemoaned the by-passing of the naming process as the media picked up The Big Belt moniker, Ann just laughed and reminded him that once a Scottish wit has come up with a clever name, it sticks: the Clyde Arc in Glasgow will forever be the Squinty Bridge; the Clyde Auditorium, supposed to look like ships' keels is known instead as the Armadillo; even the car park between those two landmarks is the Cheese Grater. Well in fact, the Queensferry Crossing is an exception to this. It's obediently referred to by its proper name, as opposed to wittier submissions like the Third Forth Bridge, but that's east-coasters for you.

As for Fraser Bam – *you'd think you'd be embarrassed to run for election with a name like that* – Tom wasn't impressed. He hadn't actually met him, but Ann had, and she hadn't warmed to him. When Tom had asked if they should be worried that the future of Mid-June could be in his hands for a long time if the tenure of Les Mitchell was anything to go by, Ann had just said, 'Maybe that's it. Maybe I'm just so used to Les. I also know Bam's fiancée Oona MacFarland – she was in Mid-June for primary school before she went off to boarding school, but she's kept in touch. She's a lovely girl and Bam is punching way above his weight there. Not to be shallow but he's a ginger who clearly wears fake tan.'

'Well I was punching too, and look how we turned out,' he had said pulling her in for a cuddle.

TOM TRIED to cut to the chase. 'So, there will be two of us this end, babysitting the lights and officers at the other end doing the same presumably?' *What a bloody waste of resources.*

'Affirmative.'

'Alright mate, I don't need the lingo. Just talk me through this ridiculous scenario. Please tell me this isn't just Fraser Bam pulling strings so he can make it up and down the Glass Pass smoothly, with this "VIP"', Tom's tone clearly conveying the sceptical ""s around VIP.

'Do I detect some cynicism towards our bold young MSP? I have to admit, that my first thought was also that he was trying to bum the whole thing up, just because he seems to have ideas above his station – he's always on show, always trying to impress. Anyway, much as I wanted to tell him where to shove it, I reached the same conclusion as you. Everyone has to be safe on that road, jumped-up important person or not, so until we get absolute certainty from the light engineers that they are fail-proof, I think this is for the best. It also turns out Bam is no longer going Up-By to collect his guest; the guest has his own driver and will be making his own way down.'

Tom knew Beattie was right. 'Well,' he sighed, 'good job I enjoy Boy Wonder's company, or it would be a long shift.'

'Calum's a good lad, isn't he?'

'He is. Knows his stuff. About the job and a lot of other things. He's a wealth of information.'

'I know what you mean. You know that I've known him since he was a wee boy, and he's always been like that. I'd go round to their house to watch the World Cup when it was in France. What year was that again?' Beattie asked.

'1998.' Tom knew he wouldn't have got that so quickly if he hadn't been around his young beat companion so much. Maybe he could develop a young man's memory again by osmosis.

'So, he was only a wee boy, what eight or nine?' Beattie continued. 'But he'd watch along with us, telling us the players' stats and what the managers' strategies were likely to be.'

'Aye, he definitely knows his football. And Ann said that at school whatever wee special subject they were covering – you know the kind of thing, local history, what it was like to live as a Victorian kid, kids being evacuated here during the war, all that – he'd go away and learn more about it on his own and come in and tell her all this extra stuff she didn't even know. We'd be having a right old chuckle if she was here, comparing notes on the marvellous brain of Calum at the end of my shifts with him.'

There was a pause before Beattie said, 'You still hanging in there Tom? You given yourself salmonella from microwave meals yet?' Another pause. 'Just kidding. Seriously, anything Kay and I can do? We miss Ann too. Still hits us now and then.'

'No, thanks for asking though. I'd let you know if I was

feeling like company. I'm not sure what's lonelier – sitting alone with the bloody cat, or the thought of being out for a Sunday lunch with you and Kay like the old days, but without Ann there.'

'Totally understand mate. You let us know. Kay sends her love.'

'Tell her thanks and that I'm asking for her too. Right, I'd best get an early night in preparation for the top policing work I have ahead of me tomorrow.'

7

Cormully

One last glance before sleep at her packed bag. It was all zipped up, and her clothes inside were wrapped around a couple of valuable essentials to protect them and prevent her from making more noise than she had to as she left in the morning. The real treasures though lay on top and practically glowed as she smiled over at them. Two trilby hats, one in electric blue, one in cerise pink. She imagined the butterflies in her chest to be a myriad of electric colours too and as she put out the light and closed her eyes, she saw the outline of the trilbies in negative behind her eyelids.

Somewhere in Mid-June

JOHN WIPED down one of his guns with a rag as he fumed. This situation had wound its way out of his grasp, and he was not relishing that feeling.

Since away back when he had perfected his authoritative persona in the school playground, running his own small version of gangs to do his bidding, John was used to people accepting he was in charge. When he set his sights on Gemma, he expected the same. In his charm offensive he had showered her with attention and having only dated people her own age until then, the grand gestures of an older man of greater means had worked. He offered her security, and she took his initial devotion and protectiveness at face value.

The age difference allowed that John to take his time deciding if he cared to have children, which as it turned out he did not. Perhaps it was this admission in the heat of a shouting match a few months ago that had changed Gemma – she hadn't seemed so trusting since, hadn't been so happy to look after his bidding when he was home, still harping on about this bloody boutique hotel malarky. Letting her take the part-time job at the pub seemed to shut her up for a bit, and he made sure he spent enough time there to keep an eye on any flirtations in either direction. Gemma was a catch. It would have been easier if she wasn't – if she was plain and meek, rather than pretty and chatty – but that would have deprived him of the thrill of the chase. Besides, he was confident that his reputation would keep any chancers at the pub at bay.

That reputation also meant that certain people counted on him to know what was going on in all nooks and crannies of life in Mid-June, and to be able to *influence* those goings-on should it be in their interests. Some deals came and went, and he would accept them if he trusted the other parties and if it was worth his while financially. A couple of his long games, though, he viewed as games of chess, and he had picked and played his pieces with great care. Unfortunately, his sphere of influence didn't extend to political rigging, so when Fraser Bam had been elected, he had unknowingly landed smack-bam into one of John's biggest and most lucrative long games. Sometimes John enjoyed a challenge, like playing the role of a man Gemma should fall for, but when it came to Fraser Bam, he had quickly grown tired of his naive intent to serve nobly. John wasn't going to let that little fuck ruin everything he'd worked on for years.

His mood was grim, but for now calm. He'd handled better and more capable people than this chump in his time. Fraser Bam was no match for John Wyllie.

PART II

AT THE GLASS PASS

8

Tom

Tom picked up the two flasks of tea and looked around to see if he was missing anything. The answer was always no: there were no brown bags of tray bakes for him to grab – Calum's mum provided the tea-break treats now.

It was in the mornings that he missed his wife the most. Evenings in front of the TV could be long, but at least he knew another day without Ann was nearly over, as opposed to just beginning. Going to bed alone was lonely but waking up alone was lonelier.

DURING THEIR MANY WORKING YEARS, doing the public sector jobs they loved, mornings had been a picture of comfortable efficiency – they moved around the kitchen like a dance they knew well, eating breakfast, preparing their packed lunches, sharing one large mug of tea and surmising what their mutual days ahead held.

When Ann retired though, she surprised Tom by embracing the lack of routine. He'd now always wake up first, that much was given. He'd slowly hoist his legs over the side of the bed and let his spine get used to a sitting position first. Then he'd push down on the bed coaxing his knees, then hips, then finally his back into an upright position. He'd even have a go at pulling his shoulders back and pushing his chest out in the short walk to the bathroom, thinking still-frames of him from bed to shower would look like Darwin's *Descent of Man*. *Welcome to your late fifties,* he'd think.

Ann's state of awake-ness would always be a wee surprise for him once he was done with his ablutions. Sometimes, he'd exit the bathroom and she'd be sitting up in bed looking at her phone, having googled something that had occurred to her seemingly in her sleep, and she'd launch in mid-subject, expecting him to have been pondering the same weekend away, or garden pond, or political question for the last fifteen minutes too. These were likely the conversations that she later referred to saying, 'I told you I was thinking of a winter weekend in Vienna, do you not listen to me?' because he hadn't managed to catch fully up before he had to leave for work.

Other times he'd encounter an empty bed, already neatly made, and have to wander into the rest of the cottage to try to find her. Only in the height of summer, which meant perhaps one or two days per year, was she ever wearing the pretty, fine-cotton pale blue kimono he had bought her in Covent Garden. The rest of the time her petite frame was swamped by a brown fleece dressing gown with a now permanently bobbly and therefore grubby-looking cream collar, that he disliked as much as she loved.

'You look like Jon Snow's wee granny in that you know' he told her.

'I don't know who you're talking about, but I don't care. It's cozy. If you will have me living in the wilds of Scotland in a stone cottage that may once have been used as a cold-storage barn for all we know, then this is how I dress in the mornings to make your tea,' she'd say smiling. She'd make their shared mug of tea and fill one thermos flask, that he'd take with him to work. In her retirement she'd taken to making tray bakes, adapting any recipes to exclude raisins, which Tom disliked, so there was also a sweet treat in a small brown sandwich bag for him to have with his tea as he sat sentry watching the kids go into school. He did enjoy her being retired, he felt very looked after.

The occasional morning, particularly when daylight was a long way from penetrating the small deep-set windows, and the thick walls gave the cottage a cave-like appeal, Ann would still be sleeping when he emerged shiny, clean and cologned from the bathroom, but with almost numb feet from standing shaving on the cold slate floor. Going around to her side of the bed and patting her hair gently, she'd roll towards him, reach up and pull him down for a cuddle. She'd feel so temptingly wrapped up in her duvet fort and sometimes she'd have a wee wriggle as she nuzzled into his neck murmuring sleepily, 'You smell good'. Then she'd make herself into a starfish shape, arms and legs wide, flat against the bed and say, 'come squash me,' which was her playful way of saying that if he had time, he could always get back into bed and warm up his feet before he put his socks on. These mornings, he appreciated the new normal even more than the tray bakes. He never properly expressed to Ann how comforted he'd felt in their new rhythm of life with her being retired. It felt old-fashioned and if he vocalised it, he worried that it would seem that he wished she'd been home all along. He certainly did not. If to change one person's life is to change the world, she had changed the world in the multiple of twenty-odd kids per year, for thirty years. Tom often joked he wished he had a pound for every time a former pupil has came up to Ann to tell her what a lasting influence she had in their lives.

They'd count down the days until his own retirement, wondering what that would look like. Would they revert to Ann being first out of bed? She doubted it. Would Tom take up tray baking? They both doubted that. They wondered how they'd find their own space in this new arrangement and Ann joked, 'Remember my limpet promise?'

'Of course, it's why we have the limpet spot.' The limpet spot was just between Tom's shoulder and his chest where Ann would often lay her head when they were in bed, him lying back and her on her side, a leg thrown over his, usually to conserve heat, as opposed to any kind of an invitation. Her limpet promise had been made quite some time before, a promise that from that horrible event on, she was going to do her best to be permanently stuck by his side.

'Well, maybe I'll go limpet on you when you retire. Stuck to you. Following you around all day. Maybe I'll be needy, not even letting you go alone to the corner shop for the rolls and papers at the weekend. Mind you, we won't even know if it's the weekend or not.'

'I think we both know it's more likely to be me that's driving you crazy by following you around. Cramping your newfound lady of leisure style.'

'I beg your pardon?' Ann said.

'My darling, you know I'm kidding. You've earned this time to yourself after years of looking after those brats.'

'*Brats* – how dare you! You're on wise-guy mode this morning, aren't you? Listen, talking of the limpet spot and brats we love, Ewan was on the phone again asking if I could talk you into accepting that latest award with him. I told him it was highly unlikely but that I'd try.'

'Not *highly unlikely* – zero chance. He's a wee rascal to phone you about it when I've already told him no,' Tom replied.

'Tom, you know he just wants you to get the recognition you deserve. There would be no Nae Patience without you – you were there from the start. Not to be dramatic, but there might not be any Ewan without you.'

'Oh hang on, now you're getting wily. I only did what anyone would do in that split second, so forgive me, but despite your caveat, you are being rather dramatic,' Tom retorted, smiling. 'Ewan deserves all the accolades, and it's you that sits on the board of Nae Patience, not me.'

'Only because you're so determined to downplay your influence in it all. I'd love to see you standing up there with Ewan, all handsome in your uniform, receiving the award with him.'

'I'm not falling for it Ann – your flattery. Just let it be.'

'OK – but you know I only keep asking because I'm so proud of you? For everything.'

'Yes I do and it means more to me than any commendation. How about we agree to just be quietly proud of each other? Come here and geez a cuddle!'

Tom pulled up outside Calum's house. Well, Calum's mum's house. Tom would only call this drizzle, but Calum ran out as if it was pouring down, protecting his hair by holding his hat above it, but also holding a folded umbrella in the other hand. He liked to keep his neat haircut dry, but also liked to avoid hat-head if he could. *But why not put the umbrella up then?* Tom wondered. Sliding into the passenger seat, Calum dumped the umbrella, scooped up the two flasks and said as he did every morning, 'Thanks for the tea Big Man,' using the term to acknowledge the older man's superior rank rather than stature. Usually that was accompanied by his holding up some Tupperware and announcing the contents courtesy of his mum.

'Oy, where's my home baking Wee Man?' asked Tom, his use of *Wee Man* ignoring Calum's lanky 6'6" frame, and conveying both keeping-him-in-his-place and a sense of affection.

'Just coming, I didn't have enough hands,' and Calum pointed to his mum running out to the car protecting her hair with the hood of an anorak, the hood over her head and the jacket just over her shoulders. She was waving the Tupperware while awkwardly holding the half-on jacket, well, half on. Again Tom wondered to himself why she just didn't put the jacket on properly.

'Morning Tom!'

'Morning Jean, thanks for running out. Can't believe the Wee Man made you come out in this dreich.'

'Och that's OK. Tiffin today. No raisins. Have a good day you two. Be good. Come in for some Second Day Soup if you want on your way home Tom.'

On the odd occasion he ventured to the pub, Tom's friends would mention Jean, saying things like 'merry widow' and 'the way to a man's heart is his stomach' but Tom knew it was a way of showing her appreciation for his mentoring relationship with Calum. As he told one of those friends, she was just a very caring, kind woman. The friend retorted, 'Exactly – just your type' and then realising he'd gone a bit too far, patted Tom on the shoulder and they both looked at the floor shaking their heads with a small sigh.

'What's the Second Day Soup then?' Tom asked.

'It's what my mum says when you have yesterday's soup today. Apparently it's a thing. Supposed to taste better the next day. I think it's just an excuse to give me leftovers.'

'I know that ya numpty. Second Day Soup is one of our national dishes. I mean what kind of soup is it, because presumably, with it rising to the honour of Second Day Soup today, you had it last night?'

'Oh right aye. Chicken.'

'Chicken? What does that mean? Chicken noodle? Cock a Leekie? Cream of chicken?'

'Oh I don't know. You know my mum dumbs down the names of things because I'm a bit suspicious of strange foods.'

Tom smiled because he did know this. It was hard to believe given the height of the young man now, but Jean had explained that Calum had been a painfully picky eater when he was a wee boy. She had been keen to point out that being wary of new foods was apparently a mark of superior intelligence, but it had meant she had to re-name anything remotely exotic sounding – spaghetti Bolognese, became just *meat pasta* or salmon teriyaki was *sticky fish*. Maybe Tom would accept Jean's invitation and find out what variation of chicken soup it was later today.

Once Calum got all the bits and pieces settled and his seat-belt on, he started driving and asked, 'what gems have you got for me today? What documentary did you subject your poor mum to last night? Let me guess, something about the proliferation of redheads in Tennessee due to Scots migration there? Or the story of the Scottish railway workers introducing football into Uruguay in their spare time between building the rail network?' These were in fact topics Calum had shared with him near the start of their working together that had caused Tom to go home and fact-check on the iPad.

'Aye, see how much I've taught you? I'm keeping your brain alert. You're welcome, by the way. Well, it was actually about railways, but not in Uruguay. It was all about the cuts in the British railways in the 1960s by some politician called Beeching.'

'Oh good – a topic I've heard of. What was his job again?'

'Yeah, my mum knew a bit about it too – she was telling me she remembered people complaining about how it affected us down here in Mid-June. Beeching was the Chairman of British Railways, whose dubious legacy was that he cut a third of the network nationwide. This documentary was showing people who live in towns in the south of England now, who have to drive to work, and it takes them two hours to drive twelve miles, but if the old railway line was reinstated it would only take them twenty minutes. It was fascinating the knock-on impacts on quality of life and the environment of decisions made fifty years ago. The Mid-June branch was one of the casualties of course. It's made me want to go a walk along the old railway line – the presenter went along one in England and found old workers huts and evidence of the old platforms and things.'

'That actually does sound quite interesting, was it BBC? Maybe I'll take a look on iPlayer. I'll ask you again – are you sure you wouldn't be more suited to a job in academia or something with all this knowledge?'

'Well that's the thing about knowledge, the more you have the more you're likely to use it. I'll never know when any of these things might come in useful, but I know lots of them will,' Calum answered simply.

'Fair enough,' Tom said, though he wondered to himself if the topics Calum seemed to become immersed in would ever be useful in this job. As well as that, both he and Jean quietly wished Calum would spend more of his time looking for a girlfriend, and he doubted these pet subjects helped much with his chat-up patter.

When Tom didn't turn towards their usual first spot in sight of the school, Calum simply held his hands up in confusion. Tom answered the silent question, 'oh sorry, I was so interested in your Beeching stories there that I forgot to tell you – we have to head to a traffic duty thing at the Glass Pass. There's a fun job of putting out the road closures signs awaiting you too.' Calum squinted out the window at the continuing rain and groaned.

9

Alec
Holding out for a Hero, Bonnie Tyler

Predictably, Alec had had stress dreams. Every potential flaw in their plan, feasible or preposterous, had reared its ugly head in his sleep: the car not starting – pretty unlikely (despite its age, it was very reliable); the road between his and Gemma's blocked by snow – highly unlikely given it was May; her husband John showing up instead of her, shotgun in hand – unfortunately, that one fell in the *somewhat likely* category. He reasoned though that Gemma would have called things off, or at least let them know, if John had ended up not being away on business last night, so he checked his phone yet again. The plan was still going ahead, thank God.

He got up and dressed in the semi-darkness before opening the curtains. Fairly anti-climactic weather he thought looking out at the slurry rain, and again he mused about the fairytale knight charging off into a colourful sunrise brandishing his sword, on an impressive steed. Instead, he was quietly tiptoeing out of the castle so as not to wake his parents, cowering under an umbrella to get to his sensible good-miles-to-the-gallon car.

Inez

'TYPICAL,' Inez thought with an internal roll of her eyes as she looked out the window. She stood for a moment, trying to decide if it was fine rain or a heavy mist. Then with a sigh decided that it didn't really matter, she was going to get just as wet either way, and turned to start loading up her car. The task would have been impossible with an umbrella and the hood of her jacket slipped off her thick hair so much she gave up pulling it back on, so she got progressively wetter each time. Katie had assured her she didn't need to worry about her hair or make up because they'd have that all done at the studio, which she was secretly excited about - she was always complimented on her hair, but it had been a while since it had been properly styled. As she came in from her final trip, she met Katie at the foot of the stairs. Her hair was up in a clip and her face, washed and moisturised, was shiny and make-up free, which was a rarity given the business she was in. Inez thought she was even more beautiful au naturel.

'Good morning pet, how are you this morning?'

'Aunt Inez, I told you I'd help you with all that! Have you loaded the whole lot up on your own? Several dozen strawberry tarts?' Katie also looked at her watch and added, 'I'm up on time aren't I? This is when we agreed we'd start loading up?'

'Och, you know me, I'm up early anyway. No point in us both getting wet.'

'You're like a drowned rat. Good job they're going to be glamming you up when we get to the studio.'

'Lord help us,' Inez said, not really disguising her smile from Katie. They were too close to each other for coyness.

'Well I cannot wait to see the transformation. Right, what did we agree were the basics? You packed the outfit we chose right? The navy, not black?'

'Yes it's hanging in the car.'

'OK, so basics would be my handbag, your scabby purse, phones, or what you think passes for a phone, your outfit and seventy-one perfectly photogenic strawberry tarts. Let's go!' Katie said racing out to the car while Inez locked up. Apparently she agreed with Inez that there was no point in them both getting soaked.

Alec
Girl Like You, Edwin Collins

Drawing to a slow stop outside Gemma's house, Alec felt his heart flutter just at the thought of seeing her. They had kept in touch by text, so she was ready and waiting, and he caught a glimpse of her leaving her vigil by the window to make her final exit out of the front door. Alec got out of the car and held open the passenger door for her, saying nothing, just smiling broadly as she met his eyes with a nervous but excited expression. He took her bag and slung it in the back, climbed in and shut the door carefully, quietly. She did same.

He was still smiling at her when she took a deep breath in and blew an exaggerated breath out, then paused for a second. Then she startled him as she suddenly stamped her feet on the floor, drummed her hands on the dashboard and made a high-pitched, gleeful *eeeh* sound. She stopped just as suddenly, turned towards the driver's side and said playfully, 'Hi you. Shall we begin the rest of our lives together today my love?'

Ravi leaned towards her, put his hands on either side of her face and drew her in for a kiss saying, 'Yes please my darling.'

Alec looked away, feeling his smile faltering.

'Good to go mate?' Ravi glanced behind into the back seat.

'Yup, all good, let's get going,' Alec replied, waving a hand in a forward direction, as settled into his new seat in the back, looking out at Gemma's marital home, he was relieved they were getting her out of there. Today he was getting her away from that bastard John and helping her and Ravi get out of Mid-June and start their new life together. He wasn't sure how he'd feel when the adrenaline faded, and the reality of what that meant for him set in, but for now, that felt like a privilege.

Jill and Ally

JILL RAN out to Ally's car, wearing the electric blue trilby and waving the cerise one. As quickly as she could she threw her bag in the back and jumped in the passenger seat to protect the hat from the rain. 'Woohoo!!! We're Thelma and Louise!'

'But with rolling Scottish countryside in the rain instead of scorching desert.'

'Yup!' Jill laughed.

'And hopefully without the suicide pact!'

'Well, OK, yes, there's that too. Let's go! Here, put your hat on,' and she leaned over and put it on Ally's head.

'Hey, I didn't hear any clinking coming from your bag. I thought you were in charge of the drinks for the hotel room? And accessories of course,' Ally said, taking off the hat and looping her hand behind the seat to place it carefully on the back seat.

'Oy, you better wear that hat at the concert!'

'Of course I will, but imagine if the Mid-June cops clock us both in those hats at this time in the morning? We'll get pulled over with them thinking we're driving home from some mad hen night,' Ally said.

'Well, the wine is all cleverly wrapped up in my pyjamas and a jumper – for a quiet exit for me and so we don't clink all the way through reception when we're checking in. One real Champagne, two cheaper Proseccos, two big bags of crisps. No glasses, so we'll be using coffee cups or plastic bathroom cups, but that's OK. And we can get drinks at the venue, right? I'm so excited! It's so nice to get away and not be a mum for a couple of days.'

'I'm excited for you too. It'll be good for you. So, first of all – did the dog steal anything out your suitcase or pee in it when it realised you were going somewhere?'

'No thank God. What kind of a life do I have that I even have to hide the fact that I'm packing from the bloody dog!'

'Well that's a good start. Second of all – how was George?' Ally knew that both Jill and George were apprehensive about him being left alone for night with their two toddlers and a dog who would be in a huff about it too.

'Och bloody miserable. You'd have thought I was leaving for a week the way he was carrying on. He'll be fine. I've left him a fifteen-minute planner.'

'You're kidding me.'

'Nope, I wish I was. You've heard about The Mental Load, right?'

'Yes.'

'Well, I guess I've accepted that the Mental Load is all on me. The only way to get him through the next thirty-six hours was to lay it out in fifteen-minute segments. I thought it was a bit offensive to put feeding the kids on the schedule, because obviously everyone knows children need to be fed, and he eats with them sometimes – evenings if he's home on time, usually at the weekends too. So he looked at the schedule that has everything on it, and I mean everything, down to bath-time, bedtime, and where I've laid their pyjamas out, as if he doesn't even live with us, and he said '*Wow, this is a lot! Anything else?*' I said, '*Well, they'll need to eat of course*' and he picked up a pen, and huffed and puffed saying, '*well what time is that? You didn't write that down.*' Jill looked over at Ally for her reaction – who was smiling but shaking her head in disbelief.

She continued. 'Honestly, I love him, but he can be a bit clueless. The other day we were trying to get the kids out for a walk, in the cold and rain of course, but I had to get them out – they're a nightmare at bedtime if they've just been trapped in the house all day. But just getting out the house is an ordeal in itself. You don't know whether to get your own layers and jacket on and sweat while you get theirs on, or the other way round so they're wee grumpy boil-in-the-bag sprouts by the time you're going out the door. Anyway, I got all their gear on and had to go out to the utility room to put the pram together – taking the car seat off, putting the rain cover on, and clipping the boogie buggy on and all that. I asked George to put the kids' wellies on, which was all that was left to do. I rolled the pram from the back door round to the front door and was waiting outside in the rain. It was belting down against my hood and I was thinking we'd have about ten minutes before it all would all start kicking off under the sweaty pram rain cover and we'd have to turn back. Not to mention I was getting soaked. I waited and waited. Finally went up and banged on the front door and George answered, surprised to see me, no shoes or jacket on himself, and the kids still just in their socks! He said, '*I told them to put their wellies on.*' I could have screamed. Does he think that's how easy it is? I just go around all day saying, *get dressed, eat your breakfast, brush your hair,* and they do it?!'

Jill had been gesticulating wildly through her story and ended with a shaking of her hands either side of her head and gave a mock scream. Then she dropped her hands on to her lap and said 'OK, well let's hope that's that out of my system!' She took a deep breath and concluded, 'Like I said, it'll be nice to be *me* for a couple of days so I'm going to try not to worry about them.'

'Yeah, try not to worry. They'll be fine. And don't worry about venting. I'm happy to listen to it all. I love George and won't judge him when you're having a much-deserved rant,' Ally looked over at Jill briefly to reassure her and then turned back to the road and gripped the steering with a thump and added, 'and what happens at Take That stays at Take That! Woohoo Thelma! We're going to see Take That! Mark, Gary, Howard, here we come! What's today going to be?'

'The *Greatest Day!*' Jill said punching the air and they broke out into song. She put George and the kids to the back of her mind and thought about their front row seats and for the hundredth time, about catching Gary Barlow's eye. His beautiful blue eyes.

10

Fraser

Fraser had been up all night poring over papers and accounts, and hadn't even managed to completely calm his thinking, never mind make any practical progress. The thought had gradually been forming in his mind that he should tell Oona everything about his dealings with Wyllie – not as a confessional, but because she might be able to help. In fact, apart from the awful thought of having to explain to her how he got into this mess, all night he'd been wishing she was there by his side.

It still astonished him sometimes that Oona was going to be his wife. His friends joked that he was punching above his weight, usually following up with some derogatory remark about gingers. Fraser was happy to take the ginger jibes because when he inspected his slightly receding hairline, he could see a future where they turned to baldy jibes instead. He was also happy to admit he was punching: a skinny ginger from a working-class background, versus Oona with her glossy dark hair, smiling blue eyes, confident posture, and assured but friendly boarding school accent. She had the ease and poise of someone whose family hadn't had to worry about money for a couple of generations. Money can't buy you happiness, but it can score a chunk of things that keep other people up at night off your list.

Hopelessly picking through layers of paper, he knew that he would have to confess to Oona at some point, and if he did it now, maybe with her level head and sharp intellect they could make some headway together. Yes, he decided, it was the right answer to tell Oona now and he fished around for his phone under the sea of paper. Every fibre of his being hoped that she wouldn't judge his initial schoolboy error too harshly – one of his main drivers in life was to impress her and the thought of going down in her estimation gutted him.

'Good morning you. This is a very early call. Are you OK?' Oona sounded sleepy. Fraser could hear the duvet rustle.

'Oona, I – I don't know where to start. I'm in a bit of a mess.'

'You're in a wee guddle then?' Oona had picked the Old Scots word up from Fraser's mum.

'A bit more serious than a wee guddle, I'm afraid. I did something stupid, and it's snowballed – can you come over? I really need to talk this through, I've been up all night.' He had been pacing, but now sat on the couch, head down, looking at his shoes, his free hand cupping the back of his head and sighed. 'Oh Oona, I don't want to let you down but you're the only person I can talk to about this.'

'OK, not going to lie, you're making me a little nervous darling, but I'm up and throwing on some clothes already. I'll be there in no time at all. Look I'll ring off to get there faster and it sounds like we'd better start at the beginning when I get there.'

. . .

Fraser wondered if he'd cry when Oona arrived, to add to his humiliation, but he didn't. They had a long cuddle and when he pulled her tighter, she squeezed back reassuringly. 'Right, shall I come away in?' she asked, mimicking another of Mrs Bam's phrases.

Fraser was prone to saying that his mum was single-handedly keeping Old Scots dialect alive, joking about it to hide how much it made him cringe. But Oona thought it was sad that in Scotland using dialect is looked down upon as being lower class – she personally felt a bit short-changed that she hadn't grown up with those Scottish words that just uniquely describe things so perfectly. There are some words that just don't have an equivalent in English. Mrs Bam had tried to explain to Oona the nuances of something being *shoogly* – meaning it could be unsteady or just not working very well – but yet the remedy was often 'gie it a wee *shoogle* and see if that helps'. Oona enjoyed the range of the word *scunnered* which was at one end, mildly fed up –

'How are you today, Mrs Bam?'

'Och just a wee bit scunnered'—to at the other end entirely sick and tired of something –

'I'm just absolutely scunnered with people giving Fraser a hard time about The Big Belt when he's only just started the job'.

Oona had thought that *gallus* was an insult when Mrs Bam had said of her young neighbour, 'He's a right *gallus* piece of work that one', but then was slightly perturbed on the campaign trail, when Fraser was petting (or rather *clapping* if she was sticking to Scots) a Jack Russell puppy and commented to the owner, 'He's a *gallus* wee thing isn't he?' Fraser had found it hard to explain but came up with similarities to *cocky* or *cheeky*, and she learned she'd have to rely on context to discern.

Under Oona's advice, Fraser had embraced the words and

phrases he grew up with and noticed that constituents warmed to it, Oona's wisdom and influence raising him up as always.

Fraser smiled a tired smile of acknowledgment in her nod to his mum, and further mimicked her saying, 'Yes, *come away in pet*,' gesturing into the living room. Oona glanced at the papers strewn all over the dining table, but did not comment on them. A sea of calm walking into a maelstrom of frantic sleuthing, she simply sat down on the couch and patted the seat beside her. Fraser accepted the invitation and sat beside her and exhaled slowly, rubbing his thighs, still wondering where to start.

Oona reached over and gently ran her hand up and down his back. 'Start at the beginning. Whatever it is, I'm sure we can work it out.'

Fraser looked into her eyes, filled with concern, and nodded, 'Right OK. Yes, the beginning. OK.' Another deep breath. 'Do you remember when Mack helped out with the application for top-up funding for The Big Belt?'

Although Fraser had inherited The Big Belt fiasco, he dived in, excited in what he saw as a great opportunity to prove himself early on in his tenure. The top-up grant was the biggest item on the agenda at that first meeting where he had encountered Wyllie, and eager to add value from the start, he had invited his friend Mack. Mack had consulted for the Scottish Government, so he had some inside knowledge about what a good funding application looked like. Everyone around the table had impressive credentials and Fraser had to fight off imposter syndrome. An engineer spoke eloquently, but at a level laymen could understand, about a technical problem they had encountered that couldn't possibly have been foreseen. An environmental impact manager spoke about numerous issues that would never have occurred to Fraser, including the long list of detrimental effects on the quality of life in Mid-June that were being endured as the project dragged on. A managing director spoke passionately about job security and the safety of his workers. Fraser enjoyed soaking in all the insights and his first experience as a politician dealing with the private sector was heartening, as successful public/private partnerships like this were at the core of his beliefs. Someone had quipped that the group was The Big Belt Round Table, which became the name they used in subsequent correspondence. Oona had heard all about that meeting of course, but in hindsight, Fraser now had a different view on one particular aspect of the meeting.

'Remember I mentioned John Wyllie was there? And remember when I mentioned that to your dad, he went all grumbly and said, '*Of course he was*'? Oona was nodding. 'Well, that should have been my warning. Looking back, I did wonder why he was there. He wasn't nearly as integral to the conversations as everyone else at the table, but he seemed to have been at all the meetings up until that point, so I just figured people's contributions ebb and flow on a huge project like this.'

He took a stilted breath, but quickly shook off the self-recriminations that he should have had sharper instincts on this. He'd run out of time on that indulgence. 'A couple of weeks after that meeting Wyllie came into my office with a cheque for me. He said the Round Tablers were paying me a finder's fee for securing Mack as our consultant.'

Oona's demeanour didn't change. She just asked, 'How much was the cheque for?'

'Twenty grand.' He looked her straight in the eye, expecting her perhaps to put her hand to her head and say quietly '*Oh Fraser*' realising that this story, wherever it was going, started with a moment of monumental stupidity.

But she just replied calmly, 'Well, given the amounts of money you and Mack were successful in helping secure, I don't suppose you found that amount shocking. We've all got used to talking in superlatives and astounding amounts of dosh with

The Big Belt, so I can see why you didn't really flinch at twenty grand.'

Lovely Oona – her answer was considered and sympathetic but also born of an upbringing where people 'didn't flinch' at twenty thousand pounds.

Fraser had flinched alright. That was a chunk of cash he could offer to contribute towards their society wedding. Oona's dad would decline of course, but there would be dignity for Fraser in the offer. Then he'd plan with Oona the honeymoon she deserved, or if she preferred, save the cash towards a bigger house one day, another thing he was sure his father-in-law already planned to take care of. Fraser had mused how satisfying it would be to decline in return any offers to help them out, telling Oona's father he already had things covered, thank you. Fraser had dreamed those dreams for a delicious moment, before he quickly realised how ridiculous it would be for him, MSP for Kilmour and Berry Valley, to accept a cheque in his name, especially for anything to do with The Big Belt.

'Well, it wasn't really the amount that was the issue Oona, it was more the impression of impropriety I was worried about. I initially turned Wyllie down flat.'

'I realise that, yes sorry. Of course you did.'

'Well, hang on, he kind of – that is, I asked him...' Fraser had to interrupt her before she went down the path of believing that the end of the story was that he had refused the cheque. If only that were true. *Honesty is the best policy*, he thought, as he took a deep breath and continued to tell the story.

Wyllie was slick. He had fully expected resistance, and just smiled knowingly when Fraser passed the envelope back across his desk. '*Oh, are you worried this is inappropriate in some way?' he asked. 'It really isn't Fraser. It's policy. They could get in trouble for* not *paying you. Can you imagine the visual of that? It's far more straight-forward to accept a payment in fair exchange for a service you provided than risk any aspersions that you're in a* you scratch my back, I'll scratch yours *relationship with them. Honestly, this way is much simpler. They were happy with the collaboration you put together, and want you to have fair reward, to keep the relationship above-board, paying you just the same as they would pay anyone else.*'

Fraser couldn't remember the exact back and forth, except that Wyllie had successfully made him feel quite naive in the ways of the business world, mentioning that others in the Round Table had received a similar recruitment fee at some stage in The Big Belt lifespan. Wyllie left the cheque on the desk saying, '*Look, just have a think about it*,' and they went on to discuss other things, including the MJY football ground plans. Fraser now realised this was a tactic to muddy the waters, so his initial hackles about the money were somewhat dulled, and over the next few days, his mind was too busy with other things to over-analyse, and he ended up depositing the cheque.

He looked sheepish, pausing at that part of the story. Oona just smiled and rubbed his back again and said, 'OK, well, we've set the scene. I'm guessing things have moved on since then?'

The relationship with the Round Tablers continued. The conditions of the Scottish Government top-up grant that Fraser and Mack helped secure included a strict timetable of progress reports and it was agreed that Fraser would review and sign off on them. The profile of Big Belt had not diminished, the public seemingly loving any chance to fold their arms, shake their heads sagely and proceed to make vacuous comments, like, *who's running that show anyway*? and *I think it's the blind leading the blind over there in Holyrood*. Given this, highlights from the progress reports found their way into the papers. Not that Fraser wouldn't have taken his role seriously, as he was enjoying this part of the job a lot, and it was furthering his belief that these kind of partnerships between politicians and business were the way forward, but knowing that the press was scouring the reports for any misstep was even more reason to be thorough in his review of them.

The tight coil that Fraser had been for the past thirty-six hours, was slowly softening, his shoulders relaxing with each part of the story he got out and with every reassuring nod or smile or touch of Oona's. He was madly in love with her, never more so than right now, but was also lucky that she had been a sounding-board and sometimes a mentor through lots of the relevant events, so he didn't need to rehash every detail.

'Remember that progress paper I was reviewing when we were at your dad's clay pigeon shooting weekend?'

'Of course. I felt terribly for you, how distracted you were all weekend. And my dad wasn't helping, loudly pointing out whenever you were absent from the party. I'm sorry.'

'Och it's not for you to feel bad about. I'm getting used to him. Let's see how we fare coming out the other side of this though. Anyway, you'll remember that I was working on it because I wasn't fully happy about how they were representing the status of a few things – they were claiming they were much further along, much closer to completion, than I understood them to be. At first, I didn't think it was a big deal – I just wanted more accuracy and maybe a little dial-back to reflect where things stood realistically. I thought it might be a language thing, not an intent to mislead. But I hit resistance at my draft revisions and the level of the resistance was a little jarring. I had to check in that it wasn't my ego getting in the way, so I sense-checked myself, but still there was an imbalance between my perception and theirs. It was the first real thing I'd dissented on; I didn't expect to be stonewalled.'

Oona cleared her throat and shifted in her chair a little. Fraser stopped and looked at her. His story was spilling out now, unlike his faltering start, watching her every expression as the words came out a few at a time. He raised his eyebrows and gave a small nod, silently asking if she was OK, if he should keep going.

Oona answered out loud in return 'I'm fine, I'm fine. I have a feeling I'm about to be very annoyed at someone or some people, but I doubt it's going to be you, my love. Go on.' She attempted a smile of encouragement.

What a trooper she was. He'd once compared her to Princess Anne, which had not gone down well, but now and then, with a secret smile he remembered the comparisons he had tried to protest at the time – compassionate, calm, fun, posh, popular, great Scottish rugby fan – and now trooper.

'I told them I'd go onsite for a tour in case things had moved along and my understanding was incorrect, but they turned me down. I said in that case I wasn't happy to put my name to the report. It's due to be submitted next week so time is running out. Surely you can guess who came to see me a couple of days ago?'

'Oh let me take a stab – Wyllie? I'm getting closer to knowing who the subject of my wrath is going to be.'

'Yup! Walked in with a gallus swagger,' (Oona knew this was not the more affectionate use of 'gallus'), 'and an envelope. It was as if he thought we both knew the script. He sat down and made a little small talk, but his manner was far from breezy. He didn't break eye-contact. Then he said *I just dropped in with a wedding present for you*, and pushed the envelope across the table. I was sweating and not really sure why, he's just that intimidating. I think I managed to keep eye contact while I pushed it back across my desk, and said that it was very generous of him, but I couldn't accept monetary gifts. The only way I can describe his reaction is to say that his face went dark. You haven't met him, but he has dark hair anyway, which he gels back as if it's the nineties, so it looks jet-black. When I say his face went dark, even his irises clouded over they were almost the same colour as his pupils. His tone stayed even and that made the whole thing even more sinister. I'm not going to lie – I was shitting it by now.' Fraser practically shuddered at the memory.

'It wasn't a sophisticated argument. He hadn't come prepared to debate and persuade like he had the first time. I think he just thought I was up for bribes. So our discussion just went along the lines of him repeating I should accept the wedding present and me saying I can't accept cash gifts. Until he grew tired of the back and forth, stood up and pushed his forefinger down hard on the envelope pushing it right over to my side of the desk, making me lean back, and said, '*But you seem to be forgetting you already have.*''

Oona's head was resting on her fist, the other arm folded across her waist. Her fist tightened, as she drew breath to speak. Had he been asked to guess, Fraser would have said the next words out of Oona's mouth might be, '*What a bounder,*' somewhat impersonating her father, or '*filthy rotten scoundrel.*' Instead, she said, in her impeccable accent, through gritted teeth, 'That dirty fucking bastard.' The unflappable Oona was cracking. *Oh dear*, Fraser thought. Wait until he got her right up to date about yesterday's email to Wyllie and the subsequent threats.

11

Inez and Katie

Inez adjusted the temperature of her heated seats now that she felt less damp. Her niece still found her choice in car amusing. 'I thought you might have fancied something vintage – a classic Mini or an MG. Nope, not for you! You choose this flashy ride. People's faces when they overtake us and see you driving are a picture.'

'Well, you should have seen the surprise on the salesman's face! I drove in to the forecourt in that old banger of Gran's and could just feel them rolling their eyes. Until I listed the specs of what I was looking for, as well as which dealership in the UK I thought had exactly the car for me, after you helped me sleuth that out on the Internet.'

'Know what you need now to go with your pimped-out car?' Katie asked.

'Aye, you've told me before. A pimped-out phone,' Inez exaggerated weariness of the topic.

'No! Not even a pimped-out phone. Just a standard smart phone of some sort. That flip phone you use could be in a museum. I saw it on a program the other night – those ones where they make fun of tech that we thought was cutting edge at the time and now is laughably out of date.'

'Listen, you can't judge a middle-aged aunt by her phone. I'm completely connected to the outside world without a smart phone thank you very much – in ways that were perfectly acceptable and sufficient not so long ago.'

As Katie plugged her own phone into the car's USB port she asked, 'now look – wouldn't you like a smartphone for this? To play music? You're such a big music lover.'

'I'm happy with the radio.'

'Oh sorry – I was going to put something on, but we can stick with the radio if you'd rather,' Katy reached to unplug her phone again.

'No that's OK, play me some tunes. How about some David Bowie, the love of my life.'

'Aww, what about Uncle ***?' Katie teased as she scrolled through her music looking for Bowie tracks. 'Seriously, please can we get you a new phone when we are in Glasgow?'

'I have two perfectly good phones.' Inez now actually was growing tired of the topic.

'What? No you don't – oh wait, are you counting your *land-line*?' Katie said emphasising the archaic nature of the word.

'Yes *landline*. Are we reverting to language from the trenches now? The gizmo you carry around has stolen the title of phone from my landline. It's an encyclopaedia, a camera, a compass, a record shop and God knows what else. It bears only a passing resemblance to a phone.'

Katie smiled conceding Inez had a point. 'How do I turn off these fancy bum warmers? I'm sweating here.' She scanned the icons trying to find the appropriate switch, then changed her mind and instead put her head back and pushed and held the buttons to put the seat back, saying as she slowly reclined, 'Mind you, it's pretty toasty, maybe I'll just get a little more beauty sleep. Don't drive too fast now.'

Despite the power under her bonnet, Inez drove slowly and carefully. One sharp brake on these winding narrow roads and all her hard work would be for naught. She couldn't risk Katie missing out on this opportunity – she had worked so hard and was so proud of what they were going to achieve with their teamwork. Inez turned down the temperature a smidgen and turned up the volume a little, glancing over at Katie to make sure *Heroes* wasn't disturbing her snooze.

The Mid-June tributary roads filtered into one road about a half of a mile before the Glass Pass, and there was a clear view of the whole stretch as the road climbed to the point where it then disappeared from sight, winding into the hills. Inez could see the approach to the Pass was clear, as it usually was when she travelled it. Being an early bird, if she was heading Up-By she'd often be among the first through the Glass Pass in the morning, driving past the early morning delivery vans on their way down into Mid-June. She noticed their absence this morning.

The last time she travelled there had been two large lit signs a hundred yards apart. The first: *Warning, single lane traffic lights ahead, queues likely*, and the second: *Beware, single lane traffic ahead*, and then in another hundred yards, as promised, were the lights.

She had heard rumours in the village shop that in advance of the tourist season a series of signs getting progressively sterner in their tone, were being erected. According to the owner's husband, who never let the whole truth get in the way of a good story, the series of signs went along the lines of *Queues likely June-August*, then *Non-essential travel discouraged June-August*, then *You've got to be mad trying your luck on the Glass Pass anytime before September*, then *Turn back now or don't blame us.*

Inez was interested to see what the signs really said, so was paying attention as she approached the first sign. It was large with, sure enough, apparently quite a wordy message on it. However, the message was obscured with a bright orange *Road closed ahead*, that had been propped up against it.

'What? No! Closed?' She muttered to herself confused, but loud enough to stir Katie, who sat up and got her bearings.

'Oh! I really did doze off. Hang on what does this sign say?'

The next sign fifty yards on, similarly had a *Road closed ahead* sign leaning against it and Katie almost echoed Inez, saying, 'What? Closed? No!'

'I don't believe this,' Inez said.

'Not today,' Katie finished for her.

Intriguingly, the third propped up sign said *Traffic likely* and gave them a little hope, but then the fourth and final sign reverted the traffic gods' decision to their initial verdict of, *Road Closed Ahead*. Then lastly, a big red traffic light glowed brightly in the gloom to punctuate the decision.

When the car rolled to a stop in front of the light, Inez and Katie both held out their open palms towards the red light asking it various questions:

'You're kidding me?'

'What, since when were you actually CLOSED?'

'Until when?'

'Can you believe this?'

They gave up on the light and looked at each other and once again, spewed various expressions of disbelief along with a few swear words for good measure. Then the police car up the hill caught Katie's eye. It was occupied and it looked like they might have spotted them, as the passenger door started to open.

'Oh good, at least they're here to tell us what's going on,' she said, gesturing towards the car.

Tom and Calum

'OK, here go you Calum. First customers of the morning. Off you go and ruin their day. And I'll tell you that whoever is in that fancy car must have some very important place to be. They're not going to be happy.'

'Aye, cheers Sarge. Thanks for the pep talk,' Calum said, grabbing the door handle with one hand and his umbrella with the other. He was glad his mum had suggested the umbrella today, though muttered dismay at the magpie pattern.

'Could be worse,' Tom said. 'Could be robins.'

'Or blue tits?' Calum asked, the question acknowledging Tom had missed as easy one.

'Oh yes, we wouldn't want you looking like a tit,' Tom chuckled.

'You know I gave you that one don't you? Right, wish me luck.' Calum opened his door and stepped one foot out, while trying, but failing, to get the magpie umbrella up in one go. What a palaver. If anyone had been watching, he must have looked like Tippy Hendren in *The Birds*, the flapping umbrella looking like a persistent, menacing flock of black and white birds snapping at his head. But it was fine, Tom didn't have that view of him from the inside, and it was unlikely the occupants of the yellow car were watching his every move. He regained his composure and straightened up.

Inez and Katie

'OH! D'YOU SEE THIS?' Katie nudged her aunt. Inez looked up in time to catch the show.

'Aww, look at the wee soul. He looks like Tippy Hendren in *The Birds*!' Inez said.

Katie laughed and looked in the other direction. She quickly took out the clip out of her hair and shook it loose.

Calum

CALUM REACHED the car and tried to hold his umbrella so that when the driver opened their window, he'd be protecting the car from the rain splashing in. As Tom said, they weren't going to welcome his news, so he should try to at least keep them dry as he explained the situation. As the window come down, he was surprised the driver was a middle-aged lady. When it was opened enough to converse through, he leaned down awkwardly, still trying to position the umbrella optimally. He began, 'Good morning ladies…' looking first at the driver and then over to the passenger, at which point he said, 'Oh hi!', with a confused tone of recognition.

She leaned over into the driver side to reply, while Calum was momentarily mute. 'Hi. Good morning to you too. What's going on here this fine day, officer?' Her tone was sarcastic.

'Oh, sorry yes, good morning ladies,' Calum cleared his throat, recovering. 'I'm afraid the road is closed.'

'We gathered that from the signs. Well, from most of the signs. One just said there might be traffic and got our hopes up.' Again it was the younger woman who spoke to him, with the older lady just looking up at him smiling.

Calum smiled apologetically. 'Yes, we ran out of signs. The roads department got a bit carried away with all the new signs and we had to cover them all up.'

'So the Glass Pass really is closed? How long for? Will it be open again soon?' the passenger questioned.

'It really is closed, and I'm afraid we can't give you too firm an idea of when it will be open again. The lights are malfunctioning and we are waiting on an engineer and safety supervisor to arrive to fix them and then go through the correct procedures for checking them. It could take some time.'

'Are the engineer and the safety officer here?'

'I'm afraid not yet, they are on their way. It may be better to leave your journey until tomorrow if you can?'

'We can't,' was the quick reply. 'We have to be in Glasgow today. A lot of planning has gone into an event we absolutely have to attend. My aunt here is filming something for a TV show.'

'Oh right, how exciting for you,' Calum smiled nervously at the aunt.

'It is quite exciting actually, a little nerve-wracking but exciting,' she said calmly in a lovely comforting tone. The niece however was clearly struggling to be pleasant about this and he couldn't say he blamed her. They were both very attractive, but more than that definitely familiar. He didn't get a chance to converse more with the aunt as the niece once more took control of the conversation.

'Right, so what's the plan now? Are you in communication with the engineer and the safety officer?'

'Not directly no, but we are being kept abreast of their arrival. They are most certainly on their way.'

'From Mid-June or from Up-By?'

'Up-By.'

'Right, will you keep us up-to-date on that too? We're the only people waiting on this side.'

'Yes indeed ma'am. My boss up there and I aren't going anywhere.' Calum gestured towards the car with Tom in it.

The aunt joined in again. 'OK, well I guess we just have to sit tight for now. Thankfully we left in plenty time.'

'Listen, again, I'm really sorry about this. Maybe we can have a word with the engineer so that when the lights come on, this side of the Pass gets opened up first, and you'll get through straight away,' Calum offered, with no idea if that was a request he could reasonably make, but he wanted to be as helpful as he could. He had addressed the aunt, but now dared to look over at the niece for her response.

'That's the least you can do...'

'That would be very kind of you thank you,' the aunt interrupted. 'Are we allowed to know your name?'

'Calum,' he replied, then he realised he sounded like a wee boy talking to a grown up. 'I mean Calum Kirkpatrick,' he corrected. *God why was he so nervous?* 'I mean Constable Kirkpatrick.' *Finally*. He paused, feeling like there was something else he should be adding, but could only come up with 'Right you are then, I'll be in touch,' and tapped the roof of the car, stood up and started to walk away.

'We're Inez and Katie Blair by the way,' he heard.

As he walked back to the squad car he replayed the exchange. Well, his part in the exchange. At first he thought he had recognised the passenger, but now he wasn't so sure. She was very pretty, so surely he'd remember who she was if they had met before.

Somehow, making his way back to sit with Tom in the car, and leaving her sitting with her aunt, he recalled a nostalgic but not pleasant turmoil he'd had on a package holiday with his parents when he was thirteen. The dining room at the large hotel in Spain had the same seating arrangements every evening of the ten-day vacation and Calum's family was placed beside a family who had a fifteen year old daughter. She was just the right amount of beautiful and just the right amount older than him that he couldn't look in her direction any more than he had dared to look directly at the solar eclipse from the school playground earlier that month – all the other kids did, but he had done his research and knew how dangerous that was. His self-consciousness the whole holiday was paralysing. He took great pains to act normally – bite his food normally, chew his food normally, use his napkin normally. If he deviated from normal, they'd all guess – his parents, her parents and her brother, as well as their waiter Miguel – would all guess how madly in love with her he was. The last day finally arrived, and he thought he'd got away with it. No one had figured it out. How could they? He'd been neutral in his every move. As the parents were saying their farewells, sensibly not pretending they were going to stay in touch, he'd overheard his mum say to the girl in a nod-and-a-wink tone, 'I think Calum's going to miss seeing you every night.' Calum was mortified and betrayed. Now he had to try to remember what walking casually looked like, as he left blushing so deeply that tears came to his eyes and his ears turned red. His ears would turn red for months to come, just at the thought of it.

Trying to shake the recurrence of that feeling, he came up with a new theory. In the few seconds' walk towards the car, his eyes had been on the driver, and he'd profiled a middle-aged lady in an unusual car for her demographic. He had expected her passenger to be someone the same age, whether male or female. In fact, he realised, he'd probably been anticipating a middle-aged husband. So that's what had caught him off-guard. It was the rational policeman in him who had been surprised. The girl was not familiar, and her attractiveness was not going to turn him into a blushing teenage boy in front of Tom.

He attempted an unselfconscious walk the rest of the way back, whatever that looked like. Inez and Katie Blair would not be looking at him anyway – they'd be back to whatever they'd been talking about when he knocked on the window. They definitely would not be watching him.

Inez and Katie

INEZ AND KATIE watched Calum as he walked away.

'Do you know him?' Inez asked.

'Nope. Pretty certain I've never seen him before in my life,' Katie replied, not taking her eyes off him as she did.

'He seemed like he was going to say hello to you, didn't he? As if you did know each other?'

'Yes, I thought that too. Fairly unlikely though – I'm not down in Mid-June nearly as often as I'd like to be.'

'He probably just fancied you.'

'Yeah, that'll be it,' Katie laughed. 'You say that about everyone!'

'Is he your age?' Inez asked, because of course it's hard to tell precise ages once you're a couple of decades past them.

'Maybe a couple of years younger? Wouldn't let that get in the way though, he's very good looking.' Katie stopped watching Calum and picked up her phone. She finished distractedly, 'Maybe I shouldn't have been so grumpy with him.'

Tom and Calum

Tom had a chuckle as Calum flapped the magpies before getting back in the car, and he thought he heard the end of a muttered expression, 'sake man' as he sat in the car a little out of sorts. Tom could just make out now, in a lull in the drizzle, that it was two women in the car, and he wondered what they'd made of the bold Calum with his mum's umbrella.

'Is that a couple of women in that boy racer car?' Tom asked incredulously.

'Yup, aunt and niece, on their way up to Glasgow to film something for the telly.'

'Really? What are they filming?'

'I wasn't there to chat Sarge. But it's not something the aunt does every day because she said she was nervous.'

'How'd they take the news?'

'The aunt was lovely. The niece isn't going to be patient for long I'd guess.'

'Did you break it to them that there's no cell service up here?'

'I did not Sarge, no,' Calum answered flatly.

'Chicken.'

They looked back down at the yellow sports car and right on cue they saw the niece standing in the open door of her passenger side. Calum gave a small groan. She was holding her handbag over her head as a makeshift rain hat and with the other hand was waving her phone and presumably mouthing something along the lines of, 'Is there no service up here?'

'Well, answer her then, you're the liaison here,' Tom was enjoying this.

'Cheers again Sarge,' and Calum opened the door and put one leg out to stand up enough to gesture back that her fears were correct, shouting, 'Sorry' as a meek consolation, as if it was Police Scotland's fault.

12

Alec, Gemma and Ravi
Me and Mrs Jones, Billy Paul

As soon as they set off, Ravi ran through a checklist with Gemma. After today, there would be literally no turning back. None of them cared to imagine how John Wyllie would react when he found out Gemma had left, so once she and Ravi had crossed the Glass Pass today, it would be a long time before they returned. Satisfied that they were truly on their way, they settled into the journey in silence at first. Small talk seemed to have no place on so momentous a journey and all the momentous conversations had been had already.

Over the prior weeks, Alec had tested and tested Ravi's commitment and understanding that he had to be very sure of what he was doing. For many reasons, both selfish and altruistic, he wanted to make sure Ravi truly believed that Gemma was who he was going to spend the rest of his life with. They also talked about the gravity of Gemma's situation once she had left. Living with a dangerous man was one thing, but running away from one put her in an even more perilous situation in lots of ways. And Ravi too.

In trying to get his head around the whole situation, Alec had often read back the texts that he and Ravi had exchanged while he was off on his travels. Deep down, he also knew it was because he hoped that the more he read the story of their falling in love, that Ravi had essentially laid out for him in real time, the more inured to his heartache he would become.

Alec had been in New York when he first heard of Gemma. It was a Friday night.

Ravi: *Fit new barmaid at the Gillie's Rest tonight.*
Ravi: *Cute too. Nice smile. You'd like her. Was chatting to her for a bit just there.*
Ravi: *Dammit. She's married. Thought I'd met The One tonight mate lol.*
Alec: *Sorry I missed these mate, was working and now out to dinner in Greenwich Village. Sorry to hear about The One too! Better luck next time.*
Ravi: *Ooft. A bit rough this morning. After the new barmaid left we had a lock in. Must have been drowning my sorrows lol.*

Their texts for couple of weeks were just the usual chit chat, no Gemma. Then one Saturday:

Alec: *How's it hanging? What have I been missing in the 'hood these past couple of weeks?*
Ravi: *Mate! Was just about to text you. All good here, a bunch of us were down the Gillie's Rest last night.*
Alec: *How's the head today then?*
Ravi: *Fine. Quite a tame one. The new barmaid (called Gemma btw)*

was working. I had a nice chat with her. Everyone asking for you btw.
Alec: *Tell them thanks. Could have murdered a pint with you all last night. A bit dry over here, in more ways than one.*
Ravi: *Will do.*
Ravi: *Wasn't the only one gutted that she's married. B looked like he was about to start putting in a shift with her until I told him.*
Alec: *Who's married?*
Alec: *Oh, the barmaid, got it. Sorry, gtg, chat soon.*

Then the following Saturday:

Ravi: *Another Friday night without you at the Gillie's. We're getting used to it you know, better get back soon.*
Ravi: *Was telling Gemma about you. She was asking about the 10k race up at the castle in a few weeks, and I told her I'm best mates with the next Laird. She was impressed!*
Alec: *You should get yourself over here and we can go on the pull with the old Laird chat up line together! Your exotic dark looks from somewhere in the far off Empire, and me with the ancient Scottish routes and a family coat of arms. We'd clean up!*
Ravi: *Less of the Empire. Still too soon my friend!*
Ravi: *Nah, I wish I could come visit. No time off work – the old man is working me hard. Anyway, I'm training for the 10k now!*
Alec: *What? You can't run the length of yourself!*
Ravi: *I dunno, just kind of fancied it when Gemma and I were talking.*
Alec: *Oh this'll be fun to follow. Let me know how the training goes Mo Farah! It'll be one of my sisters handing out medals – say hi from me. If you make it to the finish line.*

Reading back through the texts it was obvious that Ravi was mentioning Gemma more and more, consciously or subconsciously hoping Alec would prod the topic, but he didn't at first.

Ravi: *First training run done!*
Alec: *Oh here we go. Is all your chat going to be running chat now? Like when B got a road bike and Lycra.*
Ravi: *Ha!*
A few days later:
Ravi: *Starting the second week of training with a run round your gaff. Told Gemma I'd take her along that footpath your dad built along the loch. Think it's part of the route.*
Ravi: *It was to nice to be back up at the castle. I showed Gemma around a bit. Where we used to have that rope swing. Where we used to smoke. She loved it up there.*
Alec: *All I'm thinking when I read that is you took a married woman into the old summer house, you randy wee git!*

Ravi didn't reply to that. Alec later found out that was where they first kissed. The abandoned summer house had witnessed illicit activities progress with age: playing with matches; looking at a dirty magazine they had found in a workers' shed; first cigarette; first can of cider – and then, a first kiss at the start of an affair with a married woman.

There was bound to be a late-night, alcohol infused confession, and it came early one Saturday morning, or a Friday night for Alec.

Ravi: *You around mate?*
Alec: *Just caught me, I'm on my way out. What's up?*
Ravi: *It can wait.*
Alec: *No it's fine I have ten minutes.*
Ravi: *I'm in deep mate. Gemma and I are seeing each other. Not just for 10K training.*
Alec: *What? Oh mate.*

Ravi: *I know. It's a disaster. But I can't not see her. I'm in love with her Alec.*
Alec: *Jesus Ravi.*
Ravi: *I know.*
Alec: *What's the husband like?*
Ravi: *Awful. Nasty piece of work. A bad bastard.*
Alec: *You sure? No offence, but it's kind of what she would say.*
Ravi: *I'm sure. And she's not like that at all. You'll see when you meet her. You're going to love her. God, she's magic Alec.*
Alec: *What does she see in you then?*
Ravi: *Honestly I don't know. She's far too good for me. But that means she's making me a better person. I mean I'm running a 10k next week for God's sake. That's all her influence.*
Alec: *She fell for the Ravi Shah cheeky charm and looks then?*
Alec: *In all seriousness though Ravi, not gonna lie, this sounds like a bit of a mess.*
Ravi: *I know.*
Alec: *Mate, I'm sorry but I've got to go. Let's talk tomorrow.*

When they spoke on the phone the next day, Alec got the whole story. He'd never heard Ravi talk like this before – he was well and truly besotted. Ravi didn't have any answers about the future, other than he had to be with Gemma and she said she felt the same. Alec hadn't known what to make of the conversation. Before the call he'd planned to counsel Ravi to end the relationship, and after it he'd come around to somehow rooting for the star-crossed lovers. Gemma did indeed sound like something special and it was nice to hear his best friend so happy and 'settled down', as much as you can be settled down with someone you only see for training runs, her shift at the pub and the very occasional stolen chance of more amorous activities.

Once it was out in the open, Gemma would be referred to

often in their text conversations, but her circumstances were seldom mentioned.

Alec: *Was just looking at Mid-June news online to see if I could see your sorry ass struggling over the finish line at the 10k. I saw the news about the restaurant business – a collab with the Indian guy who won MasterChef? That's massive! Congrats. How did that come about?*
Ravi: *Right?! The restaurant arm of the business has been getting some long-needed TLC – we redecorated, and the chef added a few really imaginative new dishes to the menu. I'd love to expand too. Gemma has a background in the hospitality industry and had some great ideas for social media. We tagged the MasterChef guy or something in one of the posts and he reached out to us.*
Alec: *Wow! That's amazing.*
Ravi: *Gemma's amazing.*
Alec: *I'm sure she is.*
Ravi: *I can't wait for you to meet her. I know I keep saying it, but you're going to love her.*
Alec: *I'm sure I will.*

And of course, when he finally did meet her, he did.

If asked, he wasn't sure he'd be able to explain clearly why it was that as Ravi and Gemma's plan formed and iterations came and went, he had always formed a key role. He did know that whenever they protested that he was doing enough already by lending them his flat, and that they'd manage on their own, he'd insist that a plan for today with him in it, made more sense. Hell mend him then, that it was torture every time he saw them from his view in the back seat, as they smiled over at each other in quiet, nervous excitement.

13

Inez and Katie

'OK good, we're not alone. There's another car behind us now,' Inez was relieved for something else to talk about apart from the lack of cell phone service. She looked intently at the rear-view mirror watching the car come closer. She squinted. 'Good God. What's in the passenger seat? Is it a big blue cuddly toy?'

'What? You hallucinating now? Did you take a few of your special mushrooms before I got up this morning?' Katie lifted her head from her vain phone vigil, and looked over her shoulder. 'Bloody hell, right enough what is that?' She squinted and paused, then asked again, 'What the hell is that?'

The car rolled slowly to a stop, sensibly at quite a distance behind them since clearly there was no benefit in sitting on a stationary car's bumper. Inez frowned into the rear-view mirror still. Katie maintained her rear facing position but sunk down slightly, so she was partially hidden behind the sleek headrest, an instinctual reaction so as not to be caught staring. It took a few seconds, then Inez said, 'Is it –, is it just a woman in a bright blue hat?' She said it tentatively because it was almost as ridiculous as the cuddly toy theory at this hour in the morning at a traffic light at the Glass Pass.

'God you're spot on. What the hell? I think we're both hallucinating now! Was it the not-quite-ripe strawberries? I mean really! I'm trapped in Mid-June on a really important day in my career, I can't get in touch with anyone to let them know what's going on, there's a nervous but handsome policeman with dubious taste in umbrellas, and now there's some random behind us in a – what is that? An electric blue trilby. I'm waiting to feel my teeth crumbling and then I'll know it's a dream.'

Inez chuckled and patted Katie's leg, but Katie just looked ahead again and exhaled with a helpless 'honestly!'

'Oh look, here comes our friend Constable Calum again,' Inez noticed the young policeman on the move. He had decided against the umbrella this time, wisely, Inez thought. She could see enough into the police car to think that his partner was older and wondered if he had influenced this decision. Calum strode past their car with a nod and mini salute, perhaps to acknowledge they were still there, right where he'd left them.

Inez and Katie watched in their respective mirrors as he gave the car behind the bad news. The girl in the hat was gesticulating, which mainly involved pointing at her hat. 'What do you think she's saying?' Inez said with a twinkle in her eye. '*This hat is stuck on my head – I need to get to a hospital?*'

Katie laughed and counter-suggested, '*Look? Can't you see I have terrible dress sense and need to get to a Glasgow stylist immediately?*'

'She's not for taking it off though. Funny.' Inez continued to watch the exchange and said, 'Poor Calum, it's not his fault. I wonder if he's told them that their phones won't work here.' As he walked away, the passenger in the hat slumped back in her seat.

Ally and Jill

'WELL AT LEAST NO phone service means George can't get in touch with me to ask me any stupid questions like *do his own children like milk*. But – if we don't get to see Take That tonight...' Jill's voice cracked at the devastating thought.

Ally had felt a little sorry for the young policeman as Jill had grilled him. It was just because she was so excited. Ally was too, but Jill needed this night away more. She reassured Jill, 'We have absolutely tons of time to make it up to Glasgow.'

'But we wanted to get ready together, dance and sing in our pyjamas drinking fizz.'

'We'll still have plenty time for that, I'm sure. Worst comes to worst and we're running really late, you can put on your make up while I drive, crack open a bottle and crank up the tunes. Promise. We're going to see Take That tonight and it's going to be fun!'

Jill was a little consoled. 'Have you told any of the people who work for you why you're off for the next couple of days?'

'I was deliberately vague. I have the boss-woman image to maintain. Imagine if they saw us in our trilbies, sobbing that we are finally getting to see Take That after all these years of fandom?'

'Oh I'll be sobbing! Maybe Gary will pick me out of the crowd and take me away from my humdrum life.'

'Nah, that would be three more kids if you ran off with him. And he has a wife and probably a few nannies. Do you think he's heard of the mental load? Not a chance.'

'True. I'll stick with my Gary fantasies from the nineties.'

'It was always Robbie for me. Maybe that's why I'm still single. No one could ever live up.'

'That and you're too busy winning awards – Prince's Trust alum, Scottish Business Accelerators Woman-of-the-year 2015.'

Not really, more like the other way around, Ally thought. Part of the reason her business was thriving was because she had plenty time on her hands, no special-someone competing for her attention. But she couldn't complain about that to Jill, who had three people demanding all her time and energy, stretching her to her limits. Ally wasn't sure if Jill would be envious or feel sorry for her, that when she woke up at the weekends, she wondered how on earth she was going to fill two days of leisure time. Most of her friends were married with kids. She had expected to be by this age too. Despite appearances, she was sorry that it hadn't worked out that way.

'Well when you put it like that, you're right, I'm too good for Robbie anyway,' Ally said, trying not to get too embroiled in the praise. Jill was her biggest cheerleader, bragged about her to all the new friends she'd made through having the two kids, but she could get carried away. She only saw the gloss, with no idea of how hard things were behind the scenes. But she was so run-ragged and needed an escape when they got time together, that Ally stuck to the good stories or some of the more gossipy or glamorous bits of life at Alison Lees Events Management.

'Far too good for him! Do you think he'll make a surprise appearance tonight?'

'I think that's what everyone who's gone to any of their concerts has wished for and they've all been disappointed.'

'Spoil sport,' Jill pouted.

'I know, sorry, practical me as always.'

Jill returned to her original train of thought and said, 'You always did everything first. You were the leader and I was the follower. I was sure you'd be married and with kids before me. What I mean is, I always thought you'd do all that first and I could just follow along a bit later, copying everything you were doing, learning from your no doubt amazing maternal wisdom.'

'Are you kidding me? You didn't need me to be the pioneer – you're doing a stellar job of all this being a mum malarkey. It'll be the other way round, if I...' she stopped short, not really wanting to explore the possibility of having kids of her own right now. Or at all really. But Jill had stopped listening and started answering when she heard Ally saying, 'amazing job.'

'I'm really not Ally. Doing an amazing job. Far from it. The other night I was so exhausted I told them they could watch TV a bit later instead of a bedtime story because George wasn't home yet to take over. And even when he is, he'll take them to brush their teeth and before he puts them into bed for their story, he'll bring them back into the living room to kiss me goodnight and my heart sinks. My heart sinks to kiss my own kids! I just can't be near them anymore. I need some space and just an hour before I have to go to bed just zoning out, watching TV or looking at my phone. Or both.'

'I think that's reasonable, no? I don't know how you do it, without any time to yourself. I need recharging time.'

'Ha! Well don't have kids then. There's no recharging time. It's never-ending.'

Ally said nothing.

'I mean obviously I don't regret it, but no one tells you this stuff. The real stuff. I thought I knew everything from reading books and social media.'

'Social media? You know that's all fake, right?'

'Well of course I do now. I've never once breastfed with my long glossy locks over one shoulder in a gauzy dress for example.'

'Ha! Not quite! I remember you pulling lettuce out your giant bra!'

'Cabbage actually. Reduces the swelling. When the health

visitor told me that I was like, oh great, I'm haemorrhaging like no period I've ever known, covered in baby sick, the bedroom smells of nappies and now I'll smell of boob-sweat-cabbage too?'

'Boob-sweat-cabbage! Mmm, sounds lovely.'

'God! Poor George. It's been a lot for him too. Sleeping beside someone with cabbage in their bra. Honestly, it's awful. Do we keep these things a secret from couples for the survival of the human race?'

'Maybe. Look at you though. You're not even an hour away from him and now he's "poor George" and you're talking like you're in it together again. I haven't heard you talk like that lately. You need this wee break. It's good for your relationship already.'

'I really do. Well, our fate is with them for now,' she nodded towards the police car. 'Let's put on some Take That and have a wee sing-song.'

Tom and Calum

CALUM UPDATED Tom on the inhabitants of the second car, a sleek silver car, and said that they were heading Up-By to see Take That, (*Of course I've heard of Take That! I'm middle-aged, not from Mars,* Tom had puffed), which was why they had to make the journey today and couldn't postpone their trip until tomorrow.

'Is the blue hat a thing? I mean, is it because she's going to a concert?'

'I think so,' Calum replied, but not confidently. 'There was a bright pink one in the back seat anyway, so I hope it's a thing.'

'Did you get a look in the back seat of the first car?' Tom remembered that he was just as bemused by the first car, since Calum had given him a rough profile of the driver, and probably therefore the owner, of the sporty bright yellow car and it was entirely unexpected. Not to mention they were on their way to TV studios. Who knew that the residents of Mid-June had such exciting reasons to travel Up-By?

'The back seats were laid flat and it looked like lots of cake cases.'

'Cake cases? Full or empty?'

'Full, by the look of it. You getting excited there Big Man? Maybe she's a TV chef – oh, hang on, is she?' Calum pondered.

'Well, is she? You've lost me.'

'Both the aunt and the niece looked very familiar to me is all, but I can't quite place them. So I wondered if she's a cook on TV.'

'It's not just from round and about that you recognise them?' Tom asked.

'Probably. Just thought I'd place them quicker than this if it was. We even introduced ourselves and it didn't trigger any recognition.'

'What were the names?'

'Inez, aunt, Katie, niece. "Blair" is their last name. For both. Aunt would be roughly your age. Maybe a little younger.'

'Hmmm, Inez? Nope I've never known an Inez. Pretty name though.'

'She's a pretty woman too,' Calum said.

Tom replied with the five iconic notes of the intro to that famous Roy Orbison song. Then he paused. Then sang them again. Calum couldn't resist, of course. That super-memory also knew the words to any song you cared to mention. Tom sang along for a bit, then interrupted with 'Alright alright, Simon Cowell's not around. Let's save our voices for when he is.' And they resumed their quiet vigil, Tom with a quiet smile as he remembered when he used to sing the song to Ann.

14

Inez and Katie

'I'm bo-ored,' Katie exaggerated a whining tone.

Inez smiled, trying not to roll her eyes at her twenty-nine-year-old niece sounding like a kid trapped in a traffic jam at the Glasgow Fair. 'That's because you're always on that phone and don't know how to just – be.' Her tone was kind not chiding. 'We could have a wee chair dance like the car behind,' she added, nodding in the mirror at her view of the young women who appeared to be making the most of things. Katie didn't even look around.

'I'm too grumpy. Tell me a story to cheer me up. Please?' She looked at Inez imploringly.

'Och you know all my stories Katie. I'm just your plain, boring Aunt Inez.'

'Neither of those is true, and I actually don't know all the stories. When I was pitching that we could use you for this bit to my producers, I realised there were a lot of gaps. Obviously I mentioned where they might recognise you from, if they were a certain age. I hope that's OK – I thought it would save time on them all trying to place you.'

'A certain age? Cheeky!' Inez feigned offence, but said, 'I suppose it was a long time ago now. Tempus fairly fugits after all. It's a funny thing though, sometimes it seems like yesterday, sometimes it feels like it was during another era.'

'Well, I guess it was another century. Another millennium even,' Katie pointed out the obvious. 'But it feels like what happened should have been the beginning of a story, not the end.'

'I suppose it was the beginning of our friendship with *** that counts. I wouldn't change that for the world. Neither would Andy.'

'I know. It just might have launched you onto bigger things.'

'Och shoosh, I wasn't the glamor puss you thought I was when you were young. I was just a wee lassie from Berry, and Andy a wee boy from Glasgow. Still am. Well, an old lady now.'

'And Uncle Andy an old queen!' They both laughed.

'OK, well if you're not going to fantasise about what might have been, tell me about meeting Andy.'

'Ah, my Andy. Lucky me – the right time, the right place, the right scabby bus to London. Same matching set of concerned mums seeing their seventeen-year-olds on to a bus with hardly any cash in their pockets and no jobs.'

'I can't even imagine that nowadays.'

'I know, but I suppose in *their* day you left school and got jobs at fourteen or fifteen, never mind that boys went off to National Service at eighteen, so although they were clucking hens, us two numpties heading off to London wasn't as unthinkable back then. And your Gran wanted me to travel and have a bigger life than she'd had.'

Inez remembered the scene clearly. 'We were there in the bus station, pretty calm and organised as you'd expect, Gran insisting on tying her tartan scarf onto my backpack, and there they came in a flurry. Moira's bosom led the way, then the rest of her, then Andy with his 1970s electrocuted mullet, which was styled by the bold Moira herself. He had this skinny tartan scarf from a charity shop around his neck that he thought made him look like Mick Jagger. In one hand he had a dainty suitcase that Moira had been given as a wedding present. Like a trousseau thing. It was duck egg blue leather, with rounded edges and gold clasps. Wouldn't have held one pair of platform shoes, so good job he was wearing his only pair. His other bag was a carpet bag, so he looked like a cross between a wannabe Rolling Stone, a sixties Pan-Am air hostess and Mary Poppins!' They both laughed at the image.

'Moira, all five-feet-two of her was managing to outrun him, shouting behind in thick Glaswegian, "*Moan hurry up son! I told you no tae wear they stupit shoes! Yer gonnae miss yer bus tae London.*" Your Gran's ears pricked up – you know how she liked to make friends for people. She said, "*Right Inez, he might be your first new pal, as long as his daft wee mother isn't going too.*"'

'Aww, "*daft wee mother*", Katie said, 'and then they were lifelong friends. It really is such a *Sliding Doors* moment. I can't imagine any of our lives without them in it. So who spoke to whom first?'

'Oh, Moira, of course. But she always did take the scattergun approach to *a worry shared is a worry halved.* She peppered us with a dozen questions: *was this the right stop, where did we get the tickets, what had your Gran made me for my packed lunch, maybe Andy and I could sit together on the bus so neither of us got landed with some dirty old pervert.* Meanwhile Andy was flicking either his scarf or his mullet over his shoulder, trying to look cool, and standing a little bit away from the dainty duck-egg blue suitcase, pretending it wasn't his.'

'What did you make of him? I'd have loved to have known him then,' Katie asked.

'It was nice to see someone nervous. Everyone else around seemed to have done the journey before. I think I had the measure of him fairly quickly, trying to look all worldly, trying not to stand out that this was going to be his first time crossing a border. In those days someone from the East End of Glasgow like him didn't even know the same city had a West End. Although he was technically the city mouse to my country mouse, his life was pretty small. He knew one block of high-rise flats, two schools, one shop, one off-sales, one pub. It was hardly cosmopolitan. He'd never have admitted that at the time of course. He liked to make out he knew all the haunts in the centre of town and who the players were at the time, but I guessed quite quickly he was bluffing most of it. He didn't have the money to be a man about town – they didn't even have the money to get a train down to Ardrossan when the rest of Glasgow was heading there in the summer.'

'That's so sad,' said Katie.

'Well it is, but it wasn't unusual. Travel, apart from maybe to the west coast, was for middle-class people. Even the outdoors was a middle-class thing. Do you think people in Andy's dad's world had heard of Munro-bagging? They worked, and at the weekend they had football, and their local pub.'

'True. Certainly can't imagine Moira with a knapsack and hiking boots!'

'Oh God! What a sight that would have been!' Inez agreed. 'When he comes to visit now and we go off on our jaunts up the West Highland line, or over to one of the islands, he'll still say every time that he can't believe these things were always there. Then he'll imagine what Moira would have made of it and wish he'd taken her traveling before she passed away. He'll get sad that not only did she never leave Scotland, but she didn't even get to experience how beautiful her own country was. Never even went to Edinburgh.'

'So, there he was, a poor man's Marc Bolan – did you talk to him first?'

'Yes I did. I said, "*Nice shoes*".'

'Oh of course, that's why you say that to each other every time you see each other after a long time.'

'Yup!'

'He still tells me he thought you were the most stunning woman he's ever seen.'

'Och he's got as blurry a memory as you,' Inez shook her head.

'Almost turned him straight he says. Or bi at least.'

'Oh, he'd have loved to be bi – there was a lot of it around then, very fashionable,' Inez laughed. 'Mostly because we both loved Bowie, and Bowie used to tease his adoring devotees who lapped up his every word. One minute he was declaring he was gay and always had been, then being exotically bisexual, then gay again, and all-the-while women he'd been with were adamant there was nothing homosexual about him at all. So a wee bit later, in those glory days you dream of, Andy would hang off me, and wax lyrical to people calling me an exquisite being, a magnificent beauty, his muse, and hope that people would subconsciously pick up on it as enigmatic sexuality.'

'His muse? Weren't you both bartenders? What artistic endeavours of his were you inspiring?'

'Exactly! You know Andy, never let the facts get in the way of a fabulous persona he has in his head that day.' They both had a wee chuckle.

'So there you have it, the first two of the three musketeers meeting each other. We sat together on the bus and waved to your Gran and Moira until they were out of sight. He dropped whatever facade he was aiming for, and we shared our life stories, humdrum as they were, and our dreams, lofty as they were, and by the time we got off the bus, we were planning to look for a bedsit together.' Inez paused and her smile dropped slightly as the memory changed from warm reminiscing of an oft-told story to the memories of them trying to find a place. There was no need to share the grittier parts of that story with Katie. Andy wouldn't want her to either.

'OK, so I'm always confused about when you found out Andy was gay. He didn't tell you that first day?'

'Well he found his confidence to camp it up a lot more and dabble in pretending to be some kind of bi-Bowie type once we'd been in London a for a while. That day on the bus though, I just thought he was a wee bit different, and I was expecting everyone to be different to people in Mid-June – I was hoping they would be. I wasn't thinking every time I met anyone who was slightly more worldly than the other pupils at my village school, that they were gay. I think I had once asked Gran what homosexual met, and she said something like "*some men like to go out with men instead of women*". But it seemed so far-fetched, I thought she meant one in a million. Or maybe she meant in America. I had always thought the chances of me ever knowing a homosexual were slim to none.'

'But you said your favourite thing to do was watch *Top of the Pops* with Gran. Couldn't you tell that a lot of the performers must be gay?'

'No, we just thought it was fashion. Everything was so androgynous.'

'Well, yeah that's true. But Andy, really?' Katie paused, pondering her own rhetorical question. Then asked, 'What do you think people in the high-rises made of him?'

'I don't think they knew what to make of him. The grown-ups probably called him effeminate, and he says kids would yell "poof" at him, but I don't think anyone fully understood, or wanted to, what either of those meant. No one else they knew was gay, so as long as he kept himself to himself, they just put him down as a wee bit eccentric.'

'That's incredible now. He must have felt so isolated.'

'Well, that's one of the reasons he was heading to London of course, but a larger gay population there didn't make it easier at first. Their visibility meant there was more prejudice against them and walking through certain neighbourhoods Andy would get verbal abuse from a hundred yards down the road. He'd never experienced it before. And we got it the minute we got off the bus.'

'Trying to find somewhere to stay, right?' Katie had heard various snippets of the story over the years. She was always such a wee quiet listener, taking everything in.

'Yes. We had heard, I can't remember how, maybe it was just common knowledge, that people who owned bedsits or had rooms to rent came to meet the bus coming in from up north. We thought our biggest problem was going to be that people thought we were a couple, because rooms couldn't be let to unmarried couples at that time. And we looked so young, no-one would be looking for any runaway Romeo and Juliet drama.'

'You're kidding! Even in the late seventies? I mean hadn't minds been opened up after the swinging sixties?'

'You would think, but I guess laws hadn't caught up. We had a story ready that we were cousins because sharing a room was so much cheaper and seemed like fun anyway. So sure enough we got off the bus to a few people holding up handwritten rooms-for-rent signs, and we had figured we were the only brand new London imports on that bus, so we'd have our pick. We went up to them, our stories ready and couldn't believe when one-by-one they turned us down, with pretty feeble excuses.'

'And you think it's because they could tell Andy was gay?'

'Yes. As I say, there were pros and cons to a more diverse population.'

'And then you finally got something just because the landlord fancied you? Bit of a dirty old man, right? Lucky for you, you got jobs quickly and the pub had digs.'

'See?' Inez said patting Katie on the leg. 'I told you that you know all my stories already.' She turned to face forward out of the window, letting the story conclude in that simple summation and the car go quiet. Katie resumed the futile tapping on her phone, but Inez's mind was still at the bus terminus.

INEZ AND ANDY had wondered what the hell was going on and why anyone who had rooms to let would be blocking them when there wasn't a deluge of room-takers. They were wondering what to do next when someone appeared from nowhere, seemingly out of the shadows, and said, 'Hey guys, you need rooms?'

'Yes please!' they'd replied, relieved and excited, and explained they'd only need one since they were going to share.

Inez shuddered now to remember the conversation with the balding middle-aged man in his grubby cardigan as he told them he had two small rooms, but he'd charge them the same as they'd pay for one bigger room. They'd be on the same floor and sharing a bathroom, so it seemed like the best of both worlds – sharing but not sharing.

As Inez had just told Katie, she'd expected everything to be different in London, but that also meant she hadn't established a baseline for her survival instincts – who to trust, when to know when something wasn't right. The man was keen, and Inez could feel him perusing them slowly as they had a quick confab – as if they had a choice right now, late night in a strange city with nowhere to stay. They got in his car, Andy in the front, Inez in the back, and he drove them for about twenty minutes to a Victorian semi-detached house, driveway and everything. Perhaps the respectability of the house and the neighbourhood quashed any uncomfortable feelings about their new landlord, and inside the house was just as nice.

The two rooms were on a half landing and had in fact been one room which had been split down the middle, creating rooms which were the equal and opposite of each other. The bathroom was up another half-flight of stairs, where the landlord's bedroom was, but he assured them he had his own en-suite so they would only be sharing the bathroom with each other. They weren't sure of the etiquette at this point and were relieved when he acknowledged how tired they must be and he'd talk them through things like keys, transport and house rules the next day. He took an early morning walk he said, so he'd see them on his return.

Inez and Andy watched him go upstairs and shut his bedroom door and looked at each and smiled. 'First night in the big smoke then my gorgeous new friend,' Andy whispered holding his arms open for a hug. Inez hugged him and held on for a while, tired from it all – an early start and a long journey, the exhilarating feeling of fresh, new friendship and that little stressful blip at the end of their day, thinking they might be sleeping on the streets. All was well now and they separated and Andy whispered, 'Bagsy me first in the bathroom!' and dived into his room to rummage around for his wash bag.

Inez closed her door and pulled her own wash bag out and placed it on a chair that was placed by the side of the bed to serve as a bedside table, ready to use the bathroom when she heard Andy come back down the stairs. She lay back on the bed exhausted thinking she might not be able to stay awake even that long. Even though he was a new friend of less than a day, she suspected Andy would be someone who took a long time in the bathroom. She forgave herself for not brushing her teeth and washing her face, just for today, and gave in to sleep.

It was impossible to tell from such a swift descent into deep sleep how long it had been before she heard footsteps. They seemed to stop on the small landing outside both the bedroom doors. She listened carefully but didn't hear anything more. Maybe it was just a creaky old house or maybe she'd only been asleep for a few minutes and it was just Andy going to bed. Her room was pitch dark, so it was hard for her drowsy eyes to fight to stay awake to allay any niggling fears, and she gave in to sleep once more, something that she regretted to this day.

The next time she awoke was to the slam of a door downstairs, she assumed the front door. Getting her bearings she assessed the time of day by the amount of light hitting the ceiling above the window as it shone over the top of the curtains. The light was low, and she concluded their landlord was indeed taking a very early morning walk, hence the slam of the door. She didn't have time for another thought before there was a quiet but urgent knocking at the door and Andy's voice, also hushed and urgent, 'Inez, are you awake? Can I come in?'

'Yes, and yes, come in,' Inez said, sitting up as he opened the door. Andy was wide awake, fully dressed, holding the duck-egg blue suitcase, the carpet bag standing on the landing behind him.

'Are you OK? What's going on?' Inez asked, feeling her heart race.

'We need to get of here Inez. Did you sleep in your clothes? Good, just get your shoes on, and let's get going. Here...' Andy dived at her shoes and thrust them at her, then he went on to zip the unopened wash bag into her backpack. Inez took her shoes, bewildered but with a knot in the pit of her stomach telling her she shouldn't be – she knew what had happened, or could have made a good guess.

Andy's next words were confirmation. 'We need to get out of here before that dirty old bastard gets back from his walk.'

The knot tightened, and she could only say, 'Oh God Andy, I'm sorry.'

'Listen don't worry about me, I'm OK. It could have been a

lot worse. It was a short and sharp encounter – I told him to fuck off and that if he came back in the night waving that thing in my face again, I'd bite it off.'

Day two of their friendship was starting out completely differently than day one and Inez was immediately impressed at Andy's resilience. She thought she'd have died had the awful man's predilection been towards young women instead of young men, but here Andy was, all business, getting them out of their rooms quickly and efficiently. She put her hand to her mouth and thought she was going to cry and could only say again, 'Andy, I'm sorry' softly.

He stopped his busy gathering up of their things and looked at her kindly. 'Inez, I'm fine really. Let's just get out of here for now.'

That first night stayed a secret only the two of them shared. Andy refused to give the experience any emotional room in his life, saying, 'I refuse to remember that poor excuse for a willy as my first cock. The first time I have someone's cock in my face is going to be magnificent.'

Andy was more worldly than she'd given him credit for as she'd watched him self-consciously play the part of an androgynous icon at the bus station. It was Inez that lost part of her innocence in the whole experience, not Andy.

In days to come, safely in their digs that came with their new jobs at the pub, their only regret was that they didn't take five minutes that day to do something nasty to the dirty old pervert, and they'd try to outdo each other with imagined vile acts of retribution, like wiping his toothbrush round the toilet bowl, or Andy peeing a little in a carton of orange juice.

Inez glanced across at Katie, glad her thoughts of her aunt's life in London were of Tramp, Annabel's, and Inez and Andy riding along on ***'s coattails to glamorous events. She reached over again and patted her thigh.

'You twitching without your phone pet?'

'Inez, I'm going CRAZY!'

15

Alec, Gemma and Ravi
Road to Nowhere, Talking Heads

As they rounded the corner and could see the road climb towards the Glass Pass, they noticed two cars waiting at a red light, and up the hill a bit further, parked facing down towards the road, a police car.

'Oh no, what's going on here?' Gemma said.

Alec stooped to look out the windscreen from his place in the back seat and said, 'It's just cars waiting to get through. The light's at red.'

'I meant the police car Alec!' Gemma said curtly.

'That'll be nothing too. Just keeping an eye on things.' Alec said gently and touched her shoulder. 'We're not doing anything wrong. We're just going Up-By for a night in Glasgow remember. We're not on the lam,' he added trying to make her laugh.

'Not from the police we're not, but the minute John figures

out I've left, we're on the run from him. So I just want to get over the Pass and start getting some miles between us and him.'

'I know, I know,' Alec said quietly and patted her shoulder one more time.

Ravi offered his hand as he continued to drive and Gemma took it, managing a smile over at him. Alec removed his hand from her shoulder, feeling slightly foolish and reminded that he was firmly the third wheel. Would the other two even remember he was there when they reminisced about their Great Escape in their dotage? He looked ahead and his heart sank when the first sign came within reading distance.

'*Road closed ahead?*' Gemma read with a gasp.

'Oh God,' Ravi said very quietly and looked over at Gemma, whose eyes were welling up with tears. Then another sign exactly the same, confirming their fears. The small, cruel ray of hope that the yellow car and silver car ahead had similarly been subjected to at the *Traffic Likely* and then then fourth sign declaring for the third time *Road Closed Ahead* made Alec's heart sink again. Ravi tried to lift Gemma's hand to kiss it in comfort, but she drew it away and put her head in her hands and started to cry. Alec realised he had never seen her cry. He knew the tears had come fast because of the adrenaline, but his heart ached nonetheless. They drew to a halt behind the silver car.

'Oh good, look,' Ravi nodded up the hill. The policeman on the passenger side had got out and after turning back towards the car and giving a small salute, was heading towards them. 'There's a copper already heading down the hill. He must be coming to tell us what the deal is.'

'Why is that good, Ravi?' Gemma snapped, briefly lifting her head from her hands.

'Gemma, love, try to stay calm. It'll be helpful to know what's going on. After all, we won't be able to google it. There's no phone reception on this stretch.'

Alec knew this too, but looked at his phone anyway, and as it was confirmed, he slammed his phone onto the seat, rolled his head back against the headrest and let out a long quiet breath, feeling helpless. Gemma was trying to stifle sobs and grabbed a tissue to wipe her eyes as the policeman got closer. Ravi squeezed her leg, and said, 'Gemma, look at me. Look at me please love.' She composed herself and looked back into his eyes. 'It's all going to be fine. I promise you. We're not going to let anything get in the way of getting you out of here and safely up to Glasgow. There's going to be a solution to this, I promise.'

Calum

After his salute back to Tom, Calum muttered to himself, 'Bearer of bad news has to be muggins here again' as he walked down towards his latest customers of the day. A compact sensible car, unremarkable compared to the first two. No fancy extras like tinted windows on this one. In fact he could see the occupants quite clearly. The man in the driver's seat looked to be of Indian or Pakistani descent, then there was a woman in the passenger seat, and another man, taking up a lot of the small back seat, who had his head back looking at the ceiling. All a little older than himself he guessed.

Then he thought it strange what happened between the two front seat passengers. Looking at the woman, it looked like she was crying, or had been, and was trying to stop. Then the driver seemed to reach over and she immediately looked at him, face very serious, giving small nods of acknowledgement as he spoke. They did not break eye throughout. Calum felt uneasy. From here he thought the man was gripping the woman's leg. It was an intense conversation. And the big henchman type in the back remained stock-still.

The driver turned from the woman to roll down the

window as he reached the car and just before he did Calum saw the woman give her nose a quick wipe and take a deep breath.

Inez and Katie

'OH! Constable Hottie is on the move!' Katie said and gestured up the hill.

Inez looked in the rear-view mirror. 'Oh yeah, there's another car joined us.'

'Can you see who's in it?' Katie asked.

'I don't think I'd have much chance anyway, but definitely not seeing the other one behind us has put on a bright pink hat now!'

Katie looked back and laughed out loud. 'Those girls look like a hoot. I think I like them. I see they're getting a good nosey in the rear-view mirror at the car behind.'

'I see that. But do you think that's a bit pots and kettles given you'll have a crick in your neck from staring back at them?'

'True,' Katie admitted and turned to face ahead. 'Turn green!' she commanded through gritted teeth at the traffic light.

Ally and Jill

IGNORING THE PROTESTATIONS, Jill had returned the pink hat to Ally's head as they sang along to some Take That tunes. Ally abruptly turned the volume down as the car approaching behind caught her eye in the mirror.

'Aww, What did you do that for?'

'There's another car coming up behind,' Ally said, nodding at the mirror in explanation.

'Why did you turn the music down? To help you see it?'

'Yup,' Ally laughed. 'It's an age thing! Don't you turn down the music to read road signs?'

Jill gave a small nod of recognition but turned to the more important business of watching the car behind draw to a stop. 'What we got?' she asked Ally, who had the better view.

'Shitty wee car, man driving, woman in the passenger seat, and…', she squinted not wanting to jump the gun until she had sights on all the passengers and then confirmed '…and a large man in the back seat.'

'Age?'

'I dunno. Late twenties? Early thirties?'

'Our age then?'

'You wish! We'd struggle to count as mid-thirties anymore.'

'Thirty-six is still mid-thirties! God, don't depress me even more. Having the looks and life sucked out of me by those kids is bad enough. I'll be clinging on to my thirties for dear life. Anyway – so we've got somewhere around thirty. What do they look like?' Jill sunk down in her seat and smiled over conspiratorially.

Ally took the cue and gave her best private detective commentary. 'OK, driver is handsome and quite dark-skinned. At first, I thought his hair was a bit poufy, but now I think it's long, not long-long, just collar length, but pushed back. He has a very nice nose.'

'You can see his nose from here?'

'He's talking to the girl a lot, so I'm looking a lot at his profile. His nose just looks nice and straight and distinguished.'

'OK, got you. I'll turn and take a long but subtle look back to get my own visual after you've described them all. What does the girl look like?'

'They wouldn't notice you looking back. They look like they're in a bit of a flap. They're not happy about being stuck here – what a shocker, none of us are.' Ally paused to concentrate on her description of the girl. 'Ok, the girl. Brunette, very pretty from here – hair not quite shoulder length.'

'Bob?'

'What?' Ally was confused.

'Is it a bob haircut?'

'Hmmm, I suppose so, but it's wavy. Oh! I know who she looks like – one of the Jennifers.'

'What?' It was Jill's turn to be confused.

'One of the famous Jennifer actresses. I'll know it when you say it.'

'Jennifer Lawrence?'

'No, she's blonde, isn't she?'

'Jennifer Aniston?'

'Again, I'd say she's blonde. No. This Jennifer has really dark hair.'

'Jennifer Garner?'

'Which one is that again?'

'*13 Going on 30*. She was married to Ben Affleck?' Jill was running out of Jennifers, so she was answering with questions, as if to will Ally into remembering.

'Hmmm. I don't think so,' Ally replied.

'I think I've run out. Wow, what did people do before Google?' Jill had automatically reached for her phone before remembering they had no service. 'Oh –hang on…Jennifer Connelly! Beautiful and definitely brunette. Not a highlight in sight as far as I can remember.'

Ally's finger was at her pursed lips, and she was frowning in concentration. 'I can't picture Jennifer Connelly, but I have a feeling the person I'm thinking of is married to James Bond.'

'Which James Bond? This is like doing a crossword Ally!'

'The new one. Well, the one that's around just now I think. The one from the London Olympics.'

'Daniel Craig? He's married to Rachel Weisz.'

'Oh that rings a bell. Was she in that movie where Bill Nighy can turn back time?'

'No, that's Rachel McAdams.'

'That's it! Rachel McAdams – the girl behind looks like Rachel McAdams.' Ally turned and pointed at Jill as if she'd won at charades.

Jill looked at her in disbelief. 'So not Jennifer at all then!'

'You know what I meant. We got there eventually. Teamwork!'

'Honestly, if you'd pick up a celebrity gossip magazine now and then in your carefree single life! Right, I'm taking a look myself now anyway.' Jill pushed herself back up in her seat to more easily see around the headrest and looked back. 'Oh poor thing, all I can see is her hair – which by the way, does look exactly like Rachel McAdams in *About Time*. She has her head in her hands. She's upset. And poor them. They're about to hear the bad news from Calum. Here he comes.' The officer on the move had caught Jill's peripheral vision. 'Five minutes ago they were probably singing happily along, maybe to Take That, just like us.' Jill exaggerated the empathy in her tone.

'I doubt it,' said Ally. 'She's definitely crying.'

'Oh no, I feel bad for her,' Jill said, turning to look back again, this time the sympathy in her voice genuine. 'What's going on? She's in bits. Oh, poor thing.' A pause as they both watched. 'What's he doing? The driver looks like he's grabbed her leg. Shit, what's he saying to her? He looks like he's threatening her. Oh God Ally, what should we do?' There was panic in Jill's voice.

'Well Jill, there's a police officer about to knock on their window, so I'm thinking we're off the hook on being *Take That Fans to the Rescue* right now.'

'Right enough,' Jill said and turned to face forward, happy to rely on Ally's commentary now that the poor woman had the police onsite. '*Take That Fans to the Rescue*, though. That could be a reality show.'

Alec
Re-arrange, Biffy Clyro

ALEC SAW Ravi do a rapid reset and turn on the charm as he was so good at doing – he wasn't a salesman for nothing. He said cheerfully, 'Good morning officer. Say it ain't so. The Glass Pass isn't really closed is it?'

'Good morning to you all,' Calum glanced over at Gemma, who looked away as he did, and then back at Alec, who raised a hand in hello. 'Yes, I'm afraid it is. We are waiting for engineers to come and do a safety check of the lights, and until that's done, nothing is going up and nothing is coming down.'

Well that was clear enough, Alec thought.

'Oh ok, got it. Wow. So – any idea when the engineers will be here? How long the testing will take?'

'Not right now. What I suggested to the two cars in front of you is that if your journey is non-essential you perhaps consider delaying it to tomorrow instead.'

'Well, I suppose since they're still here, their journeys, like ours, are essential,' Ravi said politely.

Alec watched the officer look expectantly at Ravi, waiting for him to elaborate. He did not, which lead to a slightly awkward pause.

'Right, well, if you really have to be Up-By, I guess you're third in the queue as soon as we get the lights going,' was the young copper's way of testing if the reason for their journey was forthcoming.

It was not. Ravi simply smiled and said 'I suppose we are. Thanks so much for letting us know what's going on though. We really appreciate it. We'll try to entertain ourselves while we wait, without phone service.' Ravi gave a bigger smile and a knowing roll of the eyes.

'Oh thank goodness, I'm glad you knew that. That was the second piece of bad news I had to break to the two cars in front.'

'We're well aware. I travel up often for work. Did the other cars tell you where they're off to?' Ravi asked.

Alec smiled to himself at Ravi's winning ways and sure enough the officer started to tell Ravi about the destinations of the other two cars before he stopped himself, realising he was letting his guard down. This was classic Ravi charm. Things fell silent, and Ravi just smiled up at the policeman, who then patted the roof of the car awkwardly and said, 'Right you are then. We'll be just up the hill a bit there and we'll let you know as soon as we know anything further.'

'Thanks so much officer. We'll be right here!' Ravi grinned and kept grinning until the window was all the way up and the copper had his back to them. He turned quickly back to Gemma, reaching to hold her hand in her lap again. 'It's just a dodgy light my love. We'll be out of here before you know it. How long can it take to find someone to get a basic traffic light working again? Not long at all is my guess. Look at me.'

As Gemma looked up, he again fixed his gaze and said 'Do you think anyone loves you more in the world than me?' She shook her head and smiled. Encouraged by the smile, Ravi's tone lightened, and he said with a wink and a nod to the back seat. 'And the Laird back there, you know he loves you too, right? More than anything? So you're in good hands.' He leaned in and said, 'Come here,' pointing at his forehead. She leaned in too and gently laid her forehead against his, and as they looked into each other's eyes.

Alec had seen this little ritual before. He looked away. This time, it was his turn to feel his eyes welling up.

Ally and Jill

ALLY GAVE a commentary of the exchange between Calum and the occupants in the car behind, with Jill not being able to help looking behind every now and then for a firsthand visual. Just after Calum left, Ally said, 'What in the Svengali is he doing to her now?'

Jill's head whipped around to see the woman forehead-to-forehead with the driver. 'What the hell? I do not like this situation, Ally. Two guys and a girl in a car and strange behaviour like this?'

'Must admit it's got my radar twitching too.' Ally thought for a moment trying to see the story from the other side as she always did, which whether Jill knew it or not was the reason she could listen to all the stories about how useless George was, and not begin to dislike him. He was a good guy, and as Jill had even acknowledged, their busy, chaotic child-centric life hadn't been easy for him either.

'OK,' Ally continued, 'let's take some comfort in the fact that they are staying put, under the gaze of our friend Calum and his gaffer up the hill. If there were nefarious activities going on, they'd have done a U-turn and high-tailed it out of here.'

'That's a good way to think of it. You're right,' Jill agreed.

'But we're going to keep an eye on things from here too right?' Ally confirmed.

'Of course!' Jill replied. 'Hopefully we're putting two and two together and getting five, but we'll have a wee spy mission to keep us busy until this blasted red light turns green.'

Tom and Calum

Tom's vision of the occupants of the small car was obscured as Calum chatted with them, but he got to witness what happened when Calum started back towards him. It ended with the man in the driver's seat seemingly instructing the woman beside him to put her head against his, and they sat there for at least a couple of minutes, staring at each other. Watching Calum get into the passenger seat, he noticed that he did so easily, without the involuntary grunt that Tom emitted when he did. 'What's the story with that lot then?' he asked.

'Were you watching? That's an odd trio, isn't it?'

'Well, I don't know. It was you that was just talking to them. Who are they? Where they going? Why do they have to be Up-By so urgently that they're happy to wait on these engineers to show up? And what's the deal with the guy in the front being all over the girl?'

Calum shook his head. 'I don't know.'

'You don't know? The two cars in front practically gave you their life stories. You don't even know why they're heading up? Did you ask?'

'I did ask. Well, I kind of asked. Well, I think I asked.'

'Eh?' Tom said confused.

'The driver is a bit smooth.'

'He looks it – looked like he was casting a spell on that young woman when you turned away. He had some Svengali hypnosis thing going on there when you turned your back.'

'Really? That sounds a bit weird,' Calum replied. 'It's hard to explain. I would have said it was just that he had the gift of the gab. A big grin and all pleasantries. But he wasn't giving away where they are off to and it felt deliberate.'

'And who is in the back?' Tom asked.

'He didn't say a word. Just gestured hello when I looked in the car. Big guy, though.'

'The smooth guy's bodyguard?' Tom asked jokingly, but Calum answered seriously.

'No, that wasn't the vibe. They just seem like a strange threesome to be going on a road trip together. I mean in the first car we have a normal middle-aged lady driving that ridiculous car, dozens of cakes in the car, off to film something for TV and I thought that was pretty unusual. Then the next car we've got two best friends off to a concert, blasting music and chair-dancing in neon trilby hats, and we thought that was all a bit daft for this time in the morning. This third car is a plain wee car, no strange cargo or contents as far as we can see, and it's just made me feel a bit uneasy. Or maybe uneasy is too strong a word. Just curious I suppose. Why wouldn't he just explain where they're off to?'

Tom gave a quiet 'hmm' in acknowledgment and they both kept looking towards the third car. Calum drew breath to say something and changed his mind. Tom expected more theories or thoughts on the third car threesome and said, 'Penny for them then. Out with it.'

Calum said a little sheepishly. 'It's nothing very interesting. Just weird that you mentioned Svengali.'

'Ok, I'll bite. Why's that?' Tom smiled.

'Do you know the name of the novel Svengali appears in?'

'Calum, I wouldn't even have known he was from a book. To my wife's chagrin and eye rolls no doubt.'

'Aye, no doubt,' agreed Calum. 'Svengali appears in a nineteenth century novel called *Trilby*.'

'Well, ok yes, I'll give you that one – that is very coincidental. I can't remember the last time I said either "trilby" or "Svengali" and here we are this morning with a suspected Svengali in a car behind two trilbies. Well, Ann would have been annoyed at my lack of culture as usual, but she'd have found that funny,' he smiled. 'So I'm assuming a novel wasn't named after a hat, but was the hat named after the novel?'

'Almost. Trilby was the name of a young woman in the book, who was hypnotised by Svengali to become an amazing singer, and he was able to live well on her fortunes. Victorians were fascinated by mesmerism, so the book was really popular in Britain, and it introduced Bohemia as a way of life, so it was embraced for that on both sides of the Atlantic. But as for the hat –' he paused in dramatic effect and to make sure he still had Tom's attention, which wasn't guaranteed when he went down one of his rabbit holes, 'the hat didn't appear in the book at all.' He paused again.

'I'll never know how you can retain all the things you do. Go on, though – I'm on tenterhooks now,' Tom said.

'That style of hat first appeared in the stage version of the book in London. It was worn by the lead actress but somehow it became fashionable for men too, and the name stuck.'

'Well there you go. I'm glad I asked. I shouldn't retire, I should just keep working with you. I learn something new every day. You'd keep my brain alive.'

'Let's not get carried away now, Boss. A life of leisure awaits you, compared to a life of enthralling traffic duties like this in my future.' Calum gestured down at the conga line of three cars.

Tom sighed, 'Enthralling indeed.'

16

Alec
Watch How You Go, Keane

Alec was lost without access to his phone. He wanted to fix this and get Gemma out of here. Her anguish filled the small car, which felt more cramped by the minute. So many thoughts and ideas popped into his head, and he couldn't Google them to at least feel like he was doing something. He had dismissed the idea of the dreaded easterly route (not just because he'd never driven it, but because he knew he'd never talk Gemma and Ravi into risking turning and driving back through Mid-June) but he wished he could search to see if there were some old military roads or perhaps some drivable old railway lines left behind. Other, more wishful Google searches, ranged from the pragmatic, 'Private engineering services near me' in the hope of seeing to the lights himself, to the fantastical, 'Private helicopter services near me.'

The car was quiet. Alec could tell Ravi was nervous because he wasn't talking much. Ravi was never at a loss for words. Now and then he would catch Alec's eye in the mirror or briefly turn his head round to the back seat, conveying with a glance he was just as worried as Gemma, beseeching him silently to say something that would make them all feel better. But Alec had nothing.

ALEC HAD IMAGINED how things would pan out so any times. After a long but straightforward and fun journey up to Glasgow, all of them on a high that today was finally here, he'd turn the key to his flat, and Gemma would flop on the couch in the big, bright living room glowing with relief and happiness. After showing them around, they'd all have a cup of tea before Alec hit the road again. Picturing leaving them and closing the door on the flat was hard to do, but he knew it would be even harder in real life. Alec's part in the master plan would be over, and he'd never again get to see or text Gemma most days, as he had for the past few weeks. He had been instrumental in the journey but played no part in the journey's end.

Ravi was hoping to make things work as best he could not living in Mid-June – as long as John Wyllie was still there none of them could see a future where Ravi and Gemma returned there to live. The guy was a hot head with a real nasty streak. When Alec realised this running away idea was serious, he knew enough about John to realise this would be a devastating blow to a controlling maniac's ego. They had to weigh up what he was capable of in the heat of the moment versus how far he was likely to go in any premeditated acts of revenge. The former was serious enough that any thoughts of Gemma simply announcing she was leaving were ruled out as lunacy, never mind eventually having a public relationship with Ravi.

Ever a systematic thinker, Alec had pointed out the other extreme was moving abroad, perhaps even under pseudonyms. Although it was given some thought, it was agreed among the three of them that this was unnecessarily difficult and dramatic. Setting up home temporarily in Alec's flat would put some time and distance away from John – it was his vicious temper that was the biggest danger they needed to avoid for now.

For everyone's protection, no-one outside of the three people in this small car lined up in place at the Glass Pass had been told anything, including Ravi's family. The Shahs were a close-knit family. Ravi and his sister had gone to university – their father, Vikram, would have had it no other way – but they had come straight back to Mid-June after graduation to work in the family business. They all lived separately, but close to each other, in what Vikram proudly called the family compound.

Vikram had come to Scotland as a child in the sixties and against the odds, his parents found themselves on a train to the area now known as Mid-June and the tiny village of Cormully, and perhaps also against the odds they were accepted into the community almost without hesitation. The villagers quickly noticed exceptional and novel aromas coming from Mrs Shah's kitchen and one-by-one wangled themselves invites to sample her exotic cooking. Soon she was making meals for a new section of the Gillie's Rest menu entitled *Indian Fare* and eventually the Shahs were able to make a modest addition to their home and create a small Indian restaurant which today would be called 'boutique'. Glasgow may claim to have embraced Indian food first and be responsible for its spread to ubiquitousness throughout Scotland, but there was an Indian outpost in deepest Mid-June where the Shahs were independently converting the natives.

Vikram began working for the family restaurant straight

from school, and with the railway now gone, thanks to Dr Beeching, all supplies in were by road. Vikram's first job was as the van driver, up and down to Glasgow over the Glass Pass. When his fellow expats opened Cash and Carry wholesalers in the eighties, he noted that not all business owners from remote places like Mid-June made the journey to Glasgow, as the cost of the journey, plus time off from running their businesses, reduced or negated the benefit of wholesale pricing. He met with the wholesaler entrepreneurs and persuaded them that he could act as a distributor to such areas. In partnering up with them, he established and grew his own small empire.

Vikram remained extremely proud that he was a first-generation immigrant serving his family's adopted rural community. He did not take these ties for granted and talked often of how lucky they were. His wife Isha would tell him it wasn't luck – the Shah family were where they are today due to their initial generous gestures to new neighbours, then hard work, frugality and ingenuity. But Vikram would point out that they had been fortunate to land in a community where the denizens were curious, instead of suspicious, open-minded instead of insular.

Alec and Ravi sometimes talked about the similarities of their familial role models that seemed pretty unlikely given the stark contrasts in history and fortune between landed gentry ensconced in Mid-June for too long for anyone to know how long, and the Shahs. But both of their grandmothers had been brave immigrants after all and the impact of that bold female energy was being carried through generationally in both families. They laughed that growing up it was Mimi and the elder Mrs Shah, as well as Susan Douglas-Lauder and Isha Shah who could see right through them – suspect them of antics before those antics had even formed in their own heads. Neither of them was used to women playing a supporting role in family life or even family-business life – in their experience women weren't just intrinsic to both, they were leaders. Ravi felt the same as Alec, that finding someone who lived up to his grandmother's, mother's and now sister's example was a tall order. It was why they were both still single in their mid-thirties – they were holding out for a unicorn. But then Ravi met Gemma, who, although stifled by the man who had inexplicably managed to marry her, was caring, wise, dynamic and as sharp as a tack. She'd be welcomed with open arms as one of their own – if only Ravi could tell them about her.

Alec knew the Shahs would be devastated to not have Ravi close by and concerned at the circumstances that had taken him away. He had impressed upon Ravi that telling them was his first priority after he was safely ensconced in the flat, and Ravi assured him that he would. He had run through his side of the conversation in his head, including how he would remain an integral part of the business from Glasgow, and he could only hope the other side of the conversation lived up to his parents' wise and level-headed traits. Alec loved the Shahs and if he had to choose an extended family for Gemma, other than his own, it was them.

This whole caper, for want of a better word, had taken up so much of Alec's mental and emotional energy that he didn't know what he'd do once they were at 'mission accomplished'. He'd go back to Glenberry and increase his involvement in the running of the estate and gradually reduce his lecturing hours and travel. Being busy and not seeing Gemma every other day would surely help heal his heart. It was unimaginable right now, but maybe one day he'd get over her and be able to think about perhaps dating. He didn't want to be single and pining for the rest of his life. If he was to take on Glenberry, he needed a partner. But more than a partner, he hoped he'd find love as Ravi had. Alec knew them being in Glasgow and him far away was for the best in the long run.

. . .

Alec gave a huge sigh which turned into a groan on the way out. He felt utterly helpless. He'd been quiet when the copper came to explain the situation, and now he looked up at the police car and had to quell the urge to go up and batter on the windows, demanding a police escort through the Pass or any kind of action. The inertia was killing him.

17

Inez and Katie

Katie was restless. During breaks in the drizzle, she'd get out the car and pace around. Inez watched her and felt sorry for her – she knew this thing at the TV tonight was a great chance for her.

Katie had been interested in TV and film since she had been a wee girl. As a baby, she could be calmed quickly by placing her bouncy chair in front of the television set eyes wide open, appearing to take it all in. As a toddler Inez had taken her to see her first film at the cinema – *Beauty and the Beast*. She had fallen asleep in the car and stayed asleep as Inez lifted her out and carried her into the small cinema. The thundering noise of the adverts woke Katie up and as she lifted her head from Inez's shoulders, her eyes grew wider than she had ever seen them. She didn't take her eyes off the screen from when Inez carefully unwound her from her grasp into the seat until she picked her up again to leave. As a young kid she could, and would to the rest of the family's annoyance, recite favourite movies, like *The Parent Trap*, the whole way through.

No one was surprised when Katie opted to study Film and TV Studies at university. After a couple of summer internships at the BBC, she got her first job after uni there as a researcher, and she had progressed from there. Whenever she asked to talk to a boss about her career, they all assumed that she wanted to go into a role in front of the camera and her looks certainly were conducive to that path. But Katie wanted to work on the creative side – writing, producing, coming up with a concept and seeing it through from beginning to end. One of her female superiors recently offered a sympathetic ear and challenged her to come up with a topical segment for one of the evening shows and offered her the tip, 'Stick with what you know for your first one.'

Brainstorming ensued, Katie wanting to make her newfound mentor proud. Topical was one thing, but she knew it had to be at the more accessible end of current events, being as the article was for a magazine-type program, and then, as advised, she had to find something she could relate to personally. She did a little research into the history of the place she loved so much – Berry and the rest of Mid-June.

Berry and Glenberry had taken their names centuries ago because of the area's suitability for growing strawberries and raspberries. At the end of the nineteenth century and into the middle of the twentieth, the expansion of railways allowed growers to transport their berries by train to Glasgow to be distributed to the rest of the country. The industry thrived until train links were decimated in the sixties following the report by Lord Beeching. Local growers were hit badly due to the inadequacy of the road routes, or rather the singular route that included The Glass Pass. Other successful fruit growing areas of Scotland, like Perth and surrounds, were not deprived of their railway links and their roads were superior, so the industry soared there as it declined in Mid-June.

Among the far-reaching hopes there were for life after The Big Belt, one was among the berry growers who hoped that there would once more be national opportunities for them with a new up-to-date road system. Inez had told Katie all about it because she bought her berries for baking straight from one of the farms, enjoying the chance to go up there for a chat and a look around. This was when Katie hit upon combining the zeitgeist for home baking that had come about with the success of *The Great British Bake Off*, with that little bit of history from the place she considered home. She had a chance to perhaps raise its profile for when The Big Belt was completed, when berries could be exported out and tourists could be attracted in.

The proposal was well-received, and Katie presented it with such enthusiasm that her colleague couldn't resist suggesting she be involved in presenting it on TV too. She managed to convince Katie it wasn't because she was camera friendly, but because her personal touch would add extra appeal. In fact, would her aunt be the one to do the baking? Would her aunt be on the segment too?

Katie jumped at the chance of getting her aunt on TV such that she managed to ignore her own concerns about being in front of the camera instead of behind it. She couldn't resist an adventure and a bonding experience like this with her beloved aunt. This was going to be a great one. Until someone shut the bloody Glass Pass!

INEZ WATCHED Katie stroll towards the traffic light, looking it up and down with her arms folded, glancing up to see if the two policemen were watching and appreciating how frustrated she was to have no news. She knew exactly what Katie was up to and that it was only a matter of time before she'd have to talk her out of marching up the hill to give them a piece of her mind. In fact, she decided that that would be close to impossible, so it was more likely she'd accompany Katie and in order to be the good cop to Katie's frustrated cop, for want of a better expression.

If the real policemen in the car had a *good cop, bad cop* dynamic going on, it was surely the young man Calum they had met who was the good cop, and Inez wondered what the other one was like. A grumpy old sod probably. Doing as little as he could before he retired on a handsome pension and took a security job for some shady company. He'd sat there in his cozy car and made Calum come out in the rain to deliver the bad news. Who did he think he was?

Inez laughed at herself. She was getting as stir crazy as Katie, inventing a personality for someone she'd never even laid eyes on properly. And not a very flattering one at that. If she was going to invent a persona, it should be a nice one. Maybe he was a wise older mentor to Calum, kind and patient, passing on the knowledge from an admirable career well-spent. She looked up at the car and squinted. Hard to tell from here.

It was getting wetter outside again as the heavens turned the drizzle tap a tad left again and she knew what would get Katie back in the car. From her side, she rolled down the passenger window, satisfyingly as smooth as butter.

'Katie pet, get back in the car. You're getting wet.'

'Grr,' Katie said back, shaking her head making a face.

'C'mon and I'll tell you the real story of me and Uncle ***.'

Katie had been looking for a reason to get back in the car anyway, and jumped in immediately. Inez laughed. 'God you're easy.'

'You owe me one sordid story, Aunt Inez. Or a romantic one. Or both would be good right now frankly.'

'I was only kidding you on. For the millionth time, I swear there was never anything in it. We were always just good friends. He did the right thing by me the day we met and forever after. He's a kind, kind soul. My guardian angel. Things would have been very different for me – for Gran too, for all of us I suppose – if he hadn't stepped in and made sure I got what I was due.'

'And you were never tempted to take things further? I don't mean with ***,' she said quickly, as Inez started to protest again. 'I mean you, your career. Use it as a launching pad for, oh, I don't know – maybe acting? Modelling?'

'Acting? Ha! The closest I'd get to that was with this thing you got me involved in today and the likelihood of that happening is fading fast. And modelling? With the curves I had back then they'd only have wanted me for one kind of modelling, so no thank you. Or to try my hand at any other kind I'd have had to develop an eating disorder to make it.' Inez shook her head. 'Look, what happened was a lucky accident, though believe me, I didn't think so at the time. Can you imagine how worried I was about what Gran was going to say? I'd thought she'd be showing up in London to drag me home by my ponytail.'

Katie smiled. 'I don't know what's a funnier image. That, or Uncle *** as a guardian angel.' Then she chuckled.

'Right enough. That's quite a thought!' Inez laughed, and after trying to picture her old friend as an angel said, 'Spray-on leather trousers and angel wings! What a sight he'd be!' They both burst out laughing. They were infected by each other's laughter, stopping briefly with a sigh, then one or the other guffawed, and started them off again. It was no doubt cabin fever induced, but it felt good to laugh, and they let it take their mind off things.

Jill and Ally

ALLY HAD BEEN KEEPING a wary eye on the car behind. The female passenger looked like she was still crying intermittently. The driver every now and then would have a few words with her and she'd try to pull it together, but it wouldn't last long.

Jill had been more distracted by the yellow car passenger who would now and then get out and tramp around the car. She gave Ally a running commentary even though Ally was right there, mostly watching too, when she wasn't glancing in the mirror. It was in true commentary style. Short sentences which would tail off if the subject went on the move again. Longer musings if the subject was just standing back to them, seemingly taking in the vista.

'She's beautiful, isn't she? I bet she has no kids. Think she's old enough to have kids? I think she is. She'd be a young, yummy mum, but she's old enough. Know why I think she doesn't? Precisely because she is so beautiful – she's coiffed, she's poised, she's glowing. She hasn't had the life sucked out of her for nine months. Then ten months of breastfeeding. Times two.' A pause while they both watched their subject sidle up to the traffic light. 'Oh look at her giving the traffic light the evil eye. Ha! Now she's looking up at the police car. God, the look! Wouldn't be surprised if she gave them the finger! When all three cars get together and revolt, she'll be our leader. And you of course, Ally. You two will be a dream team. I can see it now.'

They kept watching as the driver talked her passenger into getting back in the car.

'What age do you think the driver is? Same age? They look like they have the same hair. They have the same silhouette,' Jill said.

Ally had assumed all questions remained rhetorical, so she didn't answer, but decided the likelihood was they were similar in age, perhaps sisters, and wondered if the driver was just as good-looking as the passenger. The two of them were now facing each other and apparently falling about laughing.

'That's some thigh-slapping laughter that's going on now! I wonder what they're talking about.' Jill resumed her commentary.

'I noticed,' chuckled Ally. Then chuckled again as it kept going. Apparently laughter was infectious even just watching through a windscreen and Ally and Jill shared a wee laugh. 'They're still going! I wonder what was so funny?'

'Should I go and ask?' Jill said. Ally should have known she was itching to get out and do something and to find out their story. Jill gave Ally such credit for being a successful business-woman, but of the duo it was Jill who was the people-person. The one who could illicit people's life stories out of them in a bar. Conversely, it was both how she'd been able to make so many new friends in her new world of being a mum, and why she was also struggling, because she was fed up talking about the same things to the same people.

'What? No Jill. Just stay put, it's started to drizzle again.'

'I dunno, just seems weird sitting here behind them. Aren't you curious why they haven't given up and gone back home? They must have an important reason to be Up-By today too. What do you think it is?'

'Maybe they're going to see Take That too. And then you'll have no chance of getting off with Gary with those two beauties in the audience distracting him.'

'Oh wouldn't that be funny. I thought the other one must be just as good-looking too.' A short pause before she simultaneously took a determined breath, nodded, opened her door and said 'I'm going to go and find out everything!'

Of course she is, thought Ally and before she could wonder if she should be the voice of reason, Jill was out the car, blue trilby and all. Bouncing around to the driver's side, she tapped on the window. The two yellow car women were still facing each other recovering from their giggles, and she could see that they jumped at Jill's knock, which cracked them up briefly again. By Jill's gestures, Ally could tell she was giving the somewhat redundant introduction that she was from the car behind. She rolled the window down slightly, taking a chance on the drizzle, and could just hear parts of Jill explaining their story: '*Can't believe this, can you? Take That...Yes! That's why I'm wearing this (pointing at the hat)...Glass Pass... fiasco...no phone service but at least her husband couldn't bug her, haha.*' Then she listened with concern to Jill's responses as she in turn listened to yellow car's story: '*No way! Oh poor you...What a nightmare...That's awful.*' The two occupants of the car had been cracking up for several minutes but now, according to Jill's side of the conversation, their situation was dire. Jill put her head all the way into the car and looked into the back. Then as she pulled back out: '*Well at least we'll not starve up here, ha ha! And we have lots of bubbly too, it's a party, ha ha!*'

What the hell? thought Ally. *Now we're having a party?* She looked up at the police car and wondered what they must be making of this. Worrying about a mutiny maybe. Looking in that direction, she didn't see Jill coming back to the car until she opened the back door and leaned in and said, 'Open the boot, will you,' grabbing her bag. 'They're coming back for a chat. They apologise that they can't invite us into their car. They have seventy-one strawberry tarts back there. I'll chuck my bag in the boot to make room.'

Ally was amused at the formality of the apology for not being able to issue an invitation into their car, and bemused that the reason was seventy-one strawberry tarts. As Jill slammed the boot, Ally watched the two women half jog towards her car holding their hoods up against the rain, laughing and waving. The driver was older than she'd expected and like the younger woman she was strikingly good-looking. They must be mother and daughter, not sisters.

All three got into the car and slammed their doors shut at

the same time. Jill made the introductions and briefly explained the purpose of the women's trip Up-By.

Keen to fill in all the gaps, Ally didn't miss a beat. 'Nice to meet you, what were you two cracking up about just there? You were making us smile from here!'

'Oh yeah,' Jill said, 'I didn't ask – what were you laughing at?'

'You know the film It's a Wonderful Life? Clarence the angel? Well we were just picturing *** ******* as an angel. With the wings. And with the leather pants.' Katie looked at them for confirmation of how funny this image was, but even Jill was baffled and just looked from one to the other for further explanation.

'It's a long story,' Katie conceded.

It made no sense at all, but because Inez nudged Katie shooshing her and trying to stifle a giggle, they all found themselves laughing away together anyway.

Tom and Calum

NEITHER KNEW it as they were both looking straight ahead, but Tom and Calum made exactly the same face when they saw the TV aunt and niece run back giggling to the Take That women. They both frowned, pursed their lips and drew back their heads quizzically.

'Now, what on earth is going on there?' Tom wondered.

'Think they know each other?' Calum asked.

'Nah, the Take Thats would have recognised Auntie Inez by her car by now if they knew each other. Just typical women, I think. They're much better at the empathy thing than us, Calum. Fact of life. They've probably been sitting there, worried about why the other has to be Up-By, and curiosity got the better of them. Look at them, they're getting on like a house on fire already.'

18

Inez, Katie, Ally and Jill

Inez was amused that it felt like they had a lot to catch up on even though they'd only just met. Inez and Katie filled in some details on the TV thing, and Jill and Ally shared a brief history of their Take That fandom – they'd been fans since the nineties, had never seen them live, and had bought these tickets the day they went on sale months ago. As well as being excited to see the gig, Jill needed a break from her two young kids and Ally was happy to get a short break away from her business, Alison Lees Events Management, a name Inez recognised. They both seemed like 'good people' as her mum would have said, and both seemed like fun too, with Jill being the bubblier one chatting a mile to the minute, and Ally chiming in with details Jill missed in her rush.

'Could you see into the car behind us from where you were?' Jill asked.

'No we couldn't. We saw it arrive of course, but it's directly behind you, so your car was in the way of me having a good nosey,' Inez answered, instinctively looking back for a look now.

'Right, don't all look at once. Ally and I will look straight ahead and you two take a look one at a time and get a visual of the people in the car, then we'll tell you what's been going on and see what you make of it.'

'Ooh, intrigue!' Katie said. 'You go first Inez then I'll go.'

Stealthy scanning of the car behind completed, Katie said, 'OK, a bit of a weird dynamic there. First instinct is that must be a couple in the front, but who's the big tall guy in the back? Do you know any of them?'

'We don't think so, no. Definitely not the two in the front. Harder to see the guy in the back, but we don't think so,' Ally replied.

It wasn't hard to tell the two young women had some thoughts on the occupants, so Katie followed up with a simple, 'OK, so tell us what you make of them. What have you seen and what have you figured out?'

Jill drew breath to talk, but Ally interrupted her before she started, knowing she'd give a clearer and more concise version of things. 'Well, when they drew up and presumably saw the signs and realised what was going on, the girl burst into tears,' Ally began.

'I could have too, right enough,' Jill interjected.

'Me too,' agreed Katie.

'But when they saw Calum – you know the young policeman is called Calum right?' Katie and Inez nodded that they'd been told his name too. 'Well, as Calum was coming down towards the car, the driver looked as if he'd grabbed her leg and gave her a stern talking to, to shut her up before the policeman got there.'

'What? No!' With this new insight, Katie's head snapped back to look at the driver again.

'Don't stare Katie,' Inez chided her. 'They'll guess that we're talking about them.'

'Sorry, you're right. This sleuthing took a bit of a sinister turn though. It wasn't really what I was expecting you to tell us,' Katie turned back to look at Ally.

'I know, sorry. We could just be making things up, but it's just all been a bit suspicious.' She went on to tell them the small series of events they'd witnessed from their vantage point and Inez and Katie listened, nodding a tacit 'of course' every time Ally repeated the disclaimer that they could just be letting their imaginations run away with them.

'I just can't shake the feeling that the girl is scared,' Ally concluded.

The four were silent for a moment. Then Jill asked no one in particular, 'Have we got room for her in here?'

Ally's eyes widened. 'What? Jill, no. What are you going to say? *We think you're being abused by the guy you seem to be voluntarily sitting in a car with, come and sit with us instead?*'

'I'd come up with something better than that. I just think that if she is really in trouble and we're not in fact imagining this, we'd kick ourselves for not acting on our suspicions. Bad things happen when good people do nothing, or whatever that saying is.'

Inez gave the accurate quote, '*The only thing necessary for evil to triumph in the world is that good men do nothing*,' and thought to herself that she'd guessed correctly when she thought that her mother would have liked these two. That was one of her mum's favourite quotes. 'Maybe you should go and ask her,' she said to Jill. 'They'll have noticed you come and get us out our car and back here for a chat, so they won't think it's weird. If everything is fine, no harm done and we can go back to the biggest villain around here being the engineer that we're waiting on to come fix that blasted light.'

'Good idea, I can just say we're having a girls' chat and ask if she wants to join. That'll work right?' She looked around the car to see the three other women mulling it over, and while they were, opened her car door was on her way.

'Oh God,' Ally said. 'I can't look. What's happening?'

Katie commentated the scene to Ally and Inez. 'They rolled down the window. Jill's pointing towards our car, I guess asking the girl if she want to join us. The girl's looking at the driver. He's shaking his head. Looks like Jill's being given a polite decline. Yup, she's heading back alone.' She turned back to face the front as Jill got in the car.

'OK, shady much? Did you see that? He wouldn't let her come. Jesus, what's going on back there? I don't like this one bit,' Jill said.

Against her better judgement, Inez couldn't help but be drawn into this very tenuous conspiracy theory. Granted, it was a bit odd to be invited into a stranger's car at a traffic jam, but Ally seemed to have had an eye on things, and she seemed like someone with level-headed judgement. As they were all trying to figure out what they thought of this latest turn of events, there was a knock at the window.

It was the girl. 'Sorry, offer still open? Maybe some new company will do me good. We're a bit of a solemn bunch back there.'

'Of course, come in, come in,' Katie said, moving over to make room.

'What a day this is isn't it? In more ways than one. Why are you all heading Up-By? I'm Gemma by the way.'

Inez thought she was faux-cheery, as if she was trying to compensate, trying to put a brave face on things. Had she been sent in here by those two guys to convince them nothing was amiss in the car behind? She caught herself. If she'd gone straight to that version of events, she could only imagine the wild theories Jill and Katie were silently dreaming up. She watched the girl closely as Katie and Jill shared the respective stories of their important quests Up-By.

Jill of course was first to ask, 'so who are you with and where are you all going?'

'Well, I'm with my boyfriend Ravi and his best friend Alec,' Gemma began, then stopped, hesitating.

Inez noticed Ally start a bit at the men's names and turn her head away from looking at Gemma to the rear view mirror, squinting closely, before she caught herself and turned back to the conversation.

Gemma continued, 'The story of where we're going is long and complicated. Well, it's at least complicated. We haven't told anyone else at all, so, no offence, but it would be weird to tell a car full of people I met five minutes ago. But trust me, we have to get over the Glass Pass today. I just can't –' She choked on the words and couldn't finish the rest of her sentence.

Jill caught Inez's eye. Something made Inez feel it should be her that asked what they all were thinking. She was the matriarch here, she should ask Gemma the obvious question. 'Are you OK pet? Are you safe with those two men back there? Is it Ravi and Alec?' She tried posing the question one more way – 'what I mean is, are you here by choice or are you being made to do anything against your will?'

'Ravi and Alec?' Gemma appeared confused at the question. 'Oh my God, yes. Totally safe with them. They are both sweethearts. They joked that they were going to be my knights in shining armour today. That's part of the reason it's so tense back there. They both feel they're letting me down because, well, because we just seem to be stuck here. They're feeling helpless.'

The rest of the women all struggled to turn their thoughts around to the men, especially Ravi, not being bad guys in this tale.

Jill asked the first follow up question, 'Knights in shining armour? Like they're rescuing you?'

'Yes, as I say, it's complicated. But yes, I would say they're rescuing me.'

'But you've been crying so much and it seemed like your boyfriend didn't want to let the police see you were crying and he did all the talking,' Jill's confusion came out as words.

Ally looked at Gemma apologetically and said, 'Sorry, we're just sitting here with nothing else to do except watch the bold Calum make his rounds, and I guess we took a crying girl in a car with two guys, a few gestures we only saw from afar, and somehow ended up with a theory that you were in an abusive situation and might need our help.'

Gemma shook her head. 'It's OK, don't worry, it probably does look a bit weird. And ironically enough, in a way, you're right. I am in an abusive relationship. Ravi and Alec are saving me from it – they're helping me run away from my husband.'

19

Fraser and Oona

Fraser read aloud yesterday's email to Wyllie and followed with the text Wyllie sent in return, cringing at having to say 'slimy little fuck' out loud.

When he finished, Oona's last vestiges of poise fell away. Fraser was frankly glad of the break from talking and relieved to see her erstwhile composure had been in stoic support and that she hadn't been resentfully waiting for a chance to berate him for the error of his ways. She paced the carpet, tracing the same lines he had for much of last night.

'So he's threatening you now? And we think perhaps Blah Blah too? Who's the slimy little fuck here?' Fraser cringed again at hearing those words from Oona's mouth. 'Trying to claim that you took bribes. Should I call Dad and ask him what he meant when he rolled his eyes after you first met Wyllie at The Big Belt meeting? If you want me to, I will, but not just yet, not in this state. Sorry darling, I'm just so – so – boiling mad. You don't deserve this.'

Fraser was filled with affection and gratitude for this woman, but he was a little confused as to what he should do next, as he had never seen her so furious. He had a feeling that he should just let her indignation run its course. He left her marching, as best she could in his small living room, and again felt guilty that it brought to mind a Royal in a tweed skirt venting frustration and trying to problem solve in the same way. Putting on the kettle, he went about preparing two cups of tea and some biscuits on a plate just as his mum would have done.

Oona was standing over the dining table riddled with papers, randomly picking up one, then another, only glancing, as if they were written in a foreign language. When she heard him come back into the room she said, still looking at the table, 'Now – even I know we could call this a *guddle*.' She relieved him of one of the cups of tea to allow him to put the plate of biscuits down on top of a cardstock file that had previously housed the now scattered reams. 'I'm sorry I'm still a little behind you on this darling,' she said waving a hand over the table.

'Oona, please don't apologise to me, I feel terrible that I couldn't spare you this, but the truth is I'm not really any more ahead of things than you. I was chasing my tail and you've already helped by listening to the story. It was good to lay it out play-by-play. I'm seeing slightly more clearly now, but still not sure of the next move. The closure of the Glass Pass can't last all day, even all morning ideally.'

'I think I know the answer to what I'm about to ask, but why didn't you tell Inspector Beattie about Wyllie and his threats?' Oona asked.

'I had to buy myself time to figure out who has more to lose here, Wyllie or me. That's what all these papers are – I suspect

Wyllie has more to lose. I think he's in deeper than one questionable payment to me.'

'So how is all this paperwork part of the story?' Oona scanned the table.

'I got it from Mack. But I'm afraid we're running out of time to get through so much of it.'

Oona had made it clear Fraser had nothing to fear now. She was his compadre, and he could bring her into the trenches with him. Even at this point, she seemed braver and more formidable than he was. When he began to explain how he came to ask Mack for all this data, his voice was back to its normal volume and cadence, as if they were just discussing the events of their day or some wedding plans. 'That afternoon in my office, there were no bones about it. Wyllie had taken my acceptance of the so-called finder's fee as an agreement that I was on-board for bribes. The timing of his visit two days before the progress paper was blatant. I had nowhere to turn.'

Oona's imploring look in reply to this over her mug of tea gave him a pang of guilt, considering how accepting she had been this morning. 'I felt like such a naive fool Oona, I couldn't tell you what I'd done.'

'Well yes, you could have, but who cares about *could haves*. You were getting to Mack.'

FRASER HAD BEEN at a loss as Wyllie slammed his office door on his way out and he looked down at the envelope. He picked it up and put it in his briefcase, not in case someone saw it, but simply because he needed it out of his sight. Mack was the only person he could call to get another take on Wyllie without raising suspicion.

They exchanged their usual pleasantries in the form of ribbing each other with sarcastic comments, before Mack got around to asking how things were in the world of Big Belt, to which Fraser replied that his last report signing, or lack thereof, had turned up something a bit weird. 'Nothing catastrophic, no need to call the papers, though God knows they'd love an inside scoop. It's more the handling of things that's taken a bit of a turn. What did you make of that guy John Wyllie?'

'Oh the greasy guy in a dark grey shirt, in a sea of bright sparks in crisp pastel Thomas Pinks? That's what I made of him. He didn't belong there.'

'Very astute as always. What's his role? Did you figure out it out when you were going through the numbers?' Fraser asked.

'You know, I wish I'd had more time to work that out, but we were on that deadline to get the application in so I was on a need-to-know basis. He was off that radar,' Mack replied.

'Feel like finding out? Just for fun?'

'Hmm, what you on to there Fraser Bam?'

'No need to sound so suspicious. I'll take a wee look myself and let you know if I need help. You comfortable sharing with me the information they gave you to put together the funding application?'

'Oh yeah sure. It's just a bit of a drill down into information which is public anyway.'

'Perfect.'

Fraser heard Mack opening up some files on his laptop, a small pause while he read the title or scanned the content and a few mumbles while he decided whether they were anything Fraser should see. He kept Fraser abreast of his conclusion by saying 'att-ach' as he inserted the files into an email, or, 'Nah, rubbish, nothing in there.' Among the mumbling he suddenly had a small lightbulb moment and said, 'Oh hang on, I did figure one thing out, I think that John Wyllie goes by the name of KCS, which stands for –' another pause while Mack scrolled through the spreadsheet for the key, '— Kay Consulting Services. I wish I'd had the time to do a deep dive. He's sketchy for sure. Maybe we should pull an all-nighter and figure out all his dirty secrets.'

Fraser had been aware the whole telephone conversation that someone else figuring out all of Wyllie's dirty secrets might be the last thing he wanted, since he was one of them. 'Just send me what you can, and I'll let you know if anything comes up. Do you know what consulting services he provides?'

'Well, that's one of the reasons I noticed. Usually, a services provider will only come under one category in the accounts – you know, your handyman under Repairs and Maintenance, your lawyer under Legal and Professional Fees, but KCS was scattered all over the place. I could have gone down a rabbit-hole, but I didn't have time, and ended up thinking it could be nothing, or maybe that he gets a commission for hooking the project up with the relevant contractors – like a finder's fee or recruitment fee. It's the small world of Mid-June after all – the guy could very well know all the players.' Hearing Mack say finder's fee, the term Wyllie had used to justify their own dealings, made Fraser's heart sink.

Oona and Fraser stood over the printouts of everything Mack had sent over that day.

'How far have you got?' Oona asked.

'Well, Mack was correct in that KCS is all over the place in the accounts. I was struggling where to go from there. But now I'm thinking straight, thanks to talking it out with you, I think the first step would be to see if the payments seem reasonable. You know, if we went along with the premise that he has a commission-type arrangement, we could compare the commission paid to KCS to the value of the contract he brokered. To do that though, we'd need a better breakdown than we have here.'

'What's the lowest level of detail you have?'

'That section of papers there,' Fraser pointed. 'That's every expenditure category broken down by date, supplier, then amount. I've gone through and highlighted all the payments to KCS.'

Oona sat down and picked up a few of sheets of paper from the top of the pile. 'This must have taken you ages,' she said sympathetically.

'Not really, the same suppliers' and contractors' names come up again and again as you'd expect, so it's fairly easy to scan down the entries. Your eye gets used to the patterns in the text.'

Glancing down the columns Oona said, 'I see what you mean. KCS stands out because it's so short.' She had a flick through some more pages. 'Wow, they're not very imaginative with their company names in the building industry, are they? They enjoy spelling out what the company does rather than going with something catchy. We have "McKenzie Road Services", "Caledonian Concrete", "Turnbull Traffic Lights, dash, Supply and Installation". Gosh I wonder exactly what they do!' She looked up at Fraser who was just smiling at her. 'Sorry darling, that's an inane thing to notice,' and she smiled back. 'Time is of the essence. As your mum would say, we should get our *heids doon* and get to work. Explain to me how much further detail you can get by drilling down a bit on your laptop and from there we'll – .'

Fraser's phone made a notification noise, and he knew immediately it was from the same app that Wyllie had used to text him yesterday. Oona, not realising, looked at him expectantly. He retrieved the phone from the couch and opened up the app. 'Fuck,' was all he could say and passed Oona the phone.

'Fuck,' she concurred.

Wyllie: *Good morning Mr Bam. You feeling good about risking the life of your VIP today? You'll have to open the Glass Pass at some* *point. If he makes it through are you happy with your chances over the Drover's Bridge? He'll be gone in a single blast.*

Oona looked shaken. 'Fraser.' She paused, trying to get the words out. 'God Fraser. That's a direct threat. I think you need to let Inspector Beattie know. I think you should call him now.'

'Where would I start Oona?' Fraser said, his hands placed behind his head as he paced.

'OK, let's think about this. How do you eat an elephant? One bite at a time. You don't need to tell him the whole back-story right now. Frankly he wouldn't be interested. He just needs to know that there's a threat been made on your and Blah Blah's life, and unfortunately you think it's a credible one. If you name Wyllie, maybe all it takes is sending someone round to his house to bring him in for questioning.'

'Will you help me write a quick note to get my thoughts straight?'

'I think that's an excellent idea. But we need to be quick. And I'm afraid that you'll need to come clean about who Blah Blah is. In many ways, such a big name is to our advantage here. Beattie will have to take this seriously and act straight away. And right after that call, you'll need to get in touch with Blah Blah's secretary and tell them to stay put for now.'

Oona was talking loudly and clearly, as she did when she was under stress. An English teacher at school had taught her that you can just as easily train your nervous habits to mask your discomfort, as give it away. The teacher would make them give speeches to their fellow students on ridiculous topics, encouraging them to focus only on their annunciation and projecting their voices to the back of the room, blocking out the snickering of their classmates. Oona was forever grateful to the teacher and whenever she was complimented on her poise or confidence would say modestly 'I'm bluffing you know' but stopped short of giving away her secret. Fraser was working on developing this skill but he was very much a work in progress.

Fraser had an idea. 'Maybe you should call Inspector Beattie. You're doing that thing. Where you command the room. The thing your English teacher taught you.'

Fraser could see Oona's first answer was going to be in the negative and she'd be within her rights to tell him to man up. But one business-like deep breath later, she replied, 'Actually yes, I will. I'll be quick and clear, and it will let you contact Blah Blah's people at the same time. Do you trust me?'

'Do I trust you? Oona, you've been amazing this morning. I can't believe how lucky I am to have you by my side. I love you so much...'

'I know darling, I love you too.' But Oona was already jotting down the headlines of what she was going to say to Inspector Beattie, then stopped, pen poised, and looked up at Fraser. 'Well? What's his number?' Fraser opened contacts in his phone, secretly thinking he was sure Princess Anne would be exactly the same in a crisis.

20

Tom and Calum

'Well first of all, can we just take a moment to acknowledge how ludicrous it is that Bam got his fiancée to call you. What next? A note from his mum?' Tom asked the Inspector through the radio, rolling his eyes at Calum.

Beattie had talked them through his call with Oona and the developments since. Tom had heard of John Wyllie and had the sense that he was the type of person who was probably guilty of crimes of some sort, but not the kind anyone calls the police about.

Immediately after speaking to Oona, Beattie had closed the road up to the Glass Pass half a mile before Drover's Bridge and instructed that the closure was made public through the usual channels. The background check on Wyllie showed up no previous on Wyllie, but he was registered as having a Firearms licence for two shotguns, which gave his *single blast* threat some substance. They headed to Wyllie's address, hoping against the odds that he'd just be sitting having a cuppa and watching morning TV. When there was no reply, they knocked on the neighbour's door. An older lady answered and when they asked about Wyllie she replied, 'Oh no, what has he done? Is the wee lassie OK?' The woman explained that Wyllie's wife was a lot younger than him and 'just always looked a wee bit sad.' According to her, 'people' had overheard nasty behaviour from Wyllie towards her.

Beattie replied to Tom's comment, 'I know we're all still a bit wary of Fraser Bam, but at this stage we need to all be on the same team – one that's doing everything to keep everyone safe and trying to track down John Wyllie. So in that spirit, let's start with your crew up there. Since we've closed the road before the Drover's Bridge, you won't be getting any more cars up there now. You said there are three cars – how many people is that?'

'There's an aunt and niece, two young women heading up to a concert and two men and one woman in the third car, so seven,' Tom replied.

'An aunt and niece? How old is the niece? Is there a child up there with you?'

'No, sorry, that was misleading. No children. The niece is a grown woman.'

'Thank God,' Beattie said. 'Including you and Calum, then, we have nine of you stuck there. We can't just send everyone home now, given that the only way back is over the Drover's Bridge. I'm just picturing those three cars – and you of course – lined up there like sitting ducks. We need to come up with a plan here. Calum, get your listening ears on and feel free to chime in. Let's put our heads together on this.'

'Well actually, Inspector, I know of somewhere we could take our people to,' Calum said tentatively.

That was quick! Tom thought.

'Go on,' said Beattie.

'There actually is a track that takes you further up the hill. Its entrance is hidden, but I was up it last year.'

'Drivable or just a footpath?'

'Drivable.'

'I can't picture another road up there at all. Can you Tom?'

'I cannot, no.' Tom replied.

'Where does it lead to? Just the top of the hill?' Beattie asked Calum.

'Well sort of, Inspector. It was kind of the point when they laid the road that it would be hidden.'

'When who laid it? Is this some ancient Roman road or something?'

'No, it was built during the War. There's actually an old listening station up there.'

'You're kidding! A real listening station? One of those stations that fed information to that place that was in that film I just saw? What was it called?' Beattie fired the questions through the radio as Tom looked over at Calum, partly in disbelief, partly in awe.

'I think you're probably talking about *The Imitation Game*, Inspector, about Alan Turing? HQ was called Bletchley Park and yes there's a genuine listening station at the top of this hill.'

'I have so many questions,' Beattie said.

'It's kind of a long story as to how I know about it – I'd suggest one for another day, under the circumstances,' Calum replied.

'Yes, quite right Calum. OK, take us through what the road's like and what's up there,' Beattie said, trying to get back to business.

'Well, the road is not in bad condition. Its entrance was deliberately obscured with plantings and they've obviously not been tended to for a few decades since it was abandoned,' Calum began.

'It must be pretty overgrown if it was abandoned right after the War.'

'Well, no Inspector, it was abandoned more recently than that, but again, that might be a story for a later date. I think you'd rather Sergeant Armstrong and I get these folks on the move.'

'Indeed, sorry Calum,' Beattie said. 'I'm just finding it fascinating that I've never even heard urban legends about this place. OK so talk us through navigating this.'

'Well, as I say, the entrance is hidden but the plants are just leafy, not girthy. Although they're untended, we're still just in spring, so they won't be as overgrown as they will be in a couple of months. I think we'll easily be able to clear an entranceway for the cars. Though perhaps it's best if I go up there to check that I'm right before we manoeuvre all the cars up there. I won't take me long.'

'Sounds good,' Beattie said with confidence. 'And then what – would you just park the cars on the other side?'

'Well no, I'd suggest we take everyone all the way up to the Y-station itself. It's very secure, and there's plenty room for the cars in a partial underground bunker-type area.'

'This is sounding good to me. When this wee adventure is over, I'll be buying you a pint, Calum, to hear all about how you know all this. Tom? Thoughts?' Beattie asked.

Tom had just been sitting witnessing the cogs turn in Calum's own Enigma machine of a brain. The boy never failed to impress but he was outdoing himself today. He had detailed knowledge of an old listening station even the Inspector had never heard of, he'd envisaged a solid and feasible plan in the short time it had taken to outline their troubling situation, and he had communicated it clearly and confidently to his superiors.

Tom answered his old friend and boss. 'Inspector, a bit like yourself, I have a lot of questions, but none of them relevant to our situation right now. I'm happy to take Calum's lead on this.' He looked over at Calum, who smiled in acknowledgment of the firm vote of confidence, perhaps even blushing a little.

'It sounds like you are clear on what the next steps are, and God knows I have plenty to be getting on with this end in mobilising the troops to track this psycho down. I'll leave you to it for now but will keep in touch. Thanks Calum, thanks Tom, talk soon.'

'Roger,' Tom re-placed the radio and turned to Calum. 'Son, you astound me. At the risk of sounding condescending, I'm very proud of you right now.'

'Thanks Sarge, but maybe hold your praise until we've got these people to safety. It's a bit of a long shot. What on earth are we going to tell them?'

'Well, I don't think we should tell them the whole story right now – as you said, getting them to safety is our first priority,' Tom said decidedly. He had been thinking about the logistical steps ahead of them while Beattie and Calum had been talking. 'Let's stick with the term "credible threat" and see how that goes. Let's focus on where we're moving them to and how, rather than why.'

'OK, when you say "let's", do you mean me? I'm not sure how to explain all this on my own Sarge.'

'No, I actually mean both of us this time. I'll not let you be the bearer of this news alone,' Tom looked down at their audience. 'Right, who is where now? Can you see? Were they playing musical cars again while we were on with the Inspector?'

Calum surveyed the cars. 'Looks like the aunt and niece have stayed put in the middle car and the girl in the third car has gone back there, though she's sitting in the back now. The big guy is in the front.'

'Ok, well, small mercies, the rain has gone off. Let's gather them all together so we only have to do this once and it means they all get exactly the same information at the same time. I suppose we should get going.' Tom opened his door, knowing it would take him a bit of time to unfurl after so long sitting in the car. Calum hopped out easily and waited those few seconds for Tom by the front of the car, before they started walking down together.

21

Inez, Katie, Jill and Ally

'Look!' said Jill, who first saw the policemen on the move. 'They're both coming to visit. Please make it be with good news.'

Ally turned round to see them approaching the driver's side, 'Somehow I doubt it,' she said.

'Oh – I think I know the older one. I must have met him before somehow, doing his rounds,' Inez mused.

'Or maybe we've just been here for so long everyone is starting to look familiar,' Katie replied.

'Maybe,' Inez replied, unconvinced.

Tom and Calum

THE WINDOWS of the middle car were already rolled down to

greet him when Tom reached the car, as Calum walked to the car behind to ask them to come out and join the conference.

'Good morning, ladies. I'm Sergeant Tom Armstrong. I know you've already met my colleague, Constable Kirkpatrick. He's just bringing the rest of your patient crew over for a chat. Do you want to get out the car? I think it's easier if we explain this to you all at once.'

When the whole group was assembled, Tom began, being careful to scan the group making eye contact as he spoke. 'I'm afraid I have to report that we've received a credible threat against the safety of people traveling out of Mid-June today – specifically over the Glass Pass and Drover's Bridge. The threat isn't as simple as malfunctioning lights. Unfortunately, this puts the nine of us in the position of not being able to travel back or forward.'

There were small gasps and murmurings, and the two pairs of women instinctively moved closer to their respective companions, Katie putting her arm through Inez's. Gemma buried her face into Ravi's shoulder with a sob and Alec stood alone, hands in pockets.

Tom went on, knowing the best thing to do was to get to their plan of action quickly, 'I want you to try not to worry too much. We are going to take you to safety. The Constable here has in-depth knowledge of this area and has a plan to take us to a site further up the hill, which is much less exposed. The plan has been agreed by Inspector Beattie, who is working on things on the ground to negate the threat and doing his utmost to get us out of here as soon as he possibly can. But in the meantime, your immediate safety is our top concern.' Tom took a deep breath but couldn't pause for long because he sensed the imminent onset of a deluge of questions, so he went on quickly, 'I know you have lots of questions, but can I suggest we get you to this safer location first. I'll let the Constable explain the next steps.'

Calum kept it simple, and spoke fast, similarly not allowing any opportunities for questions. 'There is a disused war station up the hill. By their nature, intelligence stations were secret and secure. We think it's an excellent option for us in this...' Calum paused, as he wasn't sure how to describe what was going on, '...situation. The road up to it is quite drivable. It's a short but steep walk up, so I'll head up for a look now to see how overgrown the entrance to the road is before we all head up there.' Unexpectedly, he turned to the two men from the third car and asked, 'Would you like to come with me actually? It'll be quicker to do any clearing with more than just me, and one of you can relay the go-ahead message back down to the rest of the group here.'

This was a subtle but clever move by Calum, Tom thought. He had immediately diffused the *them and us* dynamic which existed just in the nature of policeman vs civilians, but which was heightened by the inequity of knowledge and in one side telling the other what to do. By recruiting help from the other side, he had blurred the lines of who was 'them' and who was 'us'.

The big fella nodded and straightened his posture ready for action. His friend turned to look at the girl whose hand he was holding. He put his lips to her forehead and said 'I'll be back soon OK my love? Hopefully with good news. These two gentleman seem to know what they're doing. We're in good hands.' He kissed her hand and extricated himself.

Tom cleared his throat. 'Right, Calum and ...?' he paused waiting for names.

'Alec, Alec Douglas-Lauder,' and Alec stepped forward and offered his hand. 'We've actually met a couple of times before, Sergeant. At Glenberry. My dad is the Laird.'

'Oh yes, nice to see you again, Alec. Sorry it's under these circumstances,' Tom said, returning the handshake and doing a subconscious mental catch-up. 'And...Ravi? Nice to meet you

Ravi. So, Calum, Alec and Ravi will get on and do that. How long do you think it'll be Calum?'

'It's not far, just really well hidden. You'll be able to watch us on this clear bit here before we disappear around that rocky outcrop,' Calum gestured, sweeping his hand first to the right and then signalling a swooping change of direction to the left and almost completing a horizontal S-shape by the time he was pointing at the rock formation he referred to. This would be the route the cars would take, though on foot they could take a couple of steeper short cuts. 'If you keep an eye on us as we make our way up, you might be able to see that the route won't be as nail-biting as you might be thinking. From here it looks like you'll just be driving around the side of a hill on an angle, with your driver's side up and your passenger side down, but in fact when they built the station they regraded the hill between here and there so there's an invisible road – flat but covered in grass and moss like the rest of the hill, so you wouldn't know it was there. It's a clever optical illusion. Even I can't easily see it from here, even though I know it's there.'

Tom knew he shouldn't be excited to see this feat of surreptitious engineering, but he couldn't help it. Calum was correct in saying it was completely invisible from where they stood. Alec had quickly gone to grab a sweater out of the back of the car and came back to stand alongside Calum. With a quick salute he said, 'Ready when you are,' and the three headed off.

'It seems like you've all introduced yourselves while you've been waiting so patiently...' Tom paused, not knowing how to ask their names without sounding like a teacher at the start of the school year.

Ally came to his rescue. 'I'm Ally, and I was on my way Up-By with Jill here. This is Inez and her niece Katie. And this is Gemma.' Ally took the opportunity to step over to Gemma and link arms with her, as if it was part of the introductions, rather than a gesture meant to comfort and reassure.

Hands were shaken and how-do-you-dos said politely. Tom had been slightly mortified that he hadn't recognised Alec, the Laird-in-waiting of Glenberry – his dear wife would have chided him, but she had always been much better than him with names and faces. He concentrated on taking in the women's names and having his brain match them to the faces, and as he did he was confident he hadn't met any of the younger women before. Turning to offer his hand to Inez last, they locked eyes for a split second. Tom thought it had happened again and that she was about to tell him she'd met him several times previously. He'd be embarrassed, in fact mortified, to not remember this very pretty lady. He frantically wracked his brain to beat her to it because as he looked at her, maybe he did remember her from somewhere, but she simply said, 'Nice to meet you,' and didn't show any recognition at all. They dropped hands, not knowing what to say next since everyday social pleasantries seemed out of place right now. Instead, they tacitly turned in harmony to look up the hill and see what progress the three men were making, the sky now becoming bright enough that they had to shield their eyes with their hands on their foreheads.

Inez

Sergeant Armstrong had dark skin, which in Scotland just means that you can tell the person gets a nice tan in the sun, as opposed to just burning and/or freckling. Probably for that reason – that he had never had to be careful with his skin – his face had deep lines, to the point that he could even be described as craggy. On another day Inez would have been internally bemoaning the injustice that such marks of age were considered handsome in men compared to the standards expected for women. Sergeant Armstrong's looks would be considered rugged, rather than weathered and it probably wouldn't be long before Katie mentioned him being a 'silver fox'. Today though, Inez only studied him with curiosity, stealing sideways glances as they stood watching the goings-on of the advance team. It wasn't exactly his face that was familiar though, more just his presence, his aura. It was the same feeling as when you recognise someone on TV or in a film, and you can't remember what you've seen them in before, but you can say what kind of character they played by how you felt watching them. If she had seen him in a movie, she'd have said he made her feel safe and happy and that he made her smile. Maybe that was it – maybe he looked like an actor. She must have used up her quota of stolen glances because he caught her in her final one and looked down at her and smiled. The fleeting emotion of warmth made her catch her breath.

22

Calum, Alec and Ravi

'I see what you mean about this being an invisible road. Really clever, isn't it? It's hidden in plain sight,' Alec said to Calum who was just a couple of paces ahead leading the way.

'Well, they were pretty clever people, those that the Ministry of Defence recruited for these jobs.'

'How did you know about this place? I've never heard of it.'

'Oh I'm a bit of a history nerd,' Calum said vaguely.

'Oh really? Me too, though The War isn't my specialty,' Alec said, happy to be thinking about something other than Gemma, Ravi and the literal road block in his day. 'How many times have you been up here?'

'Only twice,' Calum said simply without offering any further information, and to his relief, Alec didn't probe further. Although Calum had just assured his boss, and his boss's boss, that he'd fill them in on how he knew about the Y-station when this was all over, he'd have to think carefully about what information he could divulge.

A YEAR AGO, Calum had watched a documentary on the top secret work that was carried out domestically in World War II, including the infiltration and code-breaking work that went on at Bletchley Park, and the listening and direction-finding stations, called Y-stations, around the country that provided the data. The Y-stations, like Bletchley Park, were strictly classified and the thousands of people around the country who worked in them were forbidden from talking about their work.

War history was one of Calum's favourite topics, not least because it felt like a connection to his dad, who had been a WWII history buff. He was particularly intrigued with this documentary because when he was younger, his dad had taken him on a trip to what was rumoured to be the site of a Y-station, explaining its situation was perfect for receiving signals and pointing out that the site appeared to have been deliberately flattened. His dad told him it had probably been to house a wooden hut type of structure, which had long since been removed. The secrecy surrounding the whole network was exciting for a young boy, as his dad told him all about the Official Secrets Act and that it had been decades before any information about it had been released.

In one segment of the documentary, the presenter went to a known former site of a Y-station to demonstrate how the locations of U-boats were determined. One Y-station could only pick up the direction from which a signal was coming, not its location. To pinpoint exactly where a U-boat was, required a second Y-station to pick up another bearing on the same transmission and where those lines crossed identified the exact location of the U-boat. At the end of the segment the presenter said modern day Bletchley Park Museum keeps a list of former Y-station sites, but knows the list is incomplete. Calum now understood that the site he visited with his dad could not have operated alone – for triangulation, there needed to be at least one other Y-station. There and then he had mentally scanned the land between home and roughly where he remembered he went with his dad. There was one glaringly obvious likely site for a second Y-station – the highest point in Mid-June, the top of the hill that The Glass Pass twisted around. Calum had felt a little thrill as well as a pang that his dad wasn't here to talk this over with. His mum humoured his stamina for documentaries and facts and figures, but his dad would have been revelling in this possible discovery.

It happened to be a holiday weekend that week, so he told his mum he was going hiking, which was the truth, but she'd have imagined somewhere slightly more welcoming and picturesque. The steepness of the hill, its dense forest on the upper half, the road that created a gash in the middle of the hill and the danger of falling rock, meant that climbing the Glass Pass hill was a common leisurely pursuit for Mid-June residents. Calum parked his car on one of the many short service roads that exist because of all the various repair work necessary along the road over the decades and headed off on his adventure, wondering what evidence he'd find confirming his hypothesis. What he found blew his mind.

The clear evidence of a driveway, along with the fact that its entrance had been camouflaged with plants that weren't quite in keeping with the landscape, would have been enough. But at the top of that, he'd found a concrete building, partially buried into the hill so that it only had one external facade. It could have been described as a bunker, except that the facade was almost art deco in style, which gave it the glamorous air of a Bond villain's lair.

Calum firstly took a look around the large area to the left of the site which he took to be a covered area for cars, since it was just an open entrance with room for, he estimated, four cars. There wasn't much to see there but he bided his time, waiting for the butterflies in his gut to calm before he dared enter the main building. The front door was centred on the windowed front and Calum couldn't believe there wasn't one broken pane. When he opened the door, there wasn't even a creak and the door closed tight into its frame behind him. Had his dad been making this intrepid trip with him, he'd no doubt have mentioned that you don't get workmanship like that anymore. Inside was brighter than one would expect and was just one large open space. It was pristine as abandoned buildings go. Looking around the floor, it looked like someone had just swept it, so Calum surmised it must still be completely watertight otherwise there would be evidence of moisture or old leaves or undergrowth blown in. Dotted across the ceiling he noticed several skylights made of glass bricks and went and stood underneath one looking up. The ground above was overgrown but looking around at the distance between them and the pattern of them, he realised if these were once fully open to the sky, they probably belonged to different rooms. The space must once have had internal walls which had been demolished and disposed of. Calum was overwhelmed with awe and allowed himself a long moment imagining what it would be like to have his dad right there alongside him, looking around in wonder too.

When he found the correct people to talk to at Bletchley Park, they did not have any record of a Y-station at that location, but when he explained what had led him to look for it there, they had to agree that it seemed very likely that that's what these buildings were. Calum was asked not to tell anyone about his discovery until Bletchley Park had sent up one of their experts to look around. He was also asked to be her escort to the site.

Dr Brooke White, the attractive WWII historian, had a

wealth of knowledge on the secret domestic war networks, and Calum couldn't get enough of her facts and figures and in-depth knowledge of the mechanics of Y-stations and some profiles of people who operated them. She was passionate about raising awareness of Y-station operators to the same level as the women and men of Bletchley Park, so they could be properly recognised for their service. Local operators at stations in the countryside like this were mostly women who were recruited if they reached a certain score on an IQ test. They were given crash courses in morse code, telephony and direction-finding equipment. Y-stations operated around the clock, and accuracy was critical, so the women showed admirable levels of stamina and concentration, all the while keeping their vital work a secret. It was impossible not to find Dr White's enthusiasm infectious.

That visit and the subsequent researching and consulting was quite a venture to keep to himself, especially from his mum, but of course he did. One of the reasons for the continued secrecy was that because of its condition and the clear access for cars, Dr White thought that the station was one of a few that had been kept in use after WWII as a monitoring station in the Cold War. She would investigate that possibility a bit further and promised to keep in touch.

At the time, Calum had been slightly dismayed that he hadn't been asked to sign the Official Secrets Act, but now that was quite a relief, given that he was about to lead a party of nine people up to the Y-station.

The last he'd heard from Dr White, the Cold War research was ongoing, but she was very excited to tell him that she was coming to Mid-June for an extended period of time over the summer, to work on the announcement and reveal of such an intact example of a Y-station, whose secrets had now been kept for eighty-ish years. The BBC was interested in putting something out around Remembrance Day.

. . .

CALUM DECIDED he would have to email Dr White to let her know what had happened today – whatever that ended up being – but given that she was coming up in a month or two to interview locals about anything they might know about local war efforts, he hoped she wouldn't be too concerned that eight other people had advance knowledge of its existence. As he approached the hidden entrance, he couldn't help hoping that she'd be impressed by his key role in this impromptu mission.

Alec and Ravi stood back while Calum had a poke around, locating the soft centre of the arboreous gateway which he knew was mostly leafy, with not too many large branches. The strategy of the original architects of the site had become apparent on his prior two trips. Two trees much taller than the others flanked the entrance. Their branches appeared to have been bound together because they were now permanently intertwined in an arch. The mid-sized trees had springy branches that had been trained to grow towards each other. Calum pulled a branch out towards him demonstrating to the other two men how malleable they were and explaining that they could be pulled back and wrapped around the trees behind. Just pulling one back allowed Alec and Ravi to see the wall of green was not as solid as it looked. The larger ferns growing on the bottom would be pulled out or just cut back by hand.

'And there's a road on the other side of this?' Alec asked.

'Yup. Shouldn't take us too long before you can get a look. I've only ever opened it enough to create a walkway through, but it was designed and engineered to let cars through, so I'm pretty sure we can make it work. Ravi, if you take the ferns, Alec can take the left side of the upper growth and I'll take right.'

'Are you calling me a short-arse there, Constable?' Ravi said.

'I just thought...'

'I'm only kidding you on. Totally makes sense. I'll admit to being a little bit closer to the ground than you two.'

After just a few minutes, Alec was able to poke his head through. 'Bloody hell. You're right. There's a proper road here.'

Ravi stood up from his hunched position pulling ferns for a look. 'Wow. Look at that! Well done Constable. This looks like a safe hiding place as long as we can get the cars through.'

The three men took a step back and looked at their progress so far. Then Alec said, 'If we can't quite get all the vine tied back or cut, we can always hold them back while people drive in. I think one way or the other we'll make it work.'

'I agree,' said Calum. 'Ravi, I think you could head back down and tell Tom – Sergeant Armstrong – that the cars can head up here. We'll keep working away and be ready by the time you've led them up.'

'Will do,' Ravi said, dusting off his clothes and hands as he left.

23

Tom and Inez

At base camp, Tom answered a few questions from the women as best he could, trying to strike a balance between not panicking them but making it clear they weren't taking safety for granted. He was also at a disadvantage that he didn't know anything about the safe-site Calum was leading them to. The younger women naturally edged towards Gemma, unintentionally leaving Tom standing apart from the group. It felt a little awkward, so he took the opportunity to wander around, up in front of the small line of cars and take in the vistas, while still keeping an eye on things.

Inez cleared her throat as she approached. 'Hi,' she said.

'Oh, hello,' Tom said surprised. He wasn't sure what to say. 'How are they holding up, do you think? Is that wee girl Gemma OK? She seems awfully upset.' He stopped short of asking the direct question, but it was clear he was concerned as to why.

Inez smiled at him uncertainly and looked back at the huddled group of people all significantly younger than herself and Tom. She backed up to the bonnet of her car, half leaning, half sitting and crossed her arms. 'I don't want to say too much, because I've only just met her, but it was really important to her that she got out of Mid-June today. She's leaving for good. Ravi and Alec have been helping her plan it for weeks.'

'Oh,' Tom said quietly. Then, 'So a bit more serious than a Take That concert, eh?'

Inez avoided divulging any more by saying, 'What are those two like – Ally and Jill? They're a hoot, I like them a lot.'

'That's certainly the impression neon trilbies first thing in the morning would give – that they're a hoot. Do they have families?'

'Jill has two young kids, so she was giddy to be getting away for a night. Ally isn't attached, but according to Jill, is married to her business. A very successful one apparently. She's a little more reserved than Jill, but as I say, I like them both. They both sprang into caring mode when Gemma was sharing her story with us in their car.'

'You and your niece have a special reason to be up in Glasgow I hear?' Tom asked.

Inez gave a small affirmative laugh, then gave Tom a quick summary of how the TV segment had come about and what it was going to cover – a cooking slot but with a bit of history about Mid-June and particularly the berry-growing industry. His ears pricked up at the last part.

'Berry growing eh? Would that be a clue as to what's in all the cases of cakes in the back?' he asked.

'Wow, great detective work between yourself and Constable Kirkpatrick there. Yes – strawberry tarts in fact. Seventy-one individual ones to be precise,' Inez replied.

'Seventy-one? Wouldn't you rather make that a round number like seventy? I could help you out there.' Tom's mouth watered as he winked, and he realised he wasn't just joking about being hungry. 'Calum's mum sent us on our way with some baked goods herself, but we haven't got around to having any in the excitement.'

'Oh, did she now? Well, it's looking less and less likely that my wares are going to make it up to Glasgow and more and more likely that they'll be lunch for the hostages, or whatever we are, so maybe Calum's mum and I will have a bake-off. Talking of Calum – what's all this about his secret listening station? I grew up in Mid-June and have never heard anything about one up there. And believe me that's a lot of years to have never even heard a rumour,' Inez added with a roll of her eyes.

It was ironic that she referenced her age in such a self-deprecating way, when Tom was finding himself looking at her a little too long. She really was extremely attractive. He assumed they were around the same age, but it was unusual to see a woman their age still wear their hair long and in loose waves. Is that what you would call a layered haircut? She looked back at him questioningly. 'Had you ever heard of a listening station up here?'

Oh yes, she'd asked him a question. He snapped back into the moment. 'Not ever. I'm not a lifer like you, but I've lived here for twenty or so years and I've never heard a peep about it. I can't believe the Wee Man didn't tell me about it. He's like a sponge that one. Knows a lot about a lot of things. I rib him about it of course, but I do enjoy listening to him and the obscure things he knows about. I suppose I'm not surprised that if there's only one person in the whole of Mid-June or even Scotland that knows about it, it's Calum.'

'The Wee Man,' Inez laughed. 'That's funny – he's so tall and lanky. I think my niece has developed a Stockholm syndrome crush on him, by the way.'

'She looks very like you,' Tom commented, and he wasn't

sure why. Maybe it was because he got to compliment her in a safe, indirect way.

'Everyone tells us so – lucky me! But she got her height from her dad's side of the family – lucky her.' She paused. 'How old is Calum?'

'Twenty-seven, but he's an old head on young shoulders. Not just how bright he is. His dad died a few years back and he's been a rock for his mum.'

'You sound very fond of him. Do you have kids of your own?' Inez asked.

'Sadly not, no,' Tom said honestly. 'Just never worked out for us. My wife and I. But Ann was a teacher at Kilmour Primary School, and the kids loved her, so we both got to be around kids a lot. It made her so happy when kids would come running over to her at local events or even invite her to their birthday parties and things. She was much-loved.' He paused and realised Inez could probably guess that Ann had passed, so to save her asking he concluded, 'She passed away last year.'

'I'm sorry to hear that. It sounds like she had a very rewarding career. Thank goodness we have people who still want to become teachers,' then added looking him directly in the eye, 'and policemen. Thank goodness there are still people who want to join the police force. Thank you for your service.'

Tom almost blushed. Not just at her words but because she said them with such warmth and grace. He felt drawn to her. She'd mentioned Stockholm syndrome, maybe that was what was happening to him too. 'Ahem, anyway,' Tom straightened up tall and looked past Inez and over the top of her car to the rest of the group, who were still taking the chance to stretch their legs and make the most of a break in the rain. 'Shall we head back to our compadres?'

Inez and Katie

INEZ SAW Katie turn to watch her and the Sergeant walking back, catching her eye and raising her eyebrows with a suggestive smile. Inez frowned and gave a mock-chiding shake of her head in reply. Tom spotted Ravi coming down the hill. 'Oh, here we go, looks like we have news,' he said to no-one in particular, and veered off to walk up to meet him.

Katie nudged Inez jostling her a step away from the rest and turned her back to them so they couldn't see her say quietly, 'What was going on there with the silver fox? Did you work out where you knew him from?' Inez just shook her head. They casually took another couple of steps away from the group, so they could speak quietly and not be heard.

'I think I might know,' Katie said in an excited whisper. 'Do you know how long he's been a policeman in Mid-June?'

'I think he said twenty years,' Inez replied.

'That would make sense, if he is who I think he is.'

'Well? Are you going to fill me in…' Inez asked, just as their tete-a-tete got interrupted.

'OK everyone! Listen up, we have a plan!' Ravi shouted. He was walking down the rest of the way towards them, while Tom was walking to the police car to update Inspector Beattie.

As Inez and Katie stepped back to the group Katie whispered quickly, 'I'll tell you if we have a minute when we're back in the car. If he's who I think he is, I don't think he'll want his story being broadcast.'

Inez was even more confused now, but went over to Gemma, put her arm around her shoulder and gave her a wee squeeze, as Ravi issued their instructions. 'We're going to turn all the cars around and head up that hill. I'll go first because I've got a take on his invisible road thing. It makes sense with manoeuvring the cars too – last in, first out, and so on. So you ladies will come after me,' he gestured towards Ally and Jill, 'then you,' turning to Inez and Katie, 'then the police car will bring up the rear. It's quite cool, actually. This little secret wartime road. I think we'll all feel much safer up there. Sergeant Armstrong is just radioing in to let HQ know the status.' Ravi had an air that a weight had been lifted off his shoulders and his confidence spread to the rest of the group who were quickly buoyed and ready to get going.

Katie said, 'It's good just to feel like we're doing something to take back control of our own destiny. Sitting stagnant was driving me crazy.'

'Really Katie? I hadn't noticed,' Inez smiled in her gentle sarcasm.

'I think we're all getting a little stir crazy,' Ally agreed. 'Ravi, are we waiting for the Sergeant? Or can we start turning the cars around now?'

'We can make a start, yes,' Ravi replied.

24

Alec and Calum

'Great job mate!' Alec said to Calum as they took a moment to catch their breath, after both peeling back an unusually weighty bow until it snapped, and they dragged it out of the way. 'That big one was the last one left getting in the way. We can just pull off these last smaller ones now, so the cars get less scratched. Not that I care about my old banger, but that lady Inez must love her wee yellow car and the middle car is quite big.' Even before he'd finished, they both got on with making the entrance neat and completely passable.

'Do you think once all the cars are through we should cover the entrance back up a bit with that big branch we just broke off?' Calum wondered.

'Wouldn't do any harm I'd say. Good idea. That's why you're in the police force and I'm just a history lecturer,' Alec said.

'You actually lecture history?' Calum asked.

'History of music. Once this is over you and I should write a paper on what they were listening to on their radios when they weren't listening for U-boats. That's what they would have done up here right?'

'Spot on,' Calum answered, wondering if Alec was serious about the collaboration. A few ideas sprang to mind already. 'Music history sounds very cool.'

Alec smiled. 'Well I like it. I'm lucky to have done something I really love before I have to take on the family business. I'm realising doing this little tree project that looking after those sprawling gardens is going to be a shock to my system – I have pretty soft hands, as they say. That wee bout of manual labour is the most I've done in a long while. Good for the soul though. I'm feeling pretty proud of this,' and he stood back for another look, surveying the roughly arched entranceway they'd created. 'It's incredible the forethought that went into all of this isn't it?'

Feeling a mixture of bonhomie towards his fellow labourer and a desire to show off a little to a history professor, Calum replied, 'I had to show a Bletchley Park historian around.' He paused waiting for the reaction which came quickly and enthusiastically.

'No way! Now *that's* cool.'

'She was fairly captivated by it all. Wait until you see the buildings and you'll see why. She said she's never seen anything like it. She's coming back in the summer. There could be a BBC documentary made about it.'

'No way!' Alec exclaimed again. 'Do you think you'll be on it? That would be really cool. If I'm around, I'd love to meet her. All us history buffs could get together. Maybe I could show her around our archives at the estate and see if this is mentioned anywhere. It was all walks of life who joined in the war efforts after all.'

Calum had a pang of regret he'd mentioned anything. Why

couldn't he have resisted his little show-off moment? Dr White wouldn't give Calum a second look with this guy showing her around his castle.

'I can hear car engines. They're on their way. We got finished just in time. And the sun's coming out too.' Alec looked up at the sky to see the clouds rolling away and bright blue skies above them, then turned around expectantly waiting to see the first car come around the curve of the hill. He saw Gemma's smiling face first, beside Ravi, who was also grinning at him. Seeing her look happier was soothing and he smiled back and made a grand sweeping gesture towards the leafy gateway and when she rolled down her window, bowed low and said, 'M'Lady. Lead the way!'

'Are you hopping in with us Alec?' Gemma asked.

'No, our man Calum should get in with you guys now.' And he stood up and talked to Calum over the car. 'Right Calum? You get in here since you've been up there before, and I'll come up last with Sergeant Armstrong, and we can cover this up a bit once we're all on the other side.'

Gemma got out the car to switch to the backseat and called to Calum. 'You can get in the front. I don't want to see you trying to fold into the back seat.'

'The cheek of it!' Alec said. 'You were OK with me squashed in back!'

Gemma looked sheepish and mouthed, 'Sorry' to him as she walked around the car and got in behind Ravi, as Calum took the front seat, pushing it all the way back.

'That's insult to injury there Calum! You're pushing the seat back too? Lap of luxury for Constable Calum there.' The window rose as Calum pressed the button and he gave Alec a cheeky smile and a wave.

Ally and Jill

'Look at this, he's funny.' In a show for the following two cars Alec had picked up a large stick and stabbed it into the ground like a staff, holding it in his left hand. His right hand was on his hip and his chest was puffed out triumphantly. Jill rolled down her window.

Alec looked straight ahead and said in a deep booming voice, 'I am man. I do manly things. I have calloused hands now.' Then broke character and looked into the car, holding out his right hand to show scratches on his palm, wrist and forearm, saying in a childish pout, 'no, really, look. Scars from my labours. See?'

Jill laughed and said, 'We are eternally grateful. This is quite amazing, isn't it?'

'Calum said the buildings are even better. I can't wait to see them. On you go then. I'll see you up there shortly.'

'I'll look forward to it,' Jill replied.

When the window was closed Ally gave an incredulous gasp and said 'Jill! Were you flirting with Laird Alec?'

'No but *you* should be! He's lovely. I like someone who makes me laugh and doesn't take himself too seriously. And it sure feels good to get a wee laugh this morning. It'll take my mind off the fact that it's looking less and less likely I'm going to get to gaze into Gary Barlow's eyes tonight.'

'True.'

'You have an easy chat up line with the Laird – tell him you have a connection! I can't believe you haven't already.'

'Jill, would you stop. When would I have mentioned that?' Ally said as she navigated the bumpy road.

'Will you tell him? Once we're settled in this mysterious hideout?'

'Maybe. If we get chatting, I might. But it's not that big a deal.'

'I'll make sure you get chatting. Leave it to me,' Jill

promised. Ally didn't protest any more than a perfunctory eye roll.

Inez and Katie

On the approach up the hill, Inez wasted no time. 'Well then – are you going to put me out my misery about where we've met Sergeant Armstrong before?'

'Oh we've never met him,' Katie said with a smile.

'Hmmm, you're enjoying this aren't you? That you've figured it out before me.'

'I am now actually yes. I'm excited to tell you that our silver fox is also a brave, selfless hero. I don't think he could be any more of a catch. Well unless he'd won the lottery. Mind you – you're loaded, so what do you care about how much money he has?'

Inez tutted, though she was amused by Katie's would-be matchmaking, which had never cropped up before now and had to admit to herself that she'd chosen a good candidate for her first foray into setting her aunt up. Tom was good-looking, easy to chat to and had a lovely mild manner. And now some heroic past. 'OK, OK, out with it! Can you please tell me who Tom Armstrong is? Before we have to say hi to the Laird up there. Look at him with his stick!'

'Right enough, sorry,' Katie realised she couldn't draw out teasing her aunt as long as she would have liked. 'Can you picture that coffee table book my dad bought for us all – the one about the history of Scottish football?'

'Of course,' Inez said in an *of-course* tone. Her brother-in-law had pre-ordered several copies way in advance of the publication date and had been giddy as he unboxed them, handing them out with flourish.

'Do you look through it often?' Katie asked.

'Well, it's been on a shelf for a wee while now, but I read it at the time. It was really well done.'

'Well, mine isn't stuck on a shelf – it's proudly on my coffee table, where it should be, and I pick it up quite often. There's a chapter on football hooliganism...'

'Yes, I remember that one. It was such a sad indictment – photos of supporters taunting and spitting at each other across barricades and pitched battles between guys with their football colours stretched across their beer bellies,' Inez recalled.

'That's the one, and yes it's pretty depressing – interviews with people whose wives left them after one too many A&E visits, or guys who left the gangs only once their sons asked where they went to after the games and they finally came to their senses. Not exactly the image we like to portray of the happy, chummy Tartan Army,' Katie didn't try to hide the disgust in her tone.

'But what's that got to do with this?' Inez asked

'Can you remember a picture of a policeman, his face completely smeared in blood? He's cradling a young boy?'

'I'm not sure I...oh hold on, maybe I can...wait...Katie you're not saying?' Trepidation filled Inez's voice as she feared where this was going.

'Inez, that's Tom Armstrong. I just know it.'

Inez swallowed as the bile she'd felt remembering that hideous chapter of an otherwise proud and patriotic coffee table book rose, thinking of that particularly harrowing image. 'But how – how could you possibly recognise him?' she asked.

'I'm not sure why it stuck with me. Maybe just because in the end it was such heartwarming story. I suppose the only reason they could include such an upsetting picture was because alongside it was the picture of the same wee boy years later, perfectly fine. He set up an anti-hooliganism movement in schools and he was proudly holding an award because it had made such a impact.'

'Oh that rings a bell. "Zero Tolerance", or something like that?' Inez asked.

'"Nae Patience,"' Katie corrected.

'Yeah, that was it. Well remembered – a great name. Even so, I can't believe you could recognise Tom Armstrong from that,' Inez said, amazed.

'You know, there's something about that portrait taken in that dreadful split second – the anger but dismay, the desperation but also...I dunno...determination...it said so much. So although it was horrific I was drawn to it somehow. I guess it stuck with me. Then when you said Tom's been here around twenty years, that fitted in too. There wasn't an up-to-date picture of the policeman in the book like there was for the wee boy. The boy mentioned the policeman and how grateful he was, but not by name, and there was a footnote clarifying that they were still closely in touch but the policeman had not wished to be named in the book, and there was something along the lines that he was alive and well had moved to the country with his wife,' Katie's voice cracked slightly and she turned to Inez with glassy eyes.

'Oh pet, don't!' Inez said. 'You'll make me cry. Quick wipe your eyes, you're going to have to roll the window down to get directions from this daft numpty brandishing a branch.'

25

GLASGOW
APRIL 1994

Ann was dotting around the kitchen nervously, taking double the steps it would usually take to make the mug of tea they'd share before Tom headed out to police the Old Firm game that afternoon. It was fair to say his reassurances had failed to reassure. 'You know I'll be worried sick until you get home. We moved back up here from London so that you wouldn't have to do duties like this anymore.'

'I know love, I'm sorry. They were short of people. I didn't feel I could let the shift down. It's bad enough getting the short straw policing an Old Firm game, without being short-handed on it too.'

Of course, there were lots of overlapping reasons that they had moved back to Scotland, but Tom couldn't deny football hooliganism was one of them. As a shiny new recruit in the late seventies, football match duty featured heavily in his shifts both north and south of the border. Hooliganism was as old as the game itself, as passions ran high and spilled over into aggression all too frequently, but in those days violence was still a by-product of the game. Disorder was spontaneous but there were well-accepted processes to minimise clashes and unwittingly the fans cooperated by wearing their team colours, so that the police could keep them segregated and man the paths to their respective watering holes after the game.

The eighties though, brought a whole new level of violence to the game – in Casual sub-culture it was no longer a by-product, but a premeditated, organised and integral part of match day. The gangs of young men shunned replica football strips and instead favoured designer gear. They would descend on their rival's town hours before kick-off with the aim of decimation to prove their superiority even before the game. These armies were recruited carefully, not just any old hoodlum was invited along. You had to be a good fighter and brave – a young man had confided to Tom in the divvy van once that he didn't have a choice but to fight, because he'd been told by his associates, '*when the fight starts you cannot and will not turn and run, or we'll turn on you.*'

The home team supporters would be just as organised, ready to defend their territory. There would be spotters at the train or bus stations and when the word went out that the enemy had arrived, they would appear from their hiding spots in trees, down alleys, up embankments, like rats from the sewers. These pitched battles were an entirely new and deadly kind of terror. And the more publicity they got, the more they wanted, and the more foot soldiers they recruited.

The forms of combat escalated too and soon the opposing sides would arrive to battle armed with petrol bombs, CS gas, clubs and knives. Every match-day shift had the potential to become a bloodbath, but so many hands were needed, it was hard to escape them. Ann hated those long days at home alone, waiting for the relief of Tom's key in the door. She knew that he loved being a copper, but she questioned that surely there must be safer places to be one. When English teams were banned from competing in Europe due to the behaviour of the fans, but not Scottish teams, it seemed like the final sign that it was time to return north, even though Tom knew from colleagues that there wasn't exactly a gulf separating Scottish and English Casual culture.

The forces were gradually getting to grips with things after a hellish decade, a lot in thanks to the installation of CCTV in town centres, around the grounds and travel routes. The thought occurred to Tom to remind Ann of that. 'Look, try not to worry. Any trouble that's happening nowadays has to happen well away from the grounds because of all these CCTV cameras we have all over the place. These idiots know where to go to find each other after the game and have their pitched battles in peace, without cameras and without us there to stop them before they even get started, because that's what we do. These guys like a proper fight, not one in front of kids. The safest place to be is outside the ground – cameras, hundreds of police and people with their kids.'

'Your speech isn't as consolatory as I think you think it is Tom,' Ann said, eyes wide, shaking her head. 'Did you seriously just say, '*They prefer to have their pitched battles in peace*?' They all sound like a bunch of maniacal bigots. I hate all of it.' She looked at him in despair, then added, 'And Tom, it's the Old Firm. We all know that's a law unto itself.'

This was true. The rivalry – a word that did nothing to convey the extent of the vitriol and malice of the supporters – between Rangers and Celtic was more than one hundred years old and outdid any other derby in Britain. A former Old Firm player who had gone south to play for an English side said his new team's local derby was like a Sunday school picnic compared to an Old Firm game.

'You know what I hate most?' Ann said passing Tom the mug of tea for his turn.

'What's that love?' Tom said patiently.

'That they hide behind tradition. They claim it's not just ignorant bigotry and blind hatred, they claim it's their roots, their heritage. Bullshit. They're just a bunch of hoodlums, not even paying attention to the game, just taunting each other with their awful songs.'

'I agree with you. Tradition is too dignified a word for them,' Tom appeased. Lots of the language used around Old Firm games irked him too. *Gladiatorial* made it sound noble and *a match that divides a country not just a city* gave credence to those who claimed it was more than just a game and bandied around instances from history that supported their stance. Even the fans who considered themselves on the more respectable side, elevated above the plebs in their hospitality boxes, similarly elevated their insults above the songs of the terracing and instead threw around baseless claims of corruption and conspiracy.

'Look, I'll be back before you know it and it'll be a long time before I'm working a footie shift again. These are exceptional circumstances. It's this damn chicken pox outbreak. Anyone with young kids has had to stay home with them – the shifts have been messed up for the last two weeks.'

'Ugh, you don't need to tell me about it. My classroom has been eerily quiet. Only six kids out of twenty-eight escaped it.'

Tom put his hands on Ann's shoulders and locked eyes. 'I'm going to be fine. Like I say, I'll be home before you know it and we can share a glass of beer instead of a tea.'

'Don't be a hero Tom. I want you back here without a scratch.'

AT EXACTLY WHEN Ann was expecting Tom home, the doorbell rang, and she could finally unclench. 'What are you ringing the bell for? Did you forget your key? You could have come round the back,' Ann called out as she walked to open the front door. She felt her limbs go limp as she did. Instead of her own police officer husband, two others stood on her doorstep, their faces grave. She had met the male officer before, but he reintroduced himself according to protocol as Sergeant Mark Bell and his female colleague as

Constable Lyndsey Lyle. Ann didn't hear a word. It was just noise as if she was swimming underwater.

'Mrs Armstrong – Ann? Can we come in? We don't want you to panic, Tom is OK. But he's been hurt in an incident.'

Ann put her hand to her face and heard a whimper and then a '*no-oooh'* which she guessed must have come from her own mouth. She stood aside to let them come in and the female officer touched her arm and said, 'I'm so sorry, but he's going to be fine. And that came straight from him. The first thing he wanted us to do is to stress to you that *he's going to be fine*.'

Ann nodded, trembling and managed a 'thank you' as they went into the living room, where she gestured them to sit as she perched on the edge of an armchair, her breathing also shaky.

Sergeant Bell took a deep breath and said, 'Firstly, what Lyndsey just said is correct. I spoke to Tom myself and he made me promise I'd start by telling you he's going to be fine. He is in the hospital though. He sustained quite a bad cut to his face, to his left cheek, and is having stitches. Given that it's his face, and that it happened in the line of duty, they've called in a specialist surgeon, so they'll not just be stitching him up any-old-how. The medical staff have confirmed blood loss is within safe limits – I think they knew that straight away given that he walked from the ambulance into the hospital. He wanted you to know that part too – he didn't want you imagining him being taken in on a stretcher or a wheelchair.'

'How…oh God…I don't know…I can't think…was it a…a… knife? Oh God, Tom. Tom,' and Ann put her head in her hands and began to cry. Asking permission from her colleague with just her eyes, Constable Lyle got up and crouched to the side of Ann's chair, putting her hand gently on Ann's knee.

'Not a knife, no. A bottle. It was thrown at him. Tom was…,' Bell was struggling to get his words out too. It was always terrible delivering bad news to relatives, but he had never had to pay this kind of visit to a colleague's wife. 'Tom was carrying an injured child at the time and we think he was struck with a broken bottle.'

Ann had been looking at the officer, her eyes filled with tears that were spilling in abundance down her cheeks. At this news she let out a sob and managed, 'A child? Oh God, is the child ok? What happened to him? Or her, I mean. What happened to them? Are they OK?' Her mind was muddled with panic, the whole thing was a blurry out-of-body experience.

'It was a boy and Tom told me that would be your next question – to ask about him,' he smiled gently. 'He also is going to be OK. Unfortunately, he got trampled when two groups of fans rushed towards each other. He's quite battered and bruised and obviously quite traumatised. Tom travelled in the same ambulance as him and said he'll go and see him once he's stitched up. Well, he said if he doesn't look too scary.' The Sergeant gave a small smile and slight roll of his eyes, hoping he was conveying that Tom was in good spirits and his sense of humour was showing through. 'Would you like us to take you to the hospital or would you prefer to travel there alone? I'm not sure if you'll be able to see him immediately, but I know you'll want to get there as soon as possible. If you come with us, we'll throw the lights on and get you there tout de suite.'

'I think that's the least I'm owed by some of the stupid people of this city tonight,' Ann said, getting up and looking around trying to get her brain to function through the fog of emotion enough to tell her what she needed to do before she left the house. She started to leave the room to go and find her shoes and handbag but turned back and said to the two officers, angrily, though they knew not at them, 'Who takes a child to an Old Firm for God's sake?' And then, pursing her lips and shaking her head trying to hold back more tears, added, 'Do you know the last thing I said to him? To Tom? Right before he left? "*Don't be a hero*".'

. . .

When Tom's plastic surgery, as he was referring to it, was done and he was checked out and free to go, he wanted to find the little boy and go and see how he was. The boy was called Ewan, and his parents were by his bedside. In their conversations as they waited for the admin to be finished up, Ann had questioned the wisdom in taking such a young child to a Rangers – Celtic game. But when she met the parents, she softened immediately and her heart went out to them. When Tom introduced himself Ewan's mum stood and hugged him and choked back her tears for just long enough to let out a small 'thank you', but had to turn away immediately as the tears rose and her shoulders racked in sobs once more.

Ann touched her gently on the shoulder and said quietly, 'Oh love, I'm so sorry. Come here.' The two women turned to face each other, and Ann hugged and stroked the hair of this stranger, the first encounter between two women who would remain close and inextricably linked for the rest of Ann's life.

Tom shook her husband's hand and asked how Ewan was doing and what the doctors had said. The overnight stay was to manage his pain and monitor any signs of concussion. It seemed to them like they would be able to take him home tomorrow but Ewan's dad, Craig, confessed 'to be honest Tom, ma heid's mince and it feels like the staff are talking in code sometimes, so we're just sitting tight and doing as we're told.'

Two more chairs were found and the four of them sat down and talked quietly around Ewan's bed. Craig explained that the season tickets they used to go to the game actually belonged to his brother and nephew. Ewan's big cousin was too busy studying for his O Grades to take time out to attend the match. 'Ewan was just beside himself to be going to a football game. When his cousin talks about the games he's enthralled – he idolises him. And his cousin is great with him – he was telling Ewan he wanted him to focus really hard on the game because he would phone him for a full match report afterwards. And he really did, the wee soul. He had a wee frown on his face he was concentrating so much. The old boys sitting beside me were nudging me, loving how absorbed he was in his first ever football match.'

'And tell them about the whistling,' Ewan's mum, Jennifer, said with a small smile.

Craig smiled too. 'Ewan had been trying to learn how to whistle through his fingers because we were taping the match on TV so he could watch it with his cousin once his exams are over. He wanted to be able to whistle so they would hear him. He hasn't mastered it yet, but I told these old boys beside me about it and they told Ewan they'd choose a quiet part in the match and whistle, so he'd be able to tell his cousin that was his new friends he made at the game. So these guys, probably hitting seventy, were sitting like wee kids conspiring the best time, and when they did they went *ready Ewan, hold your ears, one, two, three...* and let out this long whistle in unison. Ewan was quite shy of them, but I could tell he was thrilled.' They all shared a quiet chuckle.

'They still write a daily journal in Primary Three and Monday's was going to be all about today,' Jennifer said. It's not his strong suit so I asked the teacher if it was OK if he just kept writing about it until he ran out of things to say. She said yes. Apparently they just want children to get creative and enjoy it, not worrying about spelling and punctuation as much as we did, so if it got him interested and writing away, she was happy.'

Ann nodded. 'I'm actually a teacher too. Primary Four.' At hearing all the circumstances around why they were at the match and the fun and positively wholesome experience they'd had during it, Ann could see why Craig and Jennifer did not want to deny Ewan his big day. She felt guilty that she had voiced some thoughts which she now realised were tantamount to victim blaming.

'Gosh, a policeman and a teacher. Thank you for your service.' Ann and Tom had simultaneous looks of surprise and embarrassment.

'That's a lovely thing for you to say,' Ann said. 'Tom, are you often thanked for your service?'

'Em, hardly! I don't know if anyone ever has. If you could only hear the names I'm usually called. Yes, that's a very nice thing to say, but it's my privilege. I'm just glad the wee man is well. He looks nice and peaceful.'

Right on cue, Ewan started to stir. Jennifer leapt up and went to him, leaning over him so he would see her immediately when his eyes opened. Ann and Tom rose to their feet amidst protestations by Craig that they should stay. 'Absolutely not,' Ann insisted, 'he should only see his mum and dad here. Scary enough to wake up in a strange bed and remember what's happened. Can you call us tomorrow though and let us know how he is? Is it OK if I give you our number?'

For the first week, Jennifer gave Ann a daily update on Ewan. He recovered quickly enough that by midway through the week, he was mostly concerned about what he was missing at school and that he had been denied the Monday accolades he had been preparing for as the only kid in Primary Three, probably the school, who had been at the Old Firm game. Ann made a hesitant offer on the Friday that she could help Ewan make those diary entries Ewan had wanted to write. Jennifer cried at the offer, and both women knew that it ran much deeper than just helping him feel he was on top of schoolwork. Because an officer had been injured in the line of duty, Ewan and Craig had been interviewed by two different police departments. If Ann could sit down with Ewan and help him write about all the good parts of the day, perhaps it would help dilute the trauma of those moments after the game. Tom had thoroughly approved of the suggestion because he felt terrible that Ewan had to relive events in order to help with an investigation on his behalf. They both went to visit the family that first weekend, and Ewan gave Tom a homemade card thanking him for being so brave. Among the adults, there was not a dry eye in the room as he handed it over with a hug and insisted Tom read it out.

Ann and Ewan secreted themselves in another room for an hour and he emerged with a triumphant grin saying, 'I've never written so much. Mrs Armstrong helped me, but my hand is sore. Look, Mum! There's tons of words. Will you and dad read it? I can't wait to show my teacher.'

When his teacher read it, she asked Ewan if he wanted to tell his story of his first football game to the class. He declined but agreed to her reading it out, and his fellow students were suitably distracted from the sombre but scant accounts they'd heard from their parents as to why Ewan was off school for a week, and instead asked him all about things like the goals, the whistling, and the food from the concession stands.

A FIRM FRIENDSHIP WAS FORMED, even though Ann and Tom left Glasgow for Mid-June within a year. Either when she happened to be up in Glasgow visiting, or by phone, Ann continued to provide intermittent help with reading and writing if Ewan felt overwhelmed.

In Primary Seven, he had to write an essay about one thing that he would change about the world and how he'd help make it happen. 'I think I'd change the fish and mashed potatoes for school dinner on a Friday to fish and chips.'

Ann laughed and said, 'Well let's think about that. What would have to happen for that to change.'

'They'd just need to fix the deep fat fryer,' he responded simply.

'I don't think we could really write about that for the three pages your teacher has asked for. Maybe we need to think bigger?'

'Like world peace?'

'Let's try to find a balance between something personal like school dinners and something that's maybe too big. Your teacher wants you to be able to give a personal view on things. Do you think you could do that about world peace?'

'Probably not.' There was a long pause. 'I've been watching all the stuff about the Good Friday agreement and wondering if Old Firm fans will stop fighting each other now. I'd like that fighting to end.' He was mature enough to know to say the words cautiously, acknowledging the impact they were bound to have on Ann.

'I think that's the perfect balance, Ewan. Are you happy to write about that topic, though?'

'I think I am.'

Ewan's teacher ended up passing that essay around every member of staff in the school. A copy of it made its way to the neighbouring Catholic primary school where it did the rounds too. Before long, a joint assembly of the one hundred and fifty Primary Seven pupils from both schools, and their teachers and head-mistresses, was arranged. Ewan's parents were invited and they in turn invited Ann and Tom. Tom couldn't attend but Ann made the journey up from Mid-June and watched proudly as Ewan read out his essay and was interviewed by his own teacher and her counter-part from the Catholic school, before answering questions from his peers. He was incredible. Craig beamed with pride, and Jennifer and Ann linked arms and fought back tears together throughout.

Ann was staying with them that night, so a celebratory take-away was ordered from Ewan's favourite Chinese restaurant. The three adults smiled on, watching him tear into his chips and curry sauce, talking a mile-a-minute, adrenaline still coursing through his veins.

'It felt really good to talk up there. Did I sound OK? Once I got going I didn't feel nervous at all. Mind you, Mrs Fisher and I had practiced some of her questions. But I hadn't practiced the ques-tions that the teacher from the other school asked me. Or any of the ones from the kids. Can you believe how many people put their hands up to ask me questions? Boys from the other school came up to me at the end and told me '*well done mate*'. We usually cross the street away from each other when we see the other blazers coming, but there they were, patting me on the shoulder. It felt good you know? Like I'd maybe got through to people. Do you think I got through to people? Mum? Dad? Ann? Do you? Think I got through to people?'

Ann answered first. 'Ewan, there's no doubt in my mind those children will remember hearing your essay and about your experience at that Old Firm game for a long time to come. I was wishing I could have brought the P7s from my school up too. Which got me thinking…' She paused because she had a serious thought to share with Ewan and wanted to make sure he was listening. If his mind was still racing, she'd wait until a better time. But he looked up, chip in hand, signalling he was waiting to hear the end of her sentence. 'I think you could go to other schools and lead special assemblies like the one you did today.'

'Really? You really think so? I do feel great tonight after doing that. Like I don't want it to be over. I'd love to be doing it again tomorrow.'

That evening went into the wee hours as the four of them fired out ideas, scribbled notes and brainstormed names for this new venture. The seed of Ewan's mission – to educate boys and girls with roots on both sides of the Old Firm about the futility and danger of the hate associated with the old rivalry – sprouted fast. Any doubts the adults had were quashed by Ewan's innocent exuberance.

Their working name for the initiative was 'No Tolerance', but they knew it wasn't quite right. 'No tolerance' was something the kids' teachers would say to them and therefore conveyed a them-and-us, an omnipotent authority being involved, rather than change at grass roots. They decided to call Tom and tell him everything that had happened that day and evening and let Ewan do the honours. He excitedly blurted out random ideas, but somehow Tom got the gist and commended Ewan on a great idea. On the subject of a name, Tom and Ewan mulled over the dilemma of getting the right tone for a while before Ann, Jennifer and Craig watched Ewan's eyes grow wide as he bounced in his chair and said, 'Tom, you're a genius.'

And so the Nae Patience initiative was founded and named on that night. Twenty years later nearly all of the schools in the West of

Scotland and a lot in the rest of the country put aside a day at the beginning of Primary Seven and a day near the end of the school year, coinciding with the end of the football season, for their pupils to take part in the Nae Patience program. Significant annual grants from Rangers and Celtic football clubs, as well as smaller ones from other clubs, allowed Jennifer and Mrs Fisher to make the foundation their part-time jobs. Ewan went into schools as much as his own schooling allowed until he went to study law at university, after which he secured a job easily and was permitted to still be involved in Nae Patience – as pro bono work goes, his employers couldn't have asked for a higher profile cause for a West of Scotland legal firm.

Ann sat on the board of Nae Patience. Tom was eternally proud of her and, of course, young Ewan. He'd joke to them all that since his scar had been eaten up by one of the crevices in his old face, they had given him a much nicer reminder of that life-changing day.

PART III

AT THE Y-STATION

26

Calum directed the cars into place. Ravi and Ally drove their cars into the underground parking area and Inez and Tom parked directly behind them. All the occupants of the cars got out, made their way to the front of the station and stood in spontaneous shared awe. Calum looked at the group expectantly, but they seemed to be struck dumb. Mind you, he supposed he felt the same way when he first saw it. He was so happy to finally share this place with others, despite the circumstances.

Tom was speechless, shaking his head, arms folded. He caught Calum's eye and just opened his eyes wider, smiled and shook his head again. Inez was the first to break the stupefied silence. 'I can't believe it. I'm a bit overwhelmed actually. How on earth must you have felt when you first found it? Were you just on your own?'

'Yes. I was a bit nervous I must admit. I had a look around where the cars were before I plucked up the courage to go inside.'

'I'm dying to see inside, but I don't think I'd have dared on my own. Good for you!' Inez gushed. 'Are you going to give us a wee tour?'

'It would be my pleasure.' Calum held the door open, and the group filed in, Tom and Calum going in together last. The older man patted the younger man's shoulder.

'You've really surpassed yourself here Wee Man. This is incredible. What a find.'

They all marvelled at how well preserved the space was and Calum pointed out the skylights above them and that there were probably partitioned rooms when the station was in use. Perhaps there were separate spaces to catch some rest or sleep, or perhaps because the station was multi-use. He explained that due to there being two stations in the area, this was almost definitely a direction-finding station – each station identified the direction from which a signal was coming and where the two lines of direction crossed pinpointed the location. Stations could also intercept signals or indeed do some code breaking onsite, prior to the data being relayed to Bletchley Park. He told them all about Dr White and that she was coming back to Mid-June this summer and the purpose of that trip. He stopped short of mentioning that the station may have remained in use during the Cold War. Although he had not been asked to sign the Official Secrets Act, he thought that particular nugget might count as classified.

Calum's tour group was rapt, but since the sun had come out it was warmer outside than in the part-subterranean war rooms, and they were gradually tempted outside. The gravel courtyard had weeds growing through, but it was early in the growing season so they weren't too high, and there was a poignant relic of camaraderie – a picnic area made out of what must have been cable wire spools, tree stumps and wooden planks. Inez took a seat and lifted her face to the sun, but before anyone else sat down Calum quickly said, 'The best part is actually still to come. Come and see this,' and he started walking to the end of the area not yet explored.

The heather covered roof of the compound was highest over the main centre building and had two shoulders. The one on the left housed the parking area, and to the right there were some barely visible stepping-stone stairs leading up through lush ferns. Calum led the way and stopped at the clearing at the top, beside a stone pedestal, upon which was a brass sundial and compass.

It was easy to forget while going about daily life in Mid-June, with its winding gorse-lined roads, gently undulating hedgerows separating fields of cows or crops, and shallow valleys of strawberries, that as the crow – or more likely seagull – flies, only this hill range separated you from the sea. Soaring over the west edge of Mid-June, the other side of the range plunged steeply down to the sea, waves pounding relentlessly and spectacularly against the lower cliffs. The east side of the range was infamously hard to engineer a road around, but the west side was impossible, resulting in a stretch of coastline only sailors and birds saw.

One-by-one they reached the top of their short climb and formed a line along the brow of the hill. Stock-still they each allowed the view and the vastness of the open sea to both stun them and sooth them. Sunlight twinkled on the waters closest to the horizon, waves began their swell in the middle distance then formed closer to the shore, before crashing against the rocks below. Their vantage point was so high above that there was a noticeable delay between seeing the sprays of largest waves and hearing the sound of the crash that caused them. The group stood in three pairs and three singles. Ravi put his arm around Gemma's shoulder, and they tilted their heads, gently touching, experiencing the moment together. Katie put her arm around her aunt's shoulder as Inez slipped hers around Katie's waist, gently rubbing her back since no words would suffice. The third pair was Tom and Calum. Tom gave Calum another quick pat on the back and Calum gulped back a surprising ripple of emotion. In the absence of his father, Tom was the first person Calum would have brought here and he was glad Tom was as affected by it as he was.

Alec broke the silence. 'I. Am. Hungry.' He announced loudly.

Gemma laughed and chided him, 'A-lec! Way to ruin a moment!'

'What?' He said defensively. 'By now I thought I would have had a couple of rolls and sausage and tattie scone from that wee cafe just the other side of the Glass Pass.'

'You know what? I think we can help you out there!' Inez leaned forward to answer Alec from her position at the other end of the line.

'Us too!' Jill chimed in. 'We have supplies.'

'Actually we also have some home-baking.' All heads turned to look at Tom in surprise. 'Oh, not home made by me! Calum's mum is an excellent baker and sends him to work every day with a goody bag.'

Inez wasn't sure why she felt a little jealous and found herself momentarily vying for her strawberry tarts to garner more praise than whatever Calum's mum's goody bag contained, but she pushed it aside and said, 'Well, we have that perfect little picnic area down there, so let's get the loaves and fishes going.'

Alec rubbed his hands, making a show of being grateful, and stepped down the first couple of rocky stairs then stopped, turning to offer each lady a hand to lean on as they descended the rustic staircase. Calum and Tom let everyone else go first, and as they waited Calum asked, 'Loaves and fishes? What's she talking about? She doesn't really have fish, does she? Her car isn't under cover – it'll be stinking already in this sun.'

Tom looked at him to see if he was joking. 'It's biblical.

Loaves and fishes? Feeding of the five thousand?' Nothing. Tom had finally found a gap in Calum's knowledge. 'I'll tell you later,' he said, shaking his head. But Calum didn't enjoy this inequity of knowledge and had to know immediately, so as they made their way down to their car, Tom explained the parable to him.

27

Inez reached into one of her back footwells and pulled out a rectangle reusable shopping bag, whose contents were making it stand upright.

'What's in there?' Katie asked.

'Tablecloths.'

'Ha ha,' Katie waited for her aunt to tell her what was really in the bag, but Inez just continued about her tasks. 'Wait, you can't really have tablecloths in there. Why on earth..?'

'You know how I take some baking to Mrs Bailey on a Wednesday and Mr and Mrs Ingham on a Thursday, and sit and chat with them for a bit?'

'Yes, your one-woman meals-on-wheels service.'

'Well, they appreciate a nicely pressed tablecloth. So when I've washed and ironed some I just put them straight back in this bag and in the car,' Inez explained simply.

'I've got to watch this!' With everyone agog, her aunt proceeded to give the historic tables a wipe down with a tea-towel from the bag, then lay out pristine tablecloths which glowed like a laundry detergent commercial in the sunlight.

Calum offered to help, and Alec joined saying, 'You came

prepared, Inez. I'm beginning to suspect you're in cahoots with whatever plot has us hiding up here.' The feeling of a joint venture, with the sun shining and food on the way, had brought about a jovial atmosphere. Katie arrived at the table with a tray of strawberry tarts, prompting Alec to exclaim, 'You must be in on this too! It's a family affair!'

'That's only one of four trays by the way. You did say you were hungry,' she said.

'Hang on there, Alec! No pudding until you've had your savouries!' Alec looked up to see Jill carrying two brightly coloured party-sized bags of some kind of crisp or snack under one arm and what looked like a bottle of wine under the other. A plastic bag hanging from one hand held two Diet Cokes and two Irn Brus. 'The wine was for tonight, the cans were for tomorrow,' she explained. Ally followed behind with a neat cooler bag.

Jill put her fare on the table and said with a laugh, 'Got any bowls for the crisps or glasses for the wine Inez?'

'As a matter of fact...' Inez smiled.

'Surely you don't, Aunt Inez?' Katie gasped.

'You're right, I don't, but I wish I did. And you should see the look on your face.'

Ally placed her cooler on the table beside Alec and his mouth watered as he wondered what might be inside. He looked at Jill questioningly. She shrugged that she didn't know what was in there either. Alec moved to look over Ally's shoulder as the contents were revealed. First, a tea towel revealed two champagne flutes carefully wrapped inside, then another contained two knives. Next, a brown paper bag filled with something light – Alec could tell by the way it was lifted out – followed by a dish with a clear plastic lid which revealed a couple of dozen intriguing canapés. Finally, from the bottom, taking up the whole base of the cooler, a heavy looking board wrapped in foil. When it was laid in the centre of the table, Ally pulled back the foil to reveal a smorgasbord of meats, cheeses, nuts and dried fruit, exquisitely arranged. Alec had to gulp as his mouth watered even more. 'Did you just happen to pack charcuterie?' he asked in amazement.

Jill was even more surprised, 'What the...? I was supposed to be in charge of in-room snacks and drinks.'

'You did bring drinks and snacks. They're right there, 'Ally said kindly, gesturing towards Jill's contributions, 'and I'm sure they'll get eaten. I can't wait to get my hands covered in orange dust from those cheesy puffs there.'

'Did you know I was going to be lame and last-minute?' Jill asked, pouting a little.

'Not at all! I just thought I'd look after you for a change. You're always so busy looking after everyone at home. Aww, Jill it's nothing,' she said as Jill was welling up. 'The canapés are left over from an event yesterday and I asked the caterer to put together a cheese board for me. All your favourites are on it. Aww don't get all emotional, come here and let me give you a hug.'

'It's just so lovely of you. I was whining and complaining in the car, telling you we'd have to drink out of the plastic bathroom cups and all the while you had this planned for me.' Jill pulled back to look at Ally and wiped away an escapee tear. 'What did I do to deserve you?' She turned to Alec. 'Can you believe her? She's a keeper alright.'

Alec was distracted by the food. 'Well, Ally – and Inez – I can't thank you enough. No other people I'd rather be in a hostage situation with! Can we dig in?'

'Hang on,' Ally said as she rolled back the opening of the brown paper bag fashioning a makeshift breadbasket, as the bag contained perfect pre-sliced rounds of baguette.

'Carbs too? Marry me Ally! Sorry Inez, but Ally has stolen my heart with simple carbs,'Alec joked.

As Alec rubbed his hands again, wondering where to start,

behind him Jill raised her eyebrows at Ally before giving her another hug as if to thank her again, but whispering, 'He's dreamy! And he wants to marry you.'

'Stop it!' Ally said back in a sharp whisper but smiling.

'Tell him you know his mum and dad.'

'Shhh!' Ally scolded again.

TOM AND CALUM had been having a confab at the car while they retrieved their own Tupperware contribution to this impromptu feast and now approached the table.

'Bloody hell,' Tom said. 'Never mind loaves and fishes, I think you lot could turn water into wine. Where did you magic all this from? I feel like I'm at a fancy party! You'd better get in there Calum. Looks like the Laird there could give you a run for your money on being a bottomless pit.'

Calum sat down beside Alec, who held up a baguette round loaded with cheese and salted meats in a cheers motion, and said, 'May the best man win', before popping it into his mouth in a one-er.

The nine dining companions sat snugly around the long table and tucked in. They filled in the gaps each had missed about their respective missions Up-By, and conversation flowed as if this unexpectedly elegant *repas en plein air* had been planned for days.

When the savouries had been devoured, all eyes turned to Inez's strawberry tarts, gleaming in the sunlight. Calum felt a little put out on his mum's behalf, with her small Tupperware contribution relegated to almost out of sight at the very end of the table. Beside him, Alec said, 'Do we have the go-ahead Inez? Those are positively tantalising.'

'Of course!' was the reply. 'Sergeant, could you do the honours?'

'I think under the circumstances you can just call me Tom.

And my good Constable, Calum,' Tom said as he picked up the tray and passed it around.

Alec managed to get half of one in his mouth in one bite. He shut his eyes and made happy noises, and the others soon joined in.

'Oh my goodness, I think that's the best thing I've ever tasted,' Ally said. 'That crust! It's just all sorts of crisp, buttery deliciousness.'

Inez was slightly embarrassed by all the mouths-full mumbled agreements and satisfied sounds around the table. 'The crust is really just all about good, salted butter. I'm fussy about my butter,' she explained.

'What do you call the filling?' Alec managed to ask between bites.

'Creme patisserie.'

'It's so good. It's rich and creamy, but still very light. How on earth do you make it?' Alec was inspecting the insides of the half tart in his hand.

'Well the creme patisserie is a little more complicated, but lots of whisking to keep it light.'

'And it's really flavourful, not just sweet,' Alec was sounding like a *Great British Bake Off* judge.

'That's because I use a fresh vanilla pod, and I do have one secret ingredient that adds a hint of tang.'

'Which is?'

'Secret,' Inez said with a chiding smile.

'Fair enough!' Alec conceded as he took his final bite.

'And the strawberries are local?' Ally asked. In the back of her mind, she was wondering if she could hook Inez up as a niche supplier for her caterer.

'Yes, I'm proud to say they are. May our berry growers flourish and expand when we're done with The Big Belt?'

Calum continued to feel a little put out at all the attention being lavished on the strawberry tarts, but he had to feel a little guilty too, because he had to concede that they were delectable. 'Aren't you having one?' he asked Katie.

She looked a little sheepish. 'No – sorry Inez, I think I might have snuck a few too many of those when we were making them yesterday. You probably didn't notice.'

'Ya think?! And yes – I noticed!' Inez laughed.

Katie laughed and got up from her spot at the table and walked down to the end. She peered into the Tupperware. 'Ooh, is this tiffin? I like the look of your mum's tray bakes Calum.' She picked up a piece between her thumb and forefinger and popped it into her mouth. Calum was watching, hoping his mum's fare would illicit some praise from her. A split second later she made a noise that made him blush, so he guessed it was safe to say she liked it. She looked over at him and said, 'Want one?' When he nodded *yes please* she picked up two slices and went back round to his end of the table. 'Budge up, then. Let me in beside you, and you can tell me all the decadent ingredients that are in these.'

As their eating finally slowed, and they all felt the pleasant lull that comes with full bellies, the diners quietened. Alec moved from the table and lay back on a grassy bank enjoying the sunshine, while Ravi and Gemma just lifted their faces to the sun and Jill and Ally started to clean up the detritus from their feast. Tom and Inez continued to discuss the varied fortunes of local fruit growers and Katie asked Calum for another tour of the Y-station.

Inez turned to Tom when they left and asked, 'So, twenty-seven you said? Just two years younger than Katie.'

Alec was lying close enough to overhear and sat up and said in a loud whisper, 'Have we got some matchmaking going on here? Good – we need a little excitement around here. I'd like some budding romance to keep my time in captivity in an old WWII listening station, with my best friends, four strangers and two coppers, from getting boring.' Alec made everyone laugh. Jill nudged Ally, and Ally returned the gesture with a *stop nudging me* nudge.

'Wouldn't that be a great *How I Met Your Mother* story? I love it.' Alec continued to muse. 'Though God knows our stories from today are going to be hard enough to believe. What you got in mind, Inez? A game of spin the bottle?'

Another nudge from Jill as they worked their way around the table clearing up and a suggestive, 'That would be fun!'

'Oh, here they come. Shhh,' Alec said as Calum and Katie returned, walking quickly.

'Big news, everyone!' Katie announced and gestured towards Calum to deliver said news.

'Yup, big news – there's phone reception up on the roof by the compass.'

The majority of the group dispersed like there was a fire drill, except Tom and Inez, who were left sitting diagonally across from each other. Tom looked at her and rolled his eyes. 'Kids today.'

'Well, they're not exactly kids are they? What are they? About twenty-seven through to late thirties? And people ask me why I don't have a smartphone. People are addicted to those things.'

'I agree with you completely,' Tom said, 'though I suppose I'll give them the extenuating circumstances today.'

'What a bizarre day.' Inez shuffled up on the bench seat she was sitting on so that she was directly opposite him now. She leaned her chin on her hand and looked him straight in the eyes. 'Anything you can fill me in on?'

'I can't really...' Tom was more thrown by the boldness of her gaze rather than the question.

'Oh go on, I'm so curious as to what this is all about. You have to admit it's intriguing from where I stand. All questions and not very many answers.'

Tom was now avoiding her gaze and shaking his head,

getting ready to turn her down again, but she changed tack. 'I have to admit I'm a little scared too. There's never been any serious crime on Mid-June…'

'You'd be surprised. Know how many drug busts I've been involved in over the years?'

'Well, OK, but surely everything going on today is pretty unique? Surely you can understand why we're nervous. And you and I are practically the matriarch and patriarch of this motley crew. I'm worried about them all, not just my Katie.'

Tom turned and looked back at her for a long moment. He had to hand to her; she was a good negotiator. She'd pushed all the right buttons, including, if he wasn't mistaken, a little flirtation. It wouldn't do any harm to go over it with her, and it would help him firm up in his own mind where things stood right now. He sighed and changed his posture, and Inez guessed he was about to divulge, so she also changed her posture, folding her arms and resting them on the table, and leaned in, listening ears on.

'It started last night with a phone call Fraser Bam made to Inspector Beattie, indicating there was a problem with the lights on the Glass Pass.'

'That's what Calum told us at the start, only he didn't mention that Fraser Bam was involved.'

'Well yes, that's all the information we had really. Bam is involved closely with The Big Belt works, so we assumed that was where he got his information. Turns out he wasn't entirely honest with us, and the reason he needed us to close the road is actually because of threats texted to him. The person behind the threats knows Bam is bringing in his secret VIP today to open the new football stadium, and he threatened to do a damage, mentioning specifically the Glass Pass and Drover's Bridge. In a situation like this, you realise where your weaknesses are infrastructure-wise. He certainly called our Achilles heels correctly.'

'I wonder what Fraser Bam did to deserve this. Do you think he could be being blackmailed for some reason?'

'I don't know him well, but at the moment it looks like he is well-named. He isn't exactly showering himself in glory today. I'm sure we'll get to the bottom of that side of things in due course, but now the priority is to track down this guy making the threats in case he is serious.'

'You think he might not be?'

'Maybe there's a part of me that's thinking the same way as you, that these things don't happen in Mid-June, maybe the guy is bluffing.'

'Do you know who he is?'

'We do, yes.'

'Can you tell me?'

'This is all so unusual. We haven't wanted to alert the public, because we don't want our man to know Bam has come to us. Bam is stalling for time at the moment. We know our guy has guns, so we wouldn't want to risk a member of the public approaching him.'

'Surely we don't count as just members of the public any more. We're very much a part of this – whatever it is. Maybe one of us will know him – you know what a small world Mid-June can be – and could offer information about him. I understand why you're playing it safe out there in the rest of Mid-June but I think our little camp up here should know, and maybe we could help.'

'You make a very good point. I'll give the rest of them another couple of minutes, then I'll call them over.' Tom was enjoying having time alone with Inez. He didn't think another couple of minutes could do any harm. He smiled at her, and she smiled back.

'Well?' she asked.

'Well what?'

'I don't get to hear the name now? As your brand-new wingman and confidante?'

'Oh, yes, OK, his name is John Wyllie. He's a bit of a shady character – well a lot more than just shady as of today I suppose – and he's involved in The Big Belt project somehow. Apparently that's how Bam knows him. Know the name?' Tom asked.

'Not at all I'm afraid. That's the thing. Sometimes Mid-June feels like a goldfish bowl, and you see the same people each lap around it and other times it can surprise you with its amount of anonymity.'

Tom felt emboldened. She had just called herself his wingman, so he should finally get around to asking. 'It's funny you should mention that, I've been thinking you look familiar. Have we met before?' Asking out loud sounded odd, so he half--masked the question by joking, 'Maybe in one of those drug busts I mentioned? Does a criminal past precede your life as beloved aunt and excellent baker?'

Here we go. Inez was used to questions like this from strangers. 'Ha! No you've never arrested me and I've never even called out the police for hearing a bump in the night. I'm pretty sure we've never met.'

'Are you, or were you once, famous then?' Tom asked smiling.

'Famous? Where did you come up with that?' She smiled back.

'Just that Calum thought that he recognised you too.'

Inez was keen to change the subject now and said with a shake of her head, 'I think you two were just going a bit stir-crazy in that car together.'

'That's funny – we said the same. And do you know what I learned when we did? That the phrase *stir-crazy* is derived because *stir* was an old slang name for prison. So it referred to prisoners going mad after too long in the jail.'

'Well, I think by the end of today, it could be appropriately used of us all then. Calum tell you that?'

'Yup, the kid has a brain the size of Europe. His memory is incredible. I'm telling you, it'll come to him where he knows you from.'

God I hope not! Inez thought, before looking over Tom's shoulder and saying 'Talk of the devil. Here comes the strapping lad himself.'

Tom, started to get up and said, 'Right I'll just have a chat with him first. Looks like your niece and Jill and Ally are coming back anyway. I'll give the other three a shout when I come back, and we can fill them all in together.'

28

Tom intercepted Calum and ushered him past the cars far enough away that they couldn't be heard.

'Anything of interest on your phone?' Tom asked.

'Sorry Sarge I…' Calum misinterpreted Tom's tone.

'Not at all Calum, don't worry. You're never on your phone on duty. These circumstances today count as exceptional. Don't worry – if I'd have wanted you off your phone I'd have told you.'

'In no uncertain terms, I'm sure,' Calum smiled.

'Yup, you know me. Listen, I was chatting to Inez, and I think we should give the whole group a wee rundown of where we stand – why we made the decision to bring them up here and what information we're waiting for from down in Mid-June before we think it's safe for us all too finally get out of here.'

'Sounds good to me. Was it a pleasant heart-to-heart?' Calum said cheekily.

'We had a lovely chat, yes. I'm ignoring your inference it was anything more,' Tom said.

'I was texting with my mum up there,' Calum said.

'Oh, you shouldn't have worried her.'

'No, no, she's fine. I didn't tell her much, just that we have to stay put with a few cars of civilians because of a problem at The Glass Pass.'

'Well that's certainly believable.'

'Yup, she said to keep an eye on you and your hero complex though', he winked.

'Ha ha, very funny.'

'I was asking her about those two,' Calum nodded his head towards Inez and Katie, who were now sitting together at the table.

'Of course you were.'

'No, honestly, they both look so familiar, now, not just the niece. It's driving me nuts.'

'Oh aye? You were hoping for an in with Katie from your mum were you? The old, *my mum knows your auntie* chat-up line.'

'Well, if I was, mum would be no use. Didn't know the names at all. She Googled them for me though. There's a wee bit reception up there, but it's slow.'

'Oh aye?'

'Yeah, nothing on the auntie, but that's not surprising—'

'Oh, so over fifty and we're invisible, are we?'

'No need to take offence – have you seen her phone? She didn't strike me as someone who would have a massive social media footprint and there ended up being nothing on her at all. Tons on the niece though, which makes sense since she works in the telly. They'll always be having pictures taken – for their CVs and websites.'

'Lots of pictures of her all glammed up then?' Tom asked.

'Yup!' Calum smiled. One screenshot had made it through to his phone, with an accompanying text from his mum: *Omg Calum, she's gorgeous. And she's only two years older than you. Just saying.*

Tom was looking over at the two women ponderously. 'I reckon you only think you know the niece because you fancy her. And you think you know the auntie because they look so similar.'

If anything, it was the other way round – Calum had recognised Inez first. He gave a small sigh. 'I'm telling you, I keep getting wee flashbacks of her as a young woman. And they're right there on the tip of my brain, but I can't quite grab them in to keep them for a long enough to remember her. She's so familiar from when I was a wee boy.'

'Teacher?'

'My mum would've known a teacher's name. Honestly, it's been driving me mad. I've already gone through all my teachers, dinner ladies, cub leaders, bloody Clarks shoe shop assistants in my head. But I remember her as really young. Like, young enough that I had a guilty crush on her almost. It feels like our age difference shouldn't be as much as it is. I dunno', he resigned, his memory cells aching, 'maybe I knew her in a past life.'

Tom allowed himself a quick dwam. Ann used to tell him they'd known each other in a past life. It's the only way you could explain love at first sight. 'Anyway, let's go and share what we know up to now.'

OF THOSE WHO had been checking their phones, the first to make their way back to the table had actually been Alec, not Calum. He had been slowly ambling back to the table to allow Ravi and Gemma a moment to themselves. Before Inez and Tom saw him coming, he diverted into the woods to relieve himself. All those fizzy drinks – just like his mum had told him. From the woods, he had overheard part of Inez and Tom's conversation, crucially the part where John Wyllie's name was revealed.

Quietly and quickly, he retraced his steps and joined Ravi and Gemma.

'Guys, sorry – I have some bad news. I just overheard the Sergeant talking to Inez. He mentioned John's name as being the reason we're up here.'

'Shhh-itt,' Ravi lifted his hands behind his head and turned away in despair. Alec was left looking at Gemma, their eyes locked as she tried to process what this meant. When she spoke, words poured out.

'Do you think John was coming for us at the Glass Pass? How would the police know that? Why would John tell them anything? This is really strange. Of all the unhinged things we thought he might do to me, I never thought I'd find myself being held hostage – *with eight other people*. It makes no sense.'

'No sense at all,' Alec agreed. 'I think we should go down and tell Sergeant Armstrong our connection with John.'

'This is awful. I feel terrible that all these poor people are at risk and holed up here because of me.'

'It's not because of you, Gemma. It's because John is a maniac, I just can't figure out his particular maniacal involvement in all of this today. It's odd to me that Tom hasn't asked us about him already, if he knows there's a connection. Maybe there's none.'

Ravi whipped around and lashed out in his frustration. 'So it's just a coincidence that the day us two meat-heads arrange to help John's wife leave him, that he has some tie-in with road closures and nine people having to be sequestered in an abandoned top-secret building?' He shared Gemma's guilt. How could they admit to these people who were all heading Up-By on such innocent missions that theirs wasn't so innocent and, it turns out, way more dangerous than they could have imagined.

'Well, we're not going to find out if it's linked to us by making up theories here,' Alec snapped, mirroring Ravi's tone. He caught himself and took a breath and said in a more placatory voice, 'Look, I don't really think we have a choice but to go down there and tell the truth. We might be able to help get everyone else out of here at least, if we explain that we are likely John's target. Let's help get the innocent bystanders out of here.'

Their agreement was just silent nods, and they headed back to the table at the same time as Tom and Calum were approaching from the other direction.

ALEC AND RAVI made their confessional to Tom and Calum before the two policemen had time to give their group briefing. Tom headed straight to the car radio to talk to Beattie. 'You're never going to believe this. You know how I mentioned the Laird's son is here? He's here with Ravi Shah. He's the son of the Shahs who own the restaurant and distribution business, in about his mid-thirties I'd guess.'

'Yup, I know who you mean,' Beattie confirmed.

'There's also a young woman in their car. Gemma. Gemma Wyllie, wife of John Wyllie.'

'You're kidding me!'

'I'm afraid not. The three of them just came over to me like I was the headmaster and they had to confess something naughty to me. They had a similar story to the neighbour you spoke to – that Wyllie's nasty piece of work. Alec and Ravi are helping her get away from him. They did a dawn flit this morning, without telling Wyllie anything. They didn't tell me explicitly, but it doesn't take much reading between the lines that there's something going on between Ravi and her.'

'Well, you just couldn't make this up, could you?'

'I know what you mean. They overheard Wyllie's name being mentioned and got themselves all worked up that they were the cause of all this – that Wyllie is after them.'

'How likely is he to have worked out she's done a runner?'

'They don't know. She left her phone behind in an obvious spot so that it looks like she's just forgotten it, and so that he couldn't contact her.'

'I'm just thinking if he doesn't already know, the last thing we need is for this menace to find out his wife has left him. The threats he's made are already unhinged enough.'

'I know. I just had a similar discussion with them. To say they don't have a good word to say about him is an understatement. They didn't do much to allay my fears about him.'

'Jeez.' There was a pause while Beattie thought and regrouped before he got straight to business. 'Do you think she'd be able to help us track him down, though?'

'They want to do anything they can to help. I said I'd call you with this latest twist in the story and then get them in the car and on a call with you. Shall I give them a shout now?'

'Yes. Yes please Tom.'

Tom got out the car and waved the three of them over, at the same time saying to Calum and Inez, 'Between the two of you, feel free to get everyone up to date so far, and it looks like I may have an addendum to the tale after this call.'

It seemed most sensible to have Gemma in the front seat, so Ravi and Alec climbed into the back. 'In all our antics throughout our friendship, who would have thought that it would take this age to be in the back of a police car together?' Alec joked.

Tom started the radio conversation talking to both sides of the call at once. 'I have Inspector Beattie on the radio. Inspector, I'm now in the car with Gemma Wyllie, Ravi Shah and Alec Douglas-Lauder.'

'Thanks Tom. I don't know how much Sergeant Armstrong has filled you in on, but until this point, we've had no reason to think Wyllie has any motivations outside those made clear in his text threats, which are directed at our MSP Fraser Bam. Of course, finding out his wife has left won't help things, so we're on your side here trying to keep that small fact from him. What I mean is, you can speak freely. We are all striving towards the same result of getting Wyllie into custody as soon as possible. All that sound OK to you?'

Gemma nodded looking at Tom, and Tom gestured that she should speak up and say that into the radio. 'Yes, I understand, thank you.'

'Sergeant Armstrong mentioned you left your phone somewhere in the house. We have a man outside the house. Would he be able to see through a window if your phone is still there?'

'Emm, yes.' Gemma spoke thoughtfully. 'If he goes round to the back garden and looks through the kitchen window, I left it in there. He'll see a fruit bowl on the corner of the countertops, and my phone would be to the left of it – if it's still there.'

'Give me a couple of minutes everyone,' and he signed off abruptly. The car was silent for a moment until a tap on Tom's window made them jump. It was Inez, with Ally behind. *What the hell?* Tom thought as he rolled down the window.

'Sorry Tom, Ally has something to tell you...'

Ally spoke up. 'Inez explained to us some of what's going on, and we thought it might be relevant – or useful – um – well we just thought we should let you know that I'm good friends with Oona McFarland, who is engaged to Fraser Bam.' Inez and Ally looked at him expectantly, as if he had an action plan ready with this scenario in mind.

'Right, well I'm not sure what to do with this information right now. I'll explain it to the Inspector once we've dealt with the first remarkable coincidence at hand.'

'OK.' Both Inez and Ally lingered.

'So just go back and have a seat right now,' Tom told them.

'Oh yes, of course, sorry.'

The two women retreated and Tom rolled up the window. *How many more 'degrees of separation' were they going to find up here?*

'Did Ally just mention Oona McFarland?' Alec piped up from the backseat.

Oh, here we go already! 'Yes she did,' Tom said waiting for the follow up.

'I know Oona too. I didn't realise she was engaged to Fraser Bam. I was away while he was campaigning, I suppose.'

'You know Fraser Bam's fiancée?' Ravi asked somewhat sharply.

'Apparently, yes.'

'How? How do you know her?'

Tom rolled his eyes. These fully grown men were making him feel old. They sounded like kids on the playground. A combination of being lifelong friends and tensions running high, he supposed.

Alec answered Ravi, 'I can't remember if you've met her too. She's super posh, lives with her dad in the big house in Kilmour. He hosts lots of events for his business contacts and sometimes rolls out my dad to lend them some local gravitas. Oona is pretty – long dark hair.'

'How come you know her and I don't?' Ravi sounded pouty, making Tom roll his eyes further back into his head.

'I don't know what to tell you Ravi. I'm the future Laird of a money-pit of an estate, you're the latest hotshot in a highly successful immigrant entrepreneurial family. Are you jealous of me that I get to show up at things as the custodian of the ubiquitous crumbling Scottish castle? I'll switch if you want!'

'Ahem,' Tom's interruption was brief but stern as Beattie came on the radio.

'Gemma, good news, I think. Your phone is still there. What I'm thinking now is, with your permission, your phone might be helpful in communicating with Wyllie and perhaps trying to ascertain what his next move might be.'

Gemma hesitated and looked to Tom for reassurance.

'Sounds good this end,' Tom said, nodding at Gemma.

'Yes, that's OK,' Gemma agreed.

'Is there a way that he can get into the house without breaking and entering?' Beattie asked.

'Yes, there's a key for the back door under an ornamental frog, under a rose bush, by the garden gate.'

'I think the best way to do this is for the officer there to go in and retrieve your phone and bring it to me at the station. Then among us we can strategise how to communicate with him. Is that fine by you Gemma?'

'Yes, that's fine,' Gemma confirmed.

'OK, I'll pass on the information about the key and hopefully be back talking to you in ten to fifteen minutes,' Beattie said.

'Before you go, we have one more piece of information from up here that was just brought to my attention,' Tom said. 'Ally, who is one of the ladies who was supposed to be traveling up to Glasgow to see a concert tonight, is good friends with Fraser Bam's fiancée. Alec has also met her a few times.'

'Mid-June can be a small world, can't it?' Beattie replied, and Tom could almost hear him shaking his head.

'We were just saying the very same.'

'OK, that's good to know, but for now, our best lead is Gemma's phone. Speak soon.'

'Yup over and out, then,' Tom clicked off. 'Fresh air?' He said to his fellow occupants of the car as he opened his door. 'Let's go up and give the assembled company an update on these latest developments, just so everyone is in the loop. I think that's the best policy at this stage.'

29

Fraser and Oona had wasted no time in getting their *heids doon* after their respective phone calls with Blah Blah and Inspector Beattie. After a little time working through the paperwork, Oona discovered that Fraser was right, and her eye started recognising patterns, learning which parts of the reports were standard introductions, disclaimers, keys to terms, and as such could largely be ignored. She quickly developed a feel for what papers were high-level, which were the nuts and bolts, and which were somewhere in between. Fraser also explained what level of additional detail they could drill down to on his laptop. They worked mostly independently, sifting and sorting, Oona asking less questions as she found her rhythm, and Fraser occasionally pointing out something he realised he hadn't mentioned which might be helpful.

Gradually, they developed a picture of where Kay Consulting Services, mostly noted as KCS, cropped up, which as Mack had said, was often, and scattered throughout the accounts. They gathered together a large pile of the actual invoices payable to KCS. They were in order of account first, and then date, and zoning in on that, they searched for any clues as to what these payments were for, convinced that if they looked hard enough and let their brains find the patterns, they'd find evidence that they weren't all legitimate. When the clues weren't forthcoming, Oona suggested they look at the digital detail.

Fraser pulled his laptop in front of him. He looked over at the page Oona was holding, pulled up the corresponding page in the program, and clicked to reveal the payment description. 'There's only one more line, and it says, "Re: McKenzie Road Services".'

'There he is, our old imaginative friend McKenzie. OK, let's try the next one.' Oona showed him the details of the next one in her pile.

'"Re: Caledonian Concrete,"' Fraser read out.

Oona picked up a pen and noted the descriptor on each printout. They went through about a dozen this way before Oona put down her pen, slightly defeated and said, 'It's going to take ages this way.'

Fraser nodded in agreement and hit some keys, thinking it was highly unlikely that deep dives into the nuts and bolts of spreadsheets had been part of his predecessor's modus operandi. No, Les Mitchell was more of a shaking hands and holding babies kind of politician. Still, Fraser was happy to roll his sleeves up, but he just wasn't sure he had the precise skillset right now. He realised though, that he knew a man who did. 'Hang on, Mack will be able to help. Let's call him.'

Mack picked up the phone on the first ring. 'Fraser, I've been thinking about you all morning. How are things going?'

'Not going to lie, I've had better days. Hopefully we'll get to laugh about it over a pint, but we're not really there yet. Oona is here, and we wondered if you could send something else across to us.'

After a short description of what they were looking at, Mack exported the program data into a user-friendly format and forwarded it to Fraser. They were off the phone and back to work within a couple of minutes.

'Well we'll ignore these rows to there,' Oona pointed to the screen, 'because there are only one or two of each. Look at this chunk here though. They are all Caledonian Concrete and made on the twenty-first of the month every three months.' Oona jotted this down messily on the back of one of the invoices. She already suspected they were about to see more similarly regular payments because just a cursory glance showed lines and lines of the same names. 'Davidson Brothers Hauling is on the tenth of the month, a much smaller amount but monthly.'

Fraser ran his finger quickly down to the next clump. 'McKenzie Road Services' is on the twenty-fifth of the month and is quarterly, same as Caledonian Concrete.' He condensed the information he was reading out as he scanned his finger down to just 'monthly' or 'quarterly' as Oona scribbled the names looking at them on the screen. They got to eight contractors who were named on these regular invoices paid to Wyllie.

'Going back to what Wyllie said to you about a finder's fee for finding Mack. Do these businesses have their contracts renewed regularly, that Wyllie could claim he was in some way involved in securing their services or renegotiating their contracts?'

'They shouldn't, quite the contrary. Every major contractor had to sign until completion with indemnities and cross-indemnities flying around everywhere in case of losses and to help prevent bankruptcies. After everything that's gone on, we couldn't risk losing any of our providers if they decided to call it quits at the renewal of an interim contract.'

'That makes sense,' Oona nodded.

Fraser put his hands behind his head and leaned back in

his chair thinking. He was tired. His mind was foggy, but he wondered if it wasn't in fact their fault that they couldn't see a clever answer. Maybe there wasn't one. Maybe all these payments were just downright fraudulent but because they happened regularly, had a known contractor's name in the subject line and were quite small in Big Belt terms, they were hiding in plain sight.

'I think these payments are all just bogus, with no substance at all,' Oona announced decidedly.

How had she managed to read his mind? 'You read my mind, my love. If it walks like a duck and quacks like a duck...'

'Indeed. None of these payments would stand out in the grand scheme of things, but there are lots of them, so they add up for Wyllie. Can we figure out how long has this been going on?'

'Hang on...' Fraser reordered the spreadsheet by date. 'The first payment was just over a year ago,' he paused noticing something. 'Wait a minute though. It's not a payment – it's a negative amount. For two hundred thousand pounds.'

'You mean, it's a charge to Wyllie rather than a payment?' Oona came and looked over Fraser's shoulder to see for herself. '*BE Holdings*,' she read aloud from the description column. 'I don't think we've we seen that one before, have we? Let me search for that on here.'

Fraser had recognised almost all the other names as they had waded though, so he was already googling it on his phone.

'Beautiful Era Holdings,' he said out loud.

'Beautiful Era Holdings? Sounds like an assisted living place or a nursing home.' Oona was slightly distracted as she interpreted the spreadsheet with a shake of her head, and frowning, she said, 'BE Holdings received two hundred thousand pounds on the same day as KCS was charged it. What the hell?'

They both sat back in their chairs, Fraser working away on

his phone, and Oona saying quietly, 'What are you up to KCS and BE Holdings? Or should I say Beautiful Era Holdings? Ou La Belle Époque comme on dit en France.' Had he been properly listening, Fraser would have been in awe of Oona's impeccable French accent.

Deep in thought, they both got a fright when Oona's phone pinged. Oona jumped up to fetch it from the sideboard. 'It's just Ally.' She was about to put the phone to the side, too busy for social matters, but then just a glance at the message underneath on her lock screen made her open it.

Ally: *Oona, if you see this text me back ASAP. I suspect you know what it's about. Ally x*

'I should answer this,' Oona said, already doing so. She narrated the text exchange to Fraser as it happened.

Oona: *I'm here. With Fraser.*
Ally: *Do you know anything about a bunch of people stuck at The Glass Pass?*
Oona: *Yes, Fraser is in touch with the police. Well, actually I am too. We're having quite a complicated day. I'll explain another time. How do you know about that?*
Ally: *I'm one of the people!*
Oona: *You're kidding!*
Ally: *I wish I was! No Take That concert for me.*
Oona: *We were told you were going to be taken to somewhere safe. Are you OK?*
Ally: *Yes, we're fine. Everyone is quite calm. We can only get phone reception from one spot, so when I heard that Fraser was involved in this, I came up to let you know I'm here.*
Oona: *How many people are there?*
Ally: *Nine. Two policeman and there were three cars trying to get through the pass. Jill and me obviously, two women – an aunt and*

her niece, and the third car had Alec Douglas-Lauder and two of his friends in it. The three of them are with the police at the moment. Actually – I can see some activity there. I'll go down and see what's going on.
Oona: *Well Fraser and I are working away on trying to make sense of things here. Let's keep in touch and compare notes about what is going on. We're hoping this'll all be over soon.*
Ally: *Thx x*

Oona put her phone on the table and looked up wide-eyed at Fraser. 'Poor Ally! Can you believe she's one of the people we've been talking to Inspector Beattie about?'

'I feel awful. Was she heading Up-By for a concert?' Fraser asked.

'Yes – a Take That concert with her friend Jill. She's been talking about it for months. Actually, more about how good it would be for Jill to get away for the night. She has two young kids and is pretty overwhelmed I believe.'

'I feel even worse hearing that. These poor people. At least she says people are calm and feel safe,' Fraser said.

'Yes, and in a way, it's like we have boots on the ground – or an inside man. Let's keep plugging away with what we can do from here. Where were we?'

'*Beautiful Era Holdings*,' Fraser reminded her. 'And then I think you might have said something in French before Ally pinged you.'

'Ah oui, *La Belle Époque*. The English translation of that, albeit it's inadequate and quite misses the gist, is *Beautiful Era*. From *La Belle Epoque* to *Beautiful Era Holdings*. From the sublime to the frankly naff-sounding.' Fraser had to agree, particularly given how exquisite her French was – he had no idea why she was messing around with having his mum teach her old Scots when she had that elegant language at her disposal.

Oona gasped. She had Fraser's attention while her eyes

darted around trying to recall something. '*La Belle Époque*! No! Surely this can't be true,' she said, still mostly talking to herself. Then after another searching pause, she said to Fraser, 'This might be a stretch, but hear me out. It popped into my head because the last time I saw Alec Douglas-Lauder was at a retirement soirée my dad had for Les Mitchell. He gave a toast in which he wished Les and his wife Isabelle, Belle for short, lots of happy sailings on their new yacht in the South of France. Guess what the yacht was called – *La Belle Époque*!'

'No way! This can't be a coincidence.' Fraser was following along as Oona's voice got louder and more animated as she felt she was getting closer to solving a mystery.

'Les later told me the boat's name was a play on Belle's name. Belle said it was her time now, after all his long hours and years in politics. I don't think this is a coincidence either. That payment to BE Holdings of two hundred thousand pounds was about a year ago which is when Les retired. So what exactly is the connection?'

'My mind is going to straight to some pretty unsavoury connections I'm afraid. I'm going to call Mack to send us the same report as we got for KCS, but for BE Holdings this time. You see what comes up if you google BE Holdings.'

Mack confirmed what Fraser thought before he even sent the report, saying, 'This looks very like the one I sent you for KCS – the descriptions and distribution of payments look very similar, just made to BE Holdings, not KCS. I'll send it over to you for a closer look though. Let me know if there's anything else at all, and I'll get it to you right away. It sounds like you two are making headway over there. I'll let you get back to work.'

As Fraser hung up and refreshed his email, Oona held her phone up for him to see one of her search results. 'Les Mitchell's name isn't connected to BE Holdings...but Isabelle's is. Ding, ding, ding. Are you thinking what I'm thinking?'

'Well, I am if you're thinking the unthinkable – that the

dedicated and beloved public servant, the MSP for Kilmour and Berry Valley, was on the take, embezzling public funds via The Big Belt project…'

'…and that he then sold the rights to the scam to John Wyllie upon his retirement.' Oona finished Fraser's sentence. 'Yes, I'm thinking the unthinkable too, then.'

30

When Gemma's phone was deposited with the Inspector, Tom, Gemma, Alec and Ravi piled back into Tom's car.

Inspector Beattie began, 'Gemma, I can see from your home screen that it looks like Wyllie has already texted you. Are you OK to let me know your passcode and with me reading the texts to you? And to everyone that's in the car?'

'Yes, no problem. My passcode is 1908.'

'Thank you. Now let's see...' There was a pause as the Inspector opened the phone and clicked on the texts. 'There are four texts. I'll read them out.'

John: *I'm not going to make it back to the house this morning. I've got a busy day ahead. Be good.*
John: *People are idiots. Some c*nt has chosen the wrong person to fuck with today.*
John: *Why haven't you texted me back? Where are you?*
John: *Depending on how this thing goes I may to have to lay low for a bit. If anyone asks just say I'm out of town on business. You make sure and be good until I get back.*

Even though the policemen had explained that this morning's events were more likely to be as a result of Wyllie's dealings with Fraser Bam, Gemma still gave a small sigh of relief that Wyllie hadn't realised she had gone. The car was momentarily quiet as everyone processed the texts. Ravi shifted position in his seat in the back, not enjoying hearing Wyllie's voice, even through text. Alec patted him on the leg in solidarity. The Inspector spoke again. 'We need to choose our words carefully. Responding in a way that he'll believe it's you texting him back Gemma, but also in a way that'll get information out of him. Of course, he may not even look at his phone for some time, so we shouldn't get our hopes too high for an immediate response. You with me Tom?'

'Yes, just thinking it all through too and re-reading at the texts that I jotted down. We could reply to the texts individually. This is a good opportunity for us, or Gemma I mean, to find out more.'

Among them, they came up with the responses to Wyllie.

***John:** People are idiots. Some c*nt has chosen the wrong person to fuck with today.*
***Gemma:** Oh dear. Who's the unlucky person on the other end of your wrath?*
***John:** Why haven't you texted me back? Where are you?*
***Gemma:** I'm just out and about. My phone was in my handbag on silent.*
***John:** Depending on how this thing goes, I have to have to lay low for a bit. If anyone asks just say I'm out of town on business. You make sure and be good until I get back.*
***Gemma:** What thing? What do you mean by lay low? Where? Not gonna lie, you're making me nervous. Where are you just now? Still in Mid-June?*

'What do we do now? It could be a while before he reads

them. He seems to be having quite the busy day after all,' Alec asked.

'He's read them!' The Inspector's voice came through the radio. 'They're marked as read.'

'Oh, don't mind me. That was fast,' Alec murmured. The car went quiet again. After a couple of minutes, Tom couldn't resist checking in.

'Nothing yet Tom, obviously I'd…' Beattie replied.

'…tell us immediately. I know. Sorry,' Tom apologised. 'Would he usually answer texts right away Gemma?'

'He's pretty sporadic. Expects me to answer him back straight away, but has a different set of rules for him.' Gemma's reply was followed by an indistinguishable noise from Ravi in the back seat.

'Well, that's good to know,' Beattie said. 'And right now, I'd rather be feeling more productive than sitting staring at a phone. I'll turn the volume up to max and have Gemma's phone on me at all times, so I'll not miss any response. I know you guys can't exactly go off and get things done, but I'm sure even not being cooped up in a car will be a better option for you all right now. The weather still fine up there?'

'Very sunny, yes. And you wouldn't believe the set-up we have up here. We should have Calum lead us on a hike up here. It's incredible. So intact. Absolutely fascinating and the views are phenomenal.'

'Yes, we'll have to do that. I can't picture it all, and after the part it's played today, I'd love to be able to, so that when we're telling each other the story of this strange day in our dotage, I'll know what it looked like too.'

Tom laughed. 'Right you are then. We'll go back to the body of the kirk here and wait to hear from you. Roger.'

31

It had all been a bit too much for Ravi – listening to the love of his life communicate with her evil husband, even if it was just a subterfuge in aid of a higher purpose. 'I need to take a wander,' he mumbled. Alec didn't feel like going straight back to the picnic table, so he found himself venturing into the Y-station, which was much brighter now because the sun was hitting one of the skylights directly. He was surprised when Gemma followed him in.

'Oh – you again! I can't shake you it seems,' he laughed.

'Well, we're trying. Ravi and I – we're trying our best to leave you behind, you know,' she matched his jokey tone. Then more seriously, she said, 'we should be in your flat by now.'

'I know, I'm sorry,' Alec replied.

'You have absolutely no need to apologise. You've been so generous Alec. It's because of you that we plucked up the courage to make a move. And then you helped us plan it all out. We really appreciate it. I really appreciate it.'

'Well so much for all the planning. We could never have imagined this though,' Alec said.

'Nope,' Gemma said simply.

'How about that feast we managed to pull together?'

'Oh I know. Inez's strawberry tarts are the best things I've ever tasted,' Gemma answered.

Alec wasn't sure why he was making small talk. There was a long pause, and they just stood looking at each other, Alec noticing that the hazel flecks in her eyes were highlighted by the stream of sunlight.

At the same time as he began, 'What did you ever —,' Gemma said, 'You know Alec I —,' and they both halted and waited for the other to continue.

'You go first,' Gemma said. 'What were you going to ask me?'

'I was going to be quite rude and ask what did you ever see in John Wyllie, but it's really not my place, so ignore me. You go. What were you going to say?'

'Well actually, it's probably related. I was going to reassure you that I really do love Ravi, and I want to spend the rest of my life with him. I'm not just using him to escape John.'

'I never thought—'

'No, let me finish, because maybe if I tell you why I know Ravi and I are going to make it, it'll help you understand other things too.' Gemma paused and Alec nodded, listening. 'Ravi made me feel like myself again Alec. He made me like the thought of the future again. Without wanting to sound too dramatic, he made me want to live again. Properly – making plans and dreaming dreams. Bit by bit, John had taken all that away from me. I know I married him faster than you can say "daddy issues", but he managed to tap into everything that motivated me – not just with the nice house I'd never had growing up and stability in this lovely wee part of the world. I'm happy to report that there's a bit more to me than that. He knew it and used it to work against me – he used my own ambitions of starting my own business to lure me here. And once I was here – and *his*,' she flinched, 'he made a point of chipping away at my confidence. He disparaged my ideas and belittled all the research I'd done. They'd always been big dreams – a stretch that a girl from my background and with no connections could build a business as big as I was aiming for – but for the most part I believed I could achieve them. John took any tiny glimmer of self-doubt that occasionally appeared and exploited it. He was subtle and gradual, but he was thorough. My poor mum tried to keep all my aspirations alive every time she saw me but it got more and more difficult. I can't imagine how upsetting it must have been for her to witness.' The regret of putting her mum through this made her pause.

'Well, she'll be very relieved when you make it up to Glasgow and see her. And she'll love Ravi – everyone does,' Alec said. In many ways it was lucky that Gemma and Ravi had already fallen for each other, when Alec returned to Mid-June. It meant that he didn't ever have to see Gemma at her lowest – the person she was describing now. She was already on the upswing, envisioning a future where she got rid of John, daring to hope she could make one with Ravi. It made his own heart ache, to think that this vibrant confident woman could be so broken by a worthless piece of shit like John Wyllie. He couldn't imagine a mother's pain.

Gemma smiled as she spoke again. 'So that brings us to Ravi. Dear Ravi. I've never been revered before. Ravi positively reveres me – do you know how much that means? Right from the start, when we were just running buddies, he'd ask my advice – listening and taking in everything I told him, even though I'm just an enthusiastic amateur. You'll think it sounds trivial – that running tips are part of our love story. I'm not stupid, I knew he fancied me, so at first I thought it was just part of him chatting me up, something to talk about. But one night, he didn't know I'd come into the bar yet, and I overheard him talking about how much he was learning from me – about building up slowly, not overdoing it, taking rest days, etc.

Compared to John's ongoing campaign to beat me down, it felt really nice to be respected, even if just for something as small as that. Since you've been back, you've been there when we've been talking about the restaurant business and all the exciting things that are happening there. Ravi values my contributions – he doesn't make a move on any of the new social media stuff without running it past me first. Rediscovering my self-worth has been just – just incredible. It made me see how stifled I've been. Ravi and I are a team, even though we're still early days in our relationship and we've had such an unconventional start. I know you're protective of him – well, you're protective of everyone, let's face it – and I know how much his family means to you, so I suppose I felt the need to explain why I'm sure we're in this for the long-haul.'

'Thanks,' Alec wasn't sure what else to say.

'I once made you a bit emotional telling you about Anne Murray and *Danny's Song*. I'll probably do it again, so I'm sorry in advance, but the next time you listen to her sing *You Needed Me*, listen to those lyrics from my point of view. It could be my song to Ravi. Well, if he wasn't so stubbornly blinkered in his music tastes.' She gave a small laugh. 'I'll spare you my singing this time, but think of it – I know you must know the lyrics by heart. Ravi put me on a pedestal Alec, and he needs me. We need each other,' she finished quietly.

Alec had already done what Gemma was asking him to do – listened to *You Needed Me* and thought of her. A few times. Except that when he did, he imagined being the one to be holding her hand and giving her hope. That soulful voice singing such heart-tugging lyrics had pierced many a soul in all its decades, but he wondered if there had ever been this level of poignancy attached to it by anyone. What a claim to fame.

When Alec said nothing, Gemma held out her arms and said, 'What's a girl got to do around here to get a hug?'

Alec smiled and pulled her in, wrapping her up. They

stayed like that for a few seconds, Gemma smiling, Alec with his eyes closed, savouring, basking, for a moment. She pulled away but he resisted, just for a split second, almost imperceptibly, and they both could have pretended that it didn't happen. As their bodies untwined, he took her hands and they stood facing each other, eyes locked in a silent pause once again. Once again, a split-second of boldness got the better of him, and he said, 'Gemma, there's something I need to say —'

'I bet there's not, you know,' she interrupted. 'I bet there's nothing you need to tell me that I don't already know.' She kept looking at him, smiling.

Of course she knew, Alec realised. He nodded back, *ok, enough, they'd leave it at that,* and they dropped hands.

'Besides, you know your Shakespeare, Professor Douglas-Lauder. I am merely a Rosaline. Juliet is out there waiting for you. Maybe literally – Ally is very attractive in case you haven't noticed.'

'Right you – cheeky. Don't get any ideas. C'mon though – let's go and see where Ravi got to on his wander.' And they left the Y-station arm-in-arm.

32

Even though they were chatting quite easily, everyone's ears were tuned in to the sound of the police radio from the car, and they heard it at exactly the same time as Calum came running down from the roof of the Y-station where he had been manning his phone. 'We've heard back from Wyllie,' he explained gesturing towards his phone, indicating he'd had a text. 'Inspector Beattie says get to the radio.'

Tom stood up and Gemma, Alec and Ravi followed suit. 'Gents, no offence, but I think you can sit this one out. Calum, can you come with Gemma and me to the car please?'

'Yes Sarge,' Calum said, following.

Once the three of them were in the car, Tom notified Beattie of the change in personnel.

'Perfect, thanks Tom. Ok, Calum note this down on your phone and I'm sure Tom you have your notepad to hand.' Beattie read out Gemma's texts with Wyllie's replies.

***Gemma:** Oh dear. Who's the unlucky person on the other end of your wrath?*

John: *No one you know.*
Gemma: *I'm just out and about. My phone was in my handbag on silent.*
John: *I hope you're home now or going home soon. You know that I prefer to know that you're home when I'm not around. Unless you're running. Running is fine with me. Keeps you looking good. Don't want that firm body getting soft.*

Beattie's voice tailed off at the end of this text, but it was too late and everyone squirmed. He continued.

Gemma: *What thing? What do you mean by lay low? Where? Not gonna lie, you're making me nervous. Where are you just now? Still in Mid-June?*
John: *Still hoping this asshole I'm dealing with will see sense. If so I'll be at home tonight. He needs to realise he should just play ball. I'm at one of my barns just now.*

'Got all that?' Beattie asked after a pause to let them catch up. 'Gemma, what does *one of my barns* mean?'

Gemma replied, 'John bought up some derelict farm buildings when he got involved in The Big Belt. Something about either the next stage of the project, or if The Big Belt goes wrong...' Gemma hesitated. 'He bought them saying he'd make money when the government has to buy the land when this version of The Big Belt fails.'

'Classic,' Beattie sighed in tired annoyance. 'We have someone working on The Big Belt who will gain from it failing. Sounds about right with this whole palaver. Do you know where any of these barns are Gemma?'

'He's pointed out a few of them when we've been out in the car. They seem to string all through Mid-June. Some looked like little farm labourers' cottages, and some were literally barns, but he referred to them all as barns.'

'Any idea how many we're talking about?'

'Not really, I'm sorry. He never really gave me much detail about his financial dealings or investments.'

'If you had to guess? Five? A dozen? Twenty?'

'I'd guess a dozen.'

'OK, well we need to narrow that down somehow. I guess our first stab is just to go ahead and ask him which one. I guess we should pad it a bit.' Beattie read out loud as he typed, *'Well, hopefully whoever it is will see things your way. Which barn are you at?* Are you OK with me sending that Gemma?'

'Yes, that sounds fine, Gemma replied.

Beattie's voice came back through the radio in return, 'And...send.'

'Inspector?'

'Yes, Calum?'

'You might recall this too, but at one stage in The Big Belt planning phase there were two competing ideas of exactly which route it should take through Mid-June. Both routes were published in the papers. Perhaps Wyllie bought up properties in the alternative corridor for The Big Belt so that if the current project fails, he would be sitting pretty for the back-up plan. If you give me five minutes, I'll go up to the viewpoint, which is where we're all getting best reception on our phones, and I'll pull up the published drawings and compare them to Google Earth. If I take screenshots, we can take a look with Gemma and see if she recognises any of Wyllie's properties.'

'That's a great idea, Calum, yes please, go ahead and do that. Can you send them through to the station please so we're all looking at the same thing?'

'Will do. Back in five.'

Tom shook his head in admiration of his young colleague and friend as he said into the radio, 'He's some kid, isn't he? Mid-June is in safe hands when I'm retired.'

'You still want to retire after all this excitement today? Sure we can't talk you into staying?' Beattie asked.

They chatted a little awkwardly trying to include Gemma, aware that she was stuck with the two old friends while they waited for Calum, until Beattie interrupted the small talk with, 'Oh, here we go, I have several messages from Calum.' As Beattie paused to look through them, Calum arrived back at the car, passed Tom his phone and directed him through the pictures.

As well as pictures from Google Earth, Calum had also found the newspaper article he had referred to, and screen-shotted the aerial picture which had the alternative road superimposed over it in red. They spent a few minutes with everyone getting their bearings within the set of photos, and Beattie opened Google Earth so he could zoom in. It took Gemma a little longer to catch up, as she wasn't as familiar with the area as the rest of them, so they had to point out various landmarks so she could visualise where each picture was in real life.

Altogether, the pictures took them on a trail through Mid-June. Once Gemma had the gist of things, she was able to identify three, with a possible fourth, of Wyllie's 'barns'. Of the three she was confident about, two looked like rundown old animal sheds in the middle of low-lying wild land which had sheep dotted all around in the pictures. They were far from any roads and mostly roofless. Beattie and Tom surmised they weren't ideal hide outs. The third property though, Gemma remembered clearly, because it actually was quite a pretty little cottage by a babbling river. You couldn't see it from the road, but Wyllie was keen to show it off to her, so they had parked the car and walked for ten minutes or so, down a path through some woods, and the path opened up to the back of an old cottage which faced the river on the other side. Once they had helped her pick out the road she was able to locate the wood and the river and point out the small blob that was the cottage.

Beattie zoomed in and confirmed the blown-up version looked exactly like what she was describing. When he zoomed out again, he followed the river north, and his fears were confirmed.

'Tom. This cottage is just south of Drover's Bridge. It's well hidden, not too hard for Wyllie to get to, but not too easy for anyone like us trying to find him. And if you were going to choose a hide-out, one close to one of your threatened targets would make sense too.'

'Sounds to me like you might want to send someone out there for a look,' Tom said.

'I think that should be me. I'll take someone else from here with me,' Beattie replied. He spent a couple of minutes taking notes from Gemma – as much as she could remember about where they'd parked, the path down to the cottage through the woods, and what the entrances to the cottage were, front and back. 'Right, everyone, good work. It's about a fifteen-minute drive and then Gemma said a five minute walk, so I'm afraid you're just playing the waiting game for now.'

'Good luck, Inspector. Be careful.'

'Thanks Tom. Roger.'

33

Ravi stood up to hug Gemma as she and Tom and Calum made it back to the picnic spot. They stepped away a little, and she told him quietly what had gone on while Tom told everyone else the same story.

'Sounds like there could be a good chance he's in that cottage you've identified,' said Alec.

Inez, who was sitting next to him, put her hand on his forearm. 'Oh Alec, fingers crossed. I'd love for us all to get out of here safely sooner rather than later. Thank God it's May. In winter it would be getting dark soon.'

'Right enough,' he agreed. 'Anything we can do from here, Tom?'

'I think we just have to sit tight, I'm afraid,' was the reply. Followed by a cheeky look to Inez. 'What's the strawberry tart count at now?'

'Honestly, we'd have to be here for days before we run out of them. Have you seen how many there are in the back of my car? I'll go and get another tray.'

'I haven't seen how many, actually. Maybe I'll come and take a look with you and make sure they're still OK. Wouldn't mind a tour of your fancy car too.'

Calum and Katie caught eyes. They raised their eyebrows at each other and Calum rolled his eyes and towards Tom and Inez, smiling. 'I know,' Katie mouthed back at him.

Jill got up from the table. 'I'm going to phone George and the kids,' she announced. 'Gosh it's really warm now, isn't it?' And she started up the path to the roof of the station.

Ally asked Calum if she could take a closer look at the pictures of Wyllie's possible whereabouts, and Alec joined in. The three of them pointed out landmarks to each other, and after not too long, Ally and Alec had as good a take as Calum on the likely locations of John Wyllie's barns. Then Ally piped up with a change of subject – 'Alec, I've been meaning to tell you, I just haven't had the chance. I've met your mum and dad several times. My company does some work at the castle. Events organising type stuff. The 10k was my first thing, and I loved working with your mum, so we've done a few other things since then.'

'Oh wow really? You're *that* Alison? My mum has told me about you – she speaks very highly of you. Sorry – I suppose we've had a few distractions today or I might have made the connection.'

'That's OK – a few distractions, to say the least. But do you fancy a wee walk so you can tell me all the nice things your mum has said about me?'

Alec was a little surprised but as Ally was already getting up from the table he murmured, 'Um, sure,' and followed her. Calum and Katie caught each other's eyes again and smiled awkwardly.

'And then there were two,' Katie broke the silence. 'I think my Aunt Inez and Tom like each other, don't you? Tell me more about Tom...'

Once Ally and Alec were out of earshot, Ally said, 'OK, I'm not that much of a diva that I brought you over here to listen to how much your mum loves me – I think she's amazing by the way. I really do enjoy working with her, but I just had to get you alone. Oh, don't panic, nothing like that. You said earlier that you know Oona McFarland too, right? She's a good friend of mine.'

Alec wondered if this conversation would start to make sense soon.

Ally lowered her voice now to say, 'Listen, I texted Oona earlier. Told her what's going on here. She's with Fraser and working away on getting to the bottom of whatever it is that's motivating Wyllie. But tell me, what did you think about the next steps that Calum talked us through?'

'Um...' Alec was still trying to catch up on whatever journey Ally was leading him on.

'Don't you think they're putting all their eggs in one basket? Gemma estimated there to be a dozen or so places that Wyllie could be talking about, and only managed to pick out three of them. And they're going all-in on it being the *only* one of them that it could be.'

Alec didn't even try to interject. He was seeing why one of the things his mum said about Ally was that she is 'as quick as a whip' and also realising he had been recruited mostly as a sounding board, not as an active collaborator in wherever she was going with this.

'I think we should go up to the roof and get in touch with Oona and Fraser. She told me to keep in touch, so she'll be standing by her phone. That's why I asked Calum those questions about where he found that newspaper article, so Oona can google them too, and maybe we'll be able to spot other likely properties Wyllie has commandeered, in case this one they're going with is the wrong one.'

'Why didn't you mention this to Calum?'

'I didn't want to undermine what he and Gemma had achieved and be the nay-sayer who brings everyone's hopes down to earth with a bump. Besides, with the same information, Oona and Fraser can act much faster than we can here – they have laptops and Wi-Fi, and the distinct advantage that they're not stuck at a top-secret Y-station on a mountain top.'

'That is true,' Alec conceded.

'Come up with me and be a second set of ears, in case I miss out anything Calum told us. You can fill in the gaps.'

'OK, sounds good,' and Alec gestured *after you* in the direction of the roof. 'Take That eh? Interesting.'

'I won't hear a bad thing said about them, even if you are a music professor,' she said as she climbed up, then, asked cheekily, 'what did your mum say about me anyway?'

That you're very pretty, capable, impressive, that you love Glenberry Castle. She feels about you the way my grandmother Mimi felt about her. According to her you're perfect for me and I should marry you. Alec only thought this to himself even though it was true. Out loud he said, 'Lots of great things. Maybe I can tell you over a drink when all this was over.' He imagined his mother doing a happy jig.

Jill was smiling into the horizon, listening to her kids babbling nonsense into the phone. Before he put them on, George had sounded so concerned for her and seemed genuinely upset that she wasn't going to get to go to her concert. He'd even said a couple of times how much she had deserved a break, and how hard she works. Jill felt a warm glow to hear his words of appreciation, and she realised she was missing him and the kids – after not even a full day. As the chaos continued on the other end of the phone, she glanced over her shoulder in the other direction and saw Ally and Alec deep in conversation, in their own little twosome. She raised her eyebrows and smiled an even broader smile to herself. A minute later, when she saw them walking up towards her together, she said hurriedly into the phone, 'Kids...guys...listen to Mummy guys. I need to go now. I'll call you back again soon,' then as she passed Alec and Ally on her way down said breezily, 'The kids and George are off out a walk now. I'll give you two your privacy anyway.'

34

Although they would occasionally remind each other that they may be adding two and two together and getting five, Fraser and Oona couldn't help but think that they had come up with a fairly conceivable backstory as to how John Wyllie had got himself into this position. It started with having to turn everything everyone believed about solid, dependable Les Mitchell, MSP for Kilmour and Berry Valley, on its head. Then the more they unearthed about BE Holdings as they dug around the internet and a couple more reports that Mack sent them, the more they had to believe that Les Mitchell had been taking bribes, guised as various types of fees, the whole way through The Big Belt project. He had got away with it for so long that he had then been bold enough to seemingly sell the rights to these 'fees' to John Wyllie. And further, bold enough to put the transactions through the accounts, which made them think that the corruption probably ran deeper than just Les Mitchell and John Wyllie. Fraser and Oona had various guesses at how many people and in what roles must be entangled in this – accompanied by Oona frequently repeating the phrase 'how do people sleep at night?' – but they had uncovered a pretty good starting point.

When they texted Inspector Beattie that they had some information for them he replied: *I hope I will have some for you soon too. Closing in on Wyllie.*

They had been running on adrenaline for several hours and as the pieces fell into place it gradually subsided to a point where it no longer suppressed their appetites and Oona announced suddenly, 'I'm absolutely ravenous.'

'Now you mention it, me too,' Fraser replied.

'I can't even wait to cook anything. I need something now. Now now!'

'I could do you baked beans on toast with grated cheese on top?'

'Mmm,' Oona sighed longingly as if she was being offered a Michelin star meal. 'Add on a little Worcester sauce, and I'll maybe even still marry you.' She kissed Fraser on the cheek, teasing him. He grabbed her and held her tight.

'Oona. I can't even begin to tell you how amazing you've been...'

'Shoosh! I'm too hungry for you to gush. You get the beans on the stove, I'll make the toast.' Then Oona's phone rang. 'It's Ally. Looks like you're making the toast too, sorry, but hang on a sec and hear why she's calling.'

Oona hadn't expected there to be so many staggering developments since their last text exchange, or she'd have put Ally on speaker so Fraser could have heard firsthand. As it was, she relayed the information aloud, incredulously: 'The girl who was traveling Up-By with Alec Douglas-Lauder is John Wyllie's wife?' Fraser returned Oona's stunned look and waited for her to summarise the next part of the debrief. He couldn't hear what Ally was saying, but he could hear that she was downloading the information as fast as she could. 'They're in touch with Wyllie via her cell phone – I'm just giving Fraser the headlines Ally – mm-hmm...mm-hmm - hang on,' Oona directed herself at Fraser again. 'Wyllie owns properties throughout the valley, and he's holed up in one of them,' then back to Ally, 'mm-hmm, mm-hmm, I see...'

And so it went on until they got to Ally's action points for Oona and Fraser, and he was dismissed to make beans on toast, while Oona sat down at his laptop.

By the time Fraser returned with their banquet, Oona had the maps and drawings that Ally had directed her to pull up on the laptop and she briefed Fraser as they ate. 'Ally's concern is that Wyllie owns an unknown number of these properties, or *barns* as he apparently calls them, but Inspector Beattie and his people zero-ed in on one quite quickly – too quickly, Ally feels. There's a limit to what they can achieve up there with just their phones and poor cell service, so she talked me through all of this,' she waved a hand at a laptop as she cleaned her plate. 'Alec Douglas-Lauder was there too chiming in. Mmm, that was delicious thank you.'

'I'm not sure how much more successful we can be in pinpointing where Wyllie is,' Fraser said looking at the Google Earth images, as Oona cleared their plates.

'Well, we're refuelled now, so let's think logically about what we know. His string of properties start here,' Oona pointed. 'They looked at this cluster here because they're close to Drover's Bridge as mentioned in that second threat to Blah Blah, that he'd get him with a single shot or whatever the piece of shit said.'

Hearing Oona saying *single shot* was chilling. They'd been so immersed in the so-called white-collar side of things, which always implies that such crimes are victimless, that Fraser felt a knot in his chest to think of Wyllie out there, apparently armed, taking aim at Blah Blah and his driver. They were still staying put of course, so that wouldn't happen now, but that that had been his intent was just unimaginable. Oona was lost in her own contemplations, but something occurred to Fraser. He grabbed his phone and opened up Wyllie's texts to him again.

Oona was curious – 'What you up to there my love?'

'I'm looking at the Drover's Bridge text again. He doesn't say *a single shot*, he says *a single blast,*' Fraser replied, his thoughts still forming.

'OK, go on. What are you thinking? I can see the cogs turning.'

'Look, Wyllie is indeed a *piece of shit*, as you so eloquently put it, and all these fraudulent goings-on, basically ripping off the Scottish Government, though shockingly brazen, were not surprising to me. But could I see him with a gun taking aim at someone within range? I dunno – you love those true crime podcasts – surely it's quite a jump from cooking-the-books to a stone-cold shooting?'

'Well, you've met him, and I haven't, but yes, I agree with all of that. It's a leap to cold-blooded murder,' Oona said.

'That's why I wanted to read the exact wording of his text. If we put aside for now the knowledge we have about him having guns, when we read the first text we went straight to something being arranged to look like an accident. It made sense because unfortunately it's not outwith the realms of possibility for there to be a fatal accident on the Glass Pass with the state it's in at the moment. Never mind if Wyllie was able to interfere to make things even worse,' Fraser said.

'What do you mean by that?' Oona asked.

'Well, the reason I came up with the traffic lights stall was that I was wondering what Wyllie could do to ensure an accident, and rigging the lights was one that sprang to mind. But can you think how much rock blasting there's been going on lately? If the wind's blowing the wrong way, you can hear it all over Mid-June. With his fingerprints all over everything to do with The Big Belt, it's feasible that Wyllie could access those explosives. It would only take a small *blast* on one of those tights bends to send a car careering down the cliff face,' Fraser emphasised *blast*, to shortcut his theory for Oona.

'Ah, *blast*. It was muddled in with the news from Inspector Beattie about the guns, so my brain conflated things,' Oona realised. Fraser nodded and wondered where this new line of thought took them now. They both looked back at the aerial pictures on the screen.

'This is Drover's Bridge here, yes?' Fraser asked.

'Yes.'

'So if Wyllie planted explosives there, he would be able to detonate them from further away than the group of buildings Inspector Beattie focused on,' Fraser's finger widened the search orbit as he talked and then pondered. 'But he would still need a view of the bridge,' this thought narrowed his orbit again and shifted it slightly southeast. They zoomed in. A building very much in keeping with what they knew of John Wyllie's barns came into view.

'My darling, you are a genius. Let's find out who owns this wee *but n ben* then,' Oona said excitedly. A quick internet search and indeed the property was owned by John Wyllie. 'Well then, a short stop to the loo and I think I'll grab my keys.'

FRASER TOOK a second out from gripping his seat and watching the road, to look over at Oona in the driver's seat, and say, 'Well if we thought looking at The Big Belt accounts and coming up with Mid-June's answer to the Enron scandal was tenuous, this caper right now is another level.' About a year ago Oona and her dad had been invited to a driving day at a racetrack, courtesy of BMW, and Fraser hadn't exactly relished being her passenger ever since. She drove the meandering roads of Mid-June as if she was an F1 driver, and today she was clearly hell-bent on winning pole position. But she chatted as breezily as if she was a passenger on a coach tour, while she took the twists and turns at maximum throttle.

'We've done the best diligence we can on this. Beattie and his man are zeroing in on one cottage, and with the help of Ally and Alec – do you think they could be a thing? You've not met him, but I could see them together...'

'Oona, are you really matchmaking right now?' Fraser said, his eyes back on the road. It wasn't just his nerves that were challenged by Oona's driving – unmanly as he considered it to be, he had to admit he'd never got over his childhood affliction of travel sickness.

'Oh yes, sorry darling. With the help of Ally and Alec, we've worked out another likely place that Wyllie might be. We're doubling the chances of finding him. Yes, it's still a long-shot, but we're still doubling the chances.'

'What a day. I hope my days ahead as an MSP become less eventful.'

'Well at least Blah Blah was very understanding and says he can hold off until tomorrow. So tomorrow will be eventful, but in a good way. A left here, yes?' And before Fraser could answer, or more importantly, brace, the bend was taken as if it was the Brooklands corner at Silverstone.

'When we get to this place, I'm going in alone, Oona,' Fraser said, mustering some authority in his compromised state as terrified passenger.

'Why would you say that? We're in this together.'

'You've been amazing, but I have to keep you safe. If Wyllie is in there, you can make the appropriate calls and look out for the police coming from the road.'

'Actually, now that you mention it, what's the plan if we, sorry, *you*, do encounter him? We got in the car so fast we didn't have time to strategise.'

'As things stand now, he's in trouble. He's made threats on people's lives today. He's gone from corruption, all be it on a bold scale, to perhaps charges of attempted murder. My hope is he's starting to feel out of his depth. I'll tell him we've uncovered the racket that he and Les Mitchell have been running and that we know there must be more people involved. Maybe he could do himself a favour if he cooperates with the police as to how deep this thing runs and gives them names. There must be an advantage in getting this sorted out fast, so that we can get The Big Belt running efficiently and all above-board and get this behemoth of a project finished finally.'

'Well, I trust in your judgement on this.'

'That's kind of you to still have faith in my judgment after everything I've told you today.'

'You are wise person Fraser, with only good intentions for your community and admirably lofty ambitions for the place you want it to become. Your legacy has started today. You have behaved bravely and impeccably. People will finally get to see your true colours, hear about you at your best.' She paused and turned and winked at him. 'Is that enough of a fillip? You ready to go and get this madman?'

INSPECTOR BEATTIE HAD no way of knowing it, but his experience as a passenger was diametrically opposite to Fraser's. He wondered if he looked over, whether he would be able to see Constable Allen's lips miming 'mirror – signal – manoeuvre' as they crept along the almost empty roads. He'd already said, 'You could pick up the pace a bit here,' which Allen did for one short stretch and then slowed down, and stayed slow, at the next bend. Beattie realised Allen had thought he specifically meant 'here' because they were on a straight. With a deep breath and he told himself it was only a difference of a minute or so in getting there.

35

Fraser was relieved, if a little surprised, that Oona hadn't argued too much about waiting in the car. There was no sign of Wyllie's car, so perhaps this was going to be a big anti-climax, after all. They parked by the side of the road and estimated in which direction the house must lie, looking up and down from the landscape to their phones.

'It looks like it's a bit of a scramble down into those trees once I'm over those mossy rocks there. I'll *ca' canny* and I'll text you the second I know anything – if I see any sign of Wyllie or otherwise. If it's yes – if he's there – you should call Inspector Beattie. Stay in the car and direct him here.'

'Yes sir,' Oona said with a salute. Then more seriously, 'Do be careful my darling.'

Fraser's adrenaline had reached a peak. But that, and Oona's faith him, were steeling him and helping him turn his nerves into resolve. 'Don't worry. I'll be careful. I'll tell you all about my heroic capture of John Wyllie over a large glass of whisky this evening.'

'I'll hold you to that,' and Oona pulled him over for a kiss and a tight squeeze before he got out of the car and set off over the hill and out of sight.

Constable Allen drew to an excruciatingly slow stop at a passing place in the single lane road as instructed by the Inspector. Looking down in direction of the river, this seemed to be exactly the spot that Gemma had described. She had done well, and their think-tank seemed to have been successful. So far, this was the perfect place for John Wyllie to be holed up during this sinister siege he had Mid-June under. As they had practically trundled here, he had used the time to talk Constable Allen through the plan, so now, he gave him one final briefing. 'Once we are out of the car we want to move quickly but quietly. We'll go together, until we reach the cottage. As per his wife's recollection, our path down will bring us out at the back of the property. You should remain in the back, manning the rear egresses, and I'll go to the front where the main entrance is. How things pan out from there is not in our control so be ready to pivot and think *fast*.' It was the irony of him asking the constable to do anything speedily that prompted the emphasis on *fast*. 'Are we ready?'

'Yes, Inspector,' Allen replied and immediately and nimbly exited the car.

Oh good, he moves faster than he drives, Beattie thought as he followed suit. They moved through the short thicket of trees until it thinned out and the stone walls of a small single-story building became visible. They couldn't see the river, but by the babbling they could hear, it was just beyond the cottage, again as Gemma had described. Beattie indicated that they should stop behind a tree each, so that he could catch his breath and steel himself. Just as he did, there was the audible vibration of a phone. He'd have silently but pointedly scolded Constable Allen, except that he felt the vibration in his own pocket, so he instead berated himself for such a schoolboy error as he reached to change the settings. He noticed that his hand was shaking ever so slightly. It had a been a while since he'd done boots-on-the-ground work and even longer since it was anything as heart-pounding as charging the hideout of an armed perp. *There's life in the old dog yet,* he thought, though maybe not when Kay got hold of him tonight and heard what he'd been up to.

John Wyllie sat on a makeshift bench in his prized property. It wasn't unusual for him to spend time in his various holdings – he visited them regularly. Not that they changed in any way: the ones that were watertight still kept out the rain – in a couple of them, he even had a cot bed and some basic furniture and kitchen things – and the ones that were decrepit when he bought them, remained so. But every now and then, he liked to survey his genius – this was a long-game of which he was very proud.

A text made his phone vibrate: Wyllie, I'm outside. Come out and surrender yourself. You know it makes sense. A shuttered window kept him hidden but gave him a view to the front through a hole in the one knots in the wood. He gave a low groan. *For fuck's sake, how the fuck did that prick get here?*

John grabbed his shotgun.

Beattie's mistake in having a buzzing phone had actually been a fortuitous one. The notification was of a text: *Inspector Beattie, it's Oona McFarland here. We have just located John Wyllie. Please send help. Fraser is with him now. I attach our location below.*

36

It's strange that in most countries of the world, apart from the one large, staggeringly stubborn exception, people have very little chance of ever facing someone pointing a gun at them, but instinctively, they would all put their hands up. Fraser did that now, only with his hands out wide and in front of him at shoulder height as opposed to above his head.

'You've got some balls on you coming here. Or maybe you're just as stupid as you look,' Wyllie snarled the words at Fraser.

Fraser tried to remember what he told Oona he was going to say. He took a deep breath and said slowly and carefully, 'Look, I know what's been going on. You and Les Mitchell. He was on the take on The Big Belt all along, and since we're talking about having balls, he blatantly sold his rights to his nefarious activities to you when he retired. We've seen the evidence, John.'

'Who's *we*? You little fuck. Who else have you told about this?'

Fraser tried not to panic at this misstep. He didn't want Wyllie to know Oona had any knowledge of this whatsoever.

'Me and someone who has access to detailed information about everything, from the start.'

'That accountant Pollock? Well, he's in deeper than me so I don't know why he's *cliping*. Have you offered him some kind of deal? The corrupt weasel.'

The image of the person Wyllie was talking about came to Fraser immediately – he'd met him a couple of times. So they'd been correct to think there had to be more people involved in this. 'Well maybe it's you that will be able to cut a deal – if you help expose the whole fraud scheme that has a stranglehold on The Big Belt,' he tried to keep his tone even.

'Who will I be cutting a deal with? The police? Who's telling the police? You?' Wyllie asked taking a step towards Fraser who automatically took as step back.

'Look, the police already know,' Fraser said. 'They are on their way here. You forced my hand on that. But so far, this is all just about money, John. If anyone comes to harm though, you're looking at completely different charges and consequences. Why don't you put the gun down until they get here...'

'Why would I do that? I was right – you are as stupid as you look.'

Then in a flash and with a thundering battle cry ,that he would make fun of her for later, Oona came flying up around the side of the house and swung a golf club into the back of John's legs, causing him to fall to the ground.

'Bloody hell, Oona!' Fraser managed as he lurched towards John and grabbed the shotgun. 'Here, hold this,' and he passed the gun to her free hand. John's head had struck the ground with force and while he wasn't completely unconscious, he wasn't getting up any time soon, but Fraser straddled his chest anyway. 'What happened to the plan? The one where you stayed in the car?' he gasped to Oona.

'I mostly stuck to it. Apart from that one detail you chose to focus on. I've called Inspector Beattie and he'll be here any second. They were much closer than we realised as the crow flies, so he's on his way on foot. I suppose I got a little excited. It's all a bit of a blur.'

'But you had the presence of mind to grab a golf club? A sand wedge at that! That's forethought!'

'I just remembered they were in the back of the car and thought it might come in useful – and it did,' she replied casually planting the sand wedge on the grass beside her and rested her hand on it. With the other hand holding the shot gun, she looked as casual as if she was leaning on her shooting stick in a break at one of her dad's shooting parties. 'I'm sorry I deprived you of the villainous gloating though.'

'The what?'

'You know, when the hero captures the bad guy, and he arrogantly trots out all his dastardly plans and the missing parts of the plot are revealed.'

'My God Oona, you're something else,' Fraser said carrying on the conversation as easily as if he wasn't sitting astride a man's chest.

Oona this time addressed said man – 'I bet you'd do that wouldn't you, Wyllie? You lousy sod. Take your virtual lap of honour and revel in your evil genius.'

'Shhhh,' Fraser cautioned her.

'Fuck you, you entitled bitch,' Wyllie muttered.

They could hear Allen's footsteps and Beattie's panting before they saw them. The two policemen stopped at the corner of the cottage, and Beattie tried to make sense of the baffling scene before him.

37

Hearing Beattie coming through on the radio, Tom and Calum hurried to the car.

'I have good news – we have apprehended John Wyllie. We are taking him into custody at the station now. He has confessed to having laid explosives near the Drover's Bridge, though they were more to spook Bam than to do major damage. Once the site is neutralised, you'll be able to let everyone go, but I wanted to let you know as soon I could that we have him.'

'That is great news, indeed. Was he at the cottage Gemma helped us identify?'

'He was not. Wyllie was initially apprehended in a citizen's arrest type situation. Fraser Bam and his fiancée tracked him down, I believe with the help of two of your cohort up there at the Y-station. And with the help of a golf club too. A sand wedge I believe.'

Tom was intrigued, but it sounded like too long a story to go into right now. 'We have a lot of stories to catch up on about the events of today, that's for sure. We'll sit tight for now and be standing by for the all-clear and get these good folks out of here.'

On receiving the news, there was no coyness on Alec and Ally's part as to their involvement, as Alec did a fist pump with a victorious, 'Yes!' before reaching for Ally to put his arm around her shoulder, pull her close, and say, 'Bloody well done you! Great instincts! Dubious taste in bands, but great instincts.' Ally elbowed him playfully.

The rest of the group were baffled. 'Want to share what you two have been up to?' Jill was the first to ask.

Between them, Alec and Ally explained the story of their part in tracking down John, sometimes interrupting each other with a key part the other had missed, sometimes finishing each other's sentences. The intimacy of their ease with each other was not lost on anyone, apart from Alec and Ally themselves. Jill was grinning from ear to ear and caught Inez's eye, who gave her silent acknowledgment with a quick nod, which Ally just caught the end of.

'What?' she asked looking from Jill to Inez. 'What did I miss?'

Jill would have laughed if she had spoken, so Inez did her a favour and said, 'Nothing, nothing. I'm just so impressed by your detective work. What a great duo you make.' Jill had to avert her eyes from the table altogether.

Alec got up from the table, rubbing his hands. 'Anyone hungry again? If I'm not mistaken, there are still some giant packets of highly processed food purporting to be crisps, and plenty of strawberry tarts and chocolate tiffin.'

'I'm sure you don't have to ask Calum twice,' Tom said as he took a seat at the table. 'And I suppose if they're coming out anyway, it would be rude not to join in.'

'OK, Calum and I will do the honours. C'mon Calum, round two!' Alec and Calum set off to retrieve the plunder, while Inez and Jill got up to re-set the table, starting with the tablecloth which had been folded up and put to the side after the first feast, and had a quiet giggle to each other about Alec and Ally. They worked around Tom who was enjoying the element of 'a women's touch' thinking he'd never have known a tablecloth could make a meal so much more enjoyable. Ravi and Gemma quietly absented themselves up to the roof of the Y-station. Though they didn't have a clear role to play in the busy-ness, Katie and Ally stood up from the table just because inaction didn't feel right. As they stepped to the side, Katie let Ally in on the secret, 'You know my aunt and your bestie are talking about you right?'

'About me? No, why?'

'You and Alec. You told us all about your wee secret mission as if you'd known each other for years. Or even as if you were a couple.'

'Don't be silly. Inez and Jill are letting their imaginations run away with them. It's nice to finally meet him though. I've seen photos of him all over the castle when I've been working there.'

'He's certainly easy on the eye,' Katie laughed.

'Just a bit! His mum was keen to introduce me to him once he was back from the US. I mean I don't think she was trying to matchmake or anything, it was just so that I'd know him as he becomes more involved in running the estate,' Ally explained.

'I wouldn't be so sure. How old is he? Mid-thirties? His mum will be hoping he doesn't leave it too late to find someone to settle down with – someone who'll keep him in Scotland near the castle and her. And then you came along with all your gorgeousness and girl-power, adding awesome events to the estate calendar, making the castle an integral part of the Mid-June community again. I wouldn't be at all surprised if she has her eye on you for Alec. What do you think of him now you've met him? I think he seems lovely.'

Ally hesitated, but unique bonds had been formed today so

she found herself happy to confide in Katie. 'I really like him actually.' She got butterflies as she said it. 'He's lived up to the impression I had of him from his mum – caring and intelligent…'

'See? She's definitely been selling him to you! I'm sure she's pulling a Yenta.'

'Maybe. I mean I'd be looking at all these pictures of him making him seem like superman – receiving his degree, on some exotic adventure, at the top of a Munro, Mr Family-Man at the castle with his beautiful sisters. It seemed too good to be true that his mum might be thinking we should date. And now I've met him – well, he's so funny and interesting too.'

'He's big on eye contact, isn't he?' Katie commented.

'You've noticed that too?' Ally said, wide-eyed. 'When we were working through that Wyllie thing together, he was looking at me so intently I was swooning. Look – don't tell Jill any of this. I'll probably confess all on the way home, but up here, she'd be a liability if I admitted anything.'

'I won't say a word, but honestly, it's pretty obvious – you look good together and he likes you too.' Katie grinned. 'Oh look – we're all set up. Shall we join in the repeat round of our eclectic fare?' As they sat down, Ravi and Gemma came back to the table.

'There you two are,' Inez said. 'You must be happier than any of us that John Wyllie is in custody. What do you think that means for you two? Do you think you'll come back to Mid-June with the rest of us when we get the all-clear to get out of here?'

'That's what we were just talking about,' Ravi replied. 'We think we're still going to head up to Glasgow. We've been dreaming of this for so long – had a picture in our head of being far away, just the two of us starting our life together. For the first wee while anyway.'

Ally couldn't help but notice Alec's face fall. It made her sad and she wasn't sure all the reasons why. He was only sad that his best friend was leaving Mid-June, after all.

'Of course, if you can catch a ride back home, Alec, there's no need for you to come with us, now that things are a little less complicated. A little less dangerous.' Ravi was oblivious that this – the arrival of the end-end – was difficult this was for Alec to hear – *great, you get the girl and leave me carless*. 'We'll get your car back to you at some point – in the meantime use mine. I'll call my mum and explain everything tomorrow morning, so that'll be off your plate mate. Though I'm sure she'll be trying to get you to stop in for a glass of wine to hear all about today in person.'

Alec nodded his thanks and smiled.

'We'll give you a lift home!' Jill chimed in a little too loudly and enthusiastically, making things worse by adding in a suggestive tone, 'Won't we Ally?'

As Alec thanked Jill, Ally muttered to Katie under her breath, 'What did I say? Total liability!'

Gathering himself, Alec reclaimed his jovial demeanour and announced, 'Well, in that case, let's designate our drivers and get this champagne opened for those who won't be driving. Ladies, I would be more than happy to be your driver this evening to allow you to indulge. Why don't we put on a little Take That too in consideration of the dreadful sacrifice you've had to suffer today. Poor Gary Barlow doesn't know what he's missing out on – you two beautiful ladies singing up at him. Jill? I trust you have one or two Take That songs downloaded on your phone?'

Jill laughed and found her phone and started to look for a playlist as Alec got the champagne and two glass out of Ally's cooler. 'Oh, only two glasses —'

'I have cups, not fancy, but you're welcome to them,' Calum said, appearing with the plastic cups from his and Tom's flasks of tea.

'Ladies – I give you, the man, the myth, the legend that is Constable Kirkpatrick. He lead us to safety and now is gallantly giving up his Thermos cups,' Alec said as he opened the champagne, leading the cheer of *yays* and *woohoos*, which they all joined in as the cork popped. 'Actually Ally, could you do the honours and pour? We're missing one final touch.'

Alec returned from a quick trip to the cars with the two trilbies and handed Jill hers, but as Ally's hands were full pouring champagne, he placed it on her head for her, and looked into her eyes as he said, 'There you are – now you're perfect!' Katie watched the whole thing and swooned on Ally's behalf.

Inez was a firm 'no' on Katie's offer to drive. 'Sorry pet, but only I get to drive my pride and joy. You go ahead and have some bubbly.' And so it turned out that the four younger women clinked their glasses and cups of champagne together, and giggled as they transferred the trilbies from one head to the next, the loudest laugh coming when they ended up on Tom and Calum's heads, topping their sober black and white uniforms, Tom in the electric pink, Calum in the electric blue. The four men set about making a dent in the food rations. As the bubbles – or more likely the adrenaline rush – kicked in, the four imbibers got to their feet and sang the *Greatest Day* lyrics to Greatest Day at each other at the top of their lungs, 'Today this could be – the greatest day of our lives' as the afternoon sun sank a little lower in the sky.

Inez hadn't realised that she had been anxious until the tension left her body like a long, slow sigh. As she watched the girls singing along, she smiled at the irony of the hopefulness of the song and how all their plans today had been derailed, but somehow it did feel like a momentous day, and the anthemic tune was befitting. Even without champagne, she felt a tingling in her arms as she settled into her relaxed and unworried state. She looked over at the men and as Alec, Ravi and Calum continued to quietly survey the tabletop and make their choices one mouthful at a time, treating the process of nourishment from such a basic spread like an art, Tom stood up to stretch his legs. Inez knew too that the picnic table got uncomfortable more quickly in your fifties, than in your twenties and thirties.

Tom was looking over at the younger women, affectionately, she thought, perhaps even protectively. It was hard to believe she had imagined him as the surly older cop this morning – the furrow in his brow that had been visible at some points today was long gone, replaced with attractive laughter lines as he smiled warmly at the antics going on round about him. Calum made a quip, Inez didn't hear what, and Tom turned to acknowledge it with a small laugh, looking down at Calum who was still sitting. All of a sudden, Tom's face transformed in Inez's vision. She saw a much younger man, with a handsome face, sparkling eyes and a fond expression, no furrows or even laughter lines in sight. Young Tom was looking down at her instead of Calum, an entirely different anthem being sung in the background. With a jolt, Inez realised she didn't recognise him from the picture in the coffee table book at all. She knew him from somewhere else altogether.

38

They had been dismissed by Inspector Beattie with a mutter of, 'I'll deal with you two another day – I've enough to be going on with here'. Not sure what to do with themselves after all the excitement, Fraser and Oona decided to head back home for that whisky they had promised each other. As soon as they got back into the house Wi-Fi range, Fraser's phone lit up, as always. 'Can't you just pretend you're still out of range?' Oona pleaded.

Fraser had no intention of getting into any humdrum constituency business after the night and day he'd had, but he had to check to see if there was news from Inspector Beattie or Blah Blah. 'You pour the whiskies, and I'll go into the kitchen and get us a snack - I promise I'll only check the bare minimum.'

Deliberately turning her back to the mess of papers on the dining room table, Oona took a moment to appreciate the bar area she had created on an antique sideboard she had talked Fraser into buying. A little piece of Art Deco heaven in a bland new-build, though of course she had never described it that way to Fraser. He was so proud of his first house, and she was in turn proud of him for that achievement. It was no mean feat at such a young age nowadays. An inlaid woodwork tray had been 'liberated' from her dad's bar, along with some vintage glasses – four delicate champagne coups and two satisfyingly weighty, gold-rimmed whisky glasses. The twenty-one-year-old malt that was in the decanter she was reaching for now, had also been deemed surplus to her father's requirements.

Pouring herself a nip, she looked over her shoulder to make sure Fraser hadn't come back in from the kitchen without her hearing him. She took a long breath in through her nose, and exhaled slowly through her mouth, then knocked back her drink. It should have stung even just a little bit, but it didn't. Maybe this was a bottle her dad was going to miss after all, and she smiled, knowing the most trouble she'd be in would be an eyeroll. The warmth of the liquor in her chest was exactly what she needed, and she poured two proper glasses and made her way to the couch. Placing one of the tumblers and both of her feet on the coffee table, she put her own glass to her nose, this time taking time to take in the aroma with each sip. She was exhausted. Her body melted into the sofa. It felt great.

Oona wasn't sure if she heard Fraser talking as soon as he started his phone call, or if she'd been in such a state of hypnosis with relief and warm whisky comfort that he gradually came into earshot, but either way, she suspected it was hearing him saying Blah Blah's name that made her notice. He was actually speaking to Blah Blah. Or just Blah as he was calling him now. *Good God, who did Fraser think he was? He should be addressing him as Sir Blah!* Her automatic reaction would normally be to rush in and alert Fraser to his faux pas, but she noticed her glass was empty, *how did that happen?* and decided she would just listen from here. There was a recognisable nervousness in Fraser's voice, but he was in control. Or maybe that was just compared to Oona who realised she had relaxed a little too much.

'It's really nice of you to want to visit all the people who were affected by today's events, but I'm not actually very sure how to get to them...'

Did Blah blah want to go to the Y-station? She was listening carefully to Fraser's half of the conversation as closely as she could through her mild haze.

'Oh, you do? Wow, um, even Inspector Beattie isn't entirely sure of its location...Right, yes, OK. We could meet you this side of the Glass Pass. I'll have to check in with Inspector Beattie that all roads are open again...Yes, yes I can do that right away. I'll call you back. OK...OK...right, bye for now.'

Fraser appeared in the doorway. 'That was Blah Blah on the phone.'

'So I gathered. Does he want to go up to the Y-station? Surely those poor people will want to get out of there as soon as they possibly can?'

'That's what I thought, but he claims to know how to get there and wants to give it a try. He's just the other side of the Glass Pass, so if I can get the go ahead that the roads are open, he could be there quite quickly. So could we I guess. He is my guest, after all. It's slightly going to defeat the purpose if he's met a bunch of my constituents before I get a chance to do the big reveal of who my secret guest is.'

'You'd better call Inspector Beattie then. I have a small confession though. I seem to have polished off quite a large glass of very good whisky. I'm a little squiffy.'

'Oona, after the day you've had, you've earned it. And also after the day you've had, I'm not surprised it went straight to your head. Maybe just stop there though, since it seems we're not quite ready to sit with our feet up after all.'

'I'll just sit tight for now, while you make your calls.' Oona's speech wasn't quite slurred, but she wasn't too many sips away.

'You do that my love.'

Fifteen minutes later, they were in the car having received

the go ahead from Inspector Beattie that the roads were safe and opened back up, and though he couldn't quite believe it, Fraser had talked him into letting him and Blah Blah deliver the news to Y-station personally. Beattie had been reluctant because it wasn't fair on Tom and everyone else to keep them waiting while the unlikely duo of the MSP for Mid-June and a septuagenarian rock star wandered around the hillside at dusk searching for them. On the other hand, it appealed to his sense of humour and would round off a very bizarre day with a final dose of absurdity, so he suggested they all go together – Fraser and Oona, the VIP and his driver, and himself. It was a double whammy of getting to see the impromptu safe house that had him so intrigued and seeing his old pal Tom's face when the unlikely crew arrived.

Fraser smiled across at Oona as she sat with her head laid back on the headrest. She was musing about meeting Blah Blah – what he'd be wearing, if he'd be as nice as he seems on TV, why he was so confident that he could take them to the listening station – and now she was back at the beginning of why he even agreed to make this special appearance in Mid-June.

'I still find it surprising that your email made its way through Blah Blah's people to the man himself so quickly. And then for him to come up with a much more generous offer than you'd been going to suggest, was even more amazing, in the best way. How did you think of him of contacting him anyway? I don't think I've ever asked. You and I chatted in fairly fantastical ways about which celebs we could contact, and then from nowhere, you thought of him.'

'I am able to give your brilliant mind some of the credit actually, but it's really tenuous,' Fraser began. 'You'd suggested that we brainstorm famous people who might have a connection with Mid-June, unlikely as that seemed and turned out to be, but it made me think about an unlikely claim my mum makes. She tells the story that she was coming out the corner shop one day and this old banger of a car came rattling along the road – she said she heard it before she saw it and that's why she looked up. There were two women in the front, laughing, but a guy was leaning forward from the back seat in between, and she realised he must be telling them a funny story. She said that's how slowly the car had to drive, that she was able to make out exactly what was going on with all the passengers. Just as they had passed, she realised the man looked familiar and when she came home she told my dad that she just saw Blah Blah's doppelgänger. They had a good laugh, with my dad saying that must have been quite a look in Mid-June.'

Oona chuckled in acknowledgement.

'A couple of years later, she was going into the corner shop, as opposed to coming out – I'm not sure why that's important, but she always mentions it – and a car caught her attention, this time because it was big and fancy with a guy in the front in full chauffeur uniform. The tinted back window was just sliding up as the car came towards the shop, but just in that couple of seconds she claims this time it definitely was Blah Blah.'

Fraser paused, pursing his lips and raising his eyebrows at Oona, giving a small nod, that there she had the story. Then before she could react, he quickly remembered and added his mother's closing argument whenever she was telling the story, 'The fancy car and chauffeur made it credible that it would be him, and a second sighting made it credible that she'd seen him the first time.' He gave a firm nod and held out his hand to indicate, *there you have it*.

Oona replied firmly and decisively. 'I'm with your mum. It must have been Blah Blah she saw. He must have a Mid-June connection. Why else would he a) offer you such a substantial donation just right off the bat, and b) offer to come up and meet the kids and the coaches? Every step of this process you've been astounded at how easy it's been dealing with him, you said it yourself. Everyone, including, I'm sorry to say, my father, told you your first foray into your master plan for putting Mid-June on the map would be slow and a slog and it wasn't – it seemed to fall right in your lap.'

Oona caught a small shadow cross Fraser's face and said quickly, 'Not that you haven't worked hard on this, but it's definitely been a combination of a great strategy, hard work and being lucky enough – or clever enough –, ' she added touching his forearm to make the point, 'to find such a willing first target.'

'It's OK, you don't need to humour me, it was sheer luck, from just remembering a daft story of my mum's and giving it a go because of Blah Blah's connection to football. But there's no way he has a link with Mid-June.'

'Did you Google it?' Oona asked knowing the answer already.

'Of course I did, you know all the research I did when I thought I was going to be making the journey from Up-By with him, so I'd have things to talk about. There was no apparent connection to Mid-June that I could figure out.'

'OK, well it must be a secret connection. What would be so secret that you can't find it on an internet deep dive about him? So, he didn't grow up here, we know that. We know his mum is English and his dad from Edinburgh. Hmmm. There was nothing about him ever working here when he was a labourer? Picking strawberries one summer? Mind you, why would that not get a mention when he's been pretty open about his working-class roots?'

Fraser shook his head at each semi-rhetorical question.

Oona pondered and tapped her fingers. She loved a good mystery, and although she believed Fraser had done his homework, he didn't have her internet sleuthing powers – she decide she would do some digging on her phone later. What would be her key search terms? Was he old enough to have been evacuated here in the war? That's where she'd start. *'Blah Blah secret childhood Mid-June.'* It wasn't even called Mid-June then though. *'Blah Blah secret child-*...Blah Blah secret child! She gasped. 'I've got it Fraser! What's another thing about him everyone knows? He loves women! Loads of girlfriends, wives, and...?' She paused, this time looking for an answer.

Fraser ventured, 'Ex-wives?'

'No. Well yes, of course. But loads of children! What if he had a secret lovechild and the child lives in Mid-June?' Oona pointed her finger in her eureka moment.

'Wow – my mum will love this theory when you tell her,' Calum said, happy Oona was distracted, but firmly believing this explanation was as likely as his mum seeing Blah Blah twice outside the Kilmour corner shop. They were almost there. Fraser was exhausted, but still felt a little rush of excitement at the thought of finally meeting him.

39

I'm so excited! I can't wait to see you! It's been so long, and Aunt Inez and I have had quite the day. It's going to be lovely to see you at the end of it,' Katie said into her phone. She was up on the roof of the Y-station with a hand covering her mouth, on the off-chance her words would carry down to the picnic table, where her aunt was with their new group of friends. The butterflies in her tummy were out of control, thinking of how elated Inez would be when this secret collusion was revealed.

Her aunt looked so happy. She was watching Ally and Jill, who were still singing to Take That, twirling each other under their arms and laughing the lyrics to each other. In the festivities, the policemen's caps had been commandeered as part of the party headwear too, so, with the trilbies, there were now four hats being passed around the jovial ensemble. Jill took Inez's hand to try to cajole her into joining her on the imagined dance floor, but Inez demurred, shaking her head and laughing. The song changed, and Jill pointed at Inez, singing the opening lines of *Shine* to her, as she passed Tom's hat from her own head onto Inez's. Her aunt looked radiant, and Katie noticed, with a further small thrill, that Tom's eyes hadn't left Inez since she'd been watching the scene. She turned away to face the view, and told her Uncle *** and Uncle Andy, once again, how excited she was to see them soon.

TOM DIDN'T KNOW that his warm smile was betraying his fascination, as he watched Inez revel in the joy of their younger comrades. Was it inappropriate how attractive he thought she looked wearing his hat? Inez tilted back her head in laughter, and his hat slipped back, nearly falling, but she caught it and held it back in place as she turned and looked up at him, still laughing. In an instant, Tom had a rush of emotion and every tingle on his skin and nerves finally took him back to another world. His body almost folded in on itself as Inez's gaze lingered. After an age she broke eye contact, turned to Calum, and said, 'I think I'm in trouble for stealing your gaffer's hat.'

Calum gulped and stepped towards Tom, as Inez turned back to the dancing. In a loud whisper that was masked to everyone else by the music he said, 'Bloody hell Sarge, I've figured out who she is.'

Tom didn't reply but he knew exactly who Inez was too. They had met before after all, though he had never found out her name.

40

LONDON
4th JUNE 1977

'Oh go on, Inez, c'mon with us. What were the chances we'd get tickets for this? We're going to win you know. Scotland are in the World Cup and England aren't. We will win tomorrow, and we'll win the World Cup next year. Ally MacLeod says so.' Andy held his palms out and shrugged his shoulders at this soon-to-be fait accompli.

'It's not exactly what I dreamed of all these years when I yearned to move to the Big Smoke. Trudging out to Wembley with a bunch of football hooligans. Be still my beating heart.'

'We'll not be trudging, we'll be marching. We are – Ally's. Tartan. Army.' Andy punched the air three times as he said the words. 'Listen, Gorgeous, your days of hanging out with David and Angie and Mick and Bianca are coming. You'll be snapped up into their set as soon as we can afford to be anywhere close to their orbit. But in the meantime, it's a really cool crowd going to the match to watch

Uncle Ally's boys hump the English. No violence, I promise you. You think I'd be setting foot near it if I thought for a minute there would be? You're allowed to be London-cool and still be patriotic you know.'

'I've got nothing to wear,' Inez said, mostly joking, but Andy was on a roll to counter her every argument and treated it like a serious point for debate.

'Ok, again, you're not going to bump into Bianca and be embarrassed you wore the same white linen suit and floppy hat. Tee-shirt and jeans will be just fine, Gorgeous. It's even going to be a lovely sunny day. Not like getting soaked in the stands back home.'

INEZ DUG out the tartan scarf her mum had tied to her backpack the day she left and donned that, flared jeans and a white vest top. Andy asked how she managed to look so cute even going to a football game. Andy was loving all things disco just now, and approved of the way Inez's hair was growing out from its Suzi Quattro rock-chick layers into longer, softer, more feminine flicks, with a heavy fringe she cut herself every now and then. When Olivia Newton John was on Top of the Pops, he'd said, 'Ok, I think she copied your hair Inez!'

The pilgrimage to Wembley to watch Scotland play the Auld Enemy was with a motley crew of wanderers and dreamers from various parts of her homeland. Their small group got absorbed into a procession led by the bearers of the biggest flags, a giant blue saltire flanked by two yellows with Lions Rampant and 'Remember Bannockburn' emblazoned in red. The crowd was mostly men, of all ages, with lots of fathers and sons among them. The older men wore tartan scarves or bunnets, but the younger men were in Bay City Rollers inspired tartan shirts, tartan flares or both, and platform shoes. Their dads would have made fun of this garb a couple of years ago when it first appeared, along with long layered hair and sideburns, but today it made the perfect uniform for the foot soldiers of the Tartan Army. Someone in full kilt regalia joined the front line and struck up a tune on his bagpipes.

Inez felt the hairs on the back of her neck stand up. The mood was boisterous but jovial and excited. An older man put his arm around her and breathed whisky on her as he said 'How you doin' hen? Is this your first game? With a lovely wee lassie like you as our lucky mascot we're gawny thrash them! Want some?'

He was merry and harmless, and Inez said, 'Aye, why not?' and took a swig of the whisky he was offering.

'Ah, you're a good girl, hen, welcome to the Tartan Army.'

Inez extricated herself from under his arm, linking her arm through his instead, and walked in step with him to the sound of the pipes. Andy looked over, separated by a few of the Army's foot soldiers and shouted, 'Have you pulled already Inez?'

'Aye!' She shouted back.

'Told you you'd love it!'

'So you did,' she called back grinning and linked arms with the man on her other side too, neither man believing their luck that this ethereal young girl was even a small part of this magnificent day for them.

INEZ ASSUMED that when they got inside the stadium the Scottish fans would be in the minority and the impact of their blue and white, red and yellow, and tartan would be a bit lost. But when she and Andy made it to their section, the sea of flags and the sound of tens of thousands of fans singing *Flower of Scotland* filled every stand. They would read in the papers the next day that at least two-thirds of the nearly one hundred thousand crowd were Scottish. Inez felt small, but with an incredible feeling that she'd never been part of something so big. There was a tremendous sense of belonging – a new comfort in a shared experience with thousands of people. She tried to imagine life outside the stadium, outside this moment, and she couldn't. So this was what it was all about. It wasn't just about the game; it was humans connecting in the most primal of ways.

'You're glowing, Gorgeous!' Andy had to yell over the wall of noise.

'I'm buzzing! This is amazing! I had no idea,' Inez yelled back, eyes wide in wonder.

The crowd broke out into *Que Sera Sera...we're going to Argentine*, a rendition of a tune that was a very unlikely a football anthem when Doris Day sang it in a Hitchcock movie more than twenty years before. It had been ten years since Scotland had beaten England at Wembley, but you'd never have known it. Going to the World Cup the following year, especially when England wasn't, gave the Scots an air of jubilation before the game had even started. Fans knew this team was special too. Their hopes and dreams filled the stadium almost as palpably as the yellow and red flags and the melodic roar.

When the game began Inez was gripped. The pace was fast, but Scotland were in control. The crowd's roar crescendo-ed along with play when Scotland had possession, and piercing whistling replaced the roar when England had the ball. She asked Andy who number 9 was, and he laughed saying, 'Joe Jordan. I should have known you'd like him. You sure do have a type, don't you? Tall, dark and handsome, how original!' She couldn't ask many questions over the boom of *Flower of Scotland* or *Bonnie Scotland...we'll support you ever more*.

When number 5 (Gordon McQueen, Inez was informed) scored at the end of the first half, Inez and Andy hugged each other and everyone around them, and the sound of triumph was deafening.

Although the singing and celebrations did not abate during half-time, the crowd still managed to turn up the volume for the team returning to the pitch. Another goal by number 8, who ran grinning to the crowd, arms in the air. The crowd pumped their arms back at him, calling out *ya wee beauty Kenny!* and Inez realised she'd heard of him – Kenny Dalglish.

The penalty to England didn't dampen the crowd because victory was never in doubt and the whistle blew at England 1 – Scotland 2.

When her mum asked Inez later that week what had possessed her to 'storm the pitch with the rest of the hooligans' after the final whistle, Inez found it hard to explain that it wasn't like that at all. For a start, it was her first football game, and everything had been new to her, so she didn't know that going on to the pitch didn't happen after every victory. There also was no time to think or question – she just got carried along in a happy wave of jubilation.

The more exuberant fans raced the length of the pitch to climb the goal posts and gesture into the cameras, but she, Andy and the little group they had formed in the stands were just happy to be on the pitch on the edge of the throngs, holding their scarves or flags aloft, watching the players get swarmed by congratulatory fans. Inez had a sore throat from singing and cheering, sore cheeks from smiling and was filled with joy of a kind she had never experienced before.

'God you're gorgeous, Gorgeous!' Andy said as he put his hands on her cheeks and kissed her full on the lips. He hugged her and said into her ear, 'Shine your light on me always, my lovely friend.'

'You're an idiot,' she replied. 'But thanks for bringing me, it's been amazing. I think I'll remember this forever!'

Andy got pulled into a scrum of bouncing celebration, and Inez raised her tartan scarf above her head once again, twirling and smiling.

THE DAY after the big game, Inez didn't have to start work at Rab's Pub until 4pm, but Andy had to open up at noon. She didn't envy him as she heard him splashing around in the bathroom, trying to waken himself up – the boy had no shame and never shut the bathroom door. It had been a very late night, but she wasn't inclined to go over it in her head right now. Pulling the covers over her head, she fell back into a deep sleep, not waking up again until 3pm. Her dreams had been interspersed with the hall phone ringing several times, and she felt guilty that it was probably her mum calling to hear all about the football match. Vic had been excited for Inez to be doing something she'd never be able to do at home. That was the whole reason she'd encouraged Inez to go to London – new, big city experiences.

Inez didn't have time to call her back now as she had to get ready for work. It was a lucky escape hangover-wise, and after a long, hot shower, she felt human enough, all things considered. Wondering if she could get away with just pulling on yesterday's clothes, she gave them a sniff, but as she did, she remembered regretting wearing the white vest top to serve in the pub a few days before. It was just a little too bare to wear while pulling pints for the mostly male clientele, so she grabbed a cheese-cloth blouse instead, pulled on the same jeans and headed to the pub with plenty time to have a bit of a saunter there for a change.

Opening the door that was on the corner of the pub, she cast daylight into the oaky smoky bar. Andy gave an excited gasp from behind the bar, cleared his throat and said loudly with a dramatic sweep of his hand, 'Here she is! I told you not to worry gents, our star is amongst us. One at a time for autographs please.'

The pub was busier than one might have thought for a Scottish pub the day after a Scottish victory at Wembley. Surely all these guys had been out late celebrating too? They all turned to see Inez and a cheer went up first, followed by wolf whistles and clapping. Inez rolled her eyes at Andy. 'What you got going on here, ya numpty? I guess you've worked through the hangover and have contrived this nonsense for me? Well, the jokes on you, no sore head here so the racket isn't bothering me at all.'

'Oh she doesn't know,' Andy put his hand to his chest. He

turned to old Jim at his usual spot on the bar. 'She doesn't know, Jim! Oh this is gawny be good!' Andy's affected antics could verge on camp sometimes.

'What don't I know? Go on, then,' Inez said walking behind the bar and going about the business of hanging up her cloth hobo bag and putting on her apron as usual.

'Ok, I need a big reveal. Quick, come here.' He grabbed Inez by the waist, spinning her to face away from him and put his hands over her eyes.

'Eew, your hands smell of carbolic soap,' Inez complained.

'Och shoosh. Right Jim, get it ready then. Yup open it up to the right page. Yup, just there, put it there. Ready Gorgeous? Ready?'

'Ready, you absolute chopper, yes, whatever nonsense this is.'

He took his hands away with a 'ta-da', and Inez looked around, first getting her focus back, then looked at Old Jim shaking her head looking for support. Jim, a man of few words or gestures, held her gaze, then gave a nod to the newspaper in front of him. It was opened to the centrefold where there was a collage of black and white photos of yesterday's game. The biggest by far, taking up almost the whole of the right-hand page, was of Inez, holding a policeman's hat on her head with one hand, beaming up at the man in uniform who had his back to the camera, the policeman whose hat she was presumably wearing.

'Oh my God,' was all Inez could manage to say.

'Don't you love it? How great is that? You're stunning. You look like an icon. None of us can take our eyes of it.'

Inez had been thinking about her encounter with the young policeman since she woke up – tall, dark and handsome, just her type right enough. She looked at the twinkle in her eye in the photo and remembered the butterflies she had chatting to him, having to lean into his ear to be heard above the ruckus. The black and white photo showed up her layers in her hair and made it look a little darker than it was in real life. Similarly, her tan looked a little deeper in black and white, the white of her vest top probably helping too.

And there was the problem. The white vest top. With no bra. One boob's modesty, the left's, was protected by the tartan scarf, but as she held the hat on her head, the other end of the scarf was caught in her right elbow, and her boob and nipple were pretty apparent through the thin cotton. In the centrefold, ironically, of a tabloid newspaper.

Oh God, what paper was this? One of the English ones? So her mum wouldn't see it? In the instant it took her to look to the top of the page to find out, Andy said, 'Oh and your mammy called the pub phone. She's seen it too.'

41

LONDON
8th JUNE 1977

It had been quite the few days since Wembley. Inez had called her mum, not knowing what reaction to expect to her centrefold picture, as Andy insisted on calling it. Apparently, Vic had shown up at the corner shop for her paper and rolls as usual to find all the early birds still in the shop, and it quickly became clear they'd been waiting for her. The picture of Inez was revealed and the villagers coo-ed as to how beautiful she was and asked if Vic had talked to her yet. Vic had told them she'd known that Inez and her friend Andy got tickets to the game, but of course would have been too busy celebrating afterwards to call her. *Of course, of course*, was the concurrence, and discussions of the game resumed while Vic stared at the picture of her beautiful daughter.

Even Inez could appreciate she had been captured at a perfect point in time. Andy had told her she was glowing, and the photographer had obviously thought so too and had managed to capture it. Of course, in youth you don't know how precious that is and how special to have it preserved by camera, but she did rather like the picture of herself. If only her scarf had been covering both boobs.

Vic quizzed Inez about the pitch invasion and whether she'd been on the goalpost that collapsed or dug up any of the turf. In the conversations in the corner shop, the reports of vandalism were met with strong disapproval, the owner, saying that in his day the celebration would have been a simple gentleman's handshake, no need at all to be digging up the pitch. Pure vandalism. (Later, his son had arrived home on the bus from London proudly offering to transplant the Wembley penalty spot he had in his Tupperware lunch box into their front lawn.)

Once Inez assured her mum none of her group had been responsible for any destructive acts, Vic had enjoyed hearing all the stories, lapping up the awe and wonder second-hand. No mention was made of the white vest with no bra. Inez thought Vic somehow must not have noticed, but in fact, Vic, no longer in her youth, did in fact know how precious it is, and had only sighed to herself, *White vest and no bra? Those were the days! Good for you, Inez, why not?*

Every local at Rab's seemed to have managed to get their hands on a copy of *The Record*, and every one of them thought they were being original and funny asking Inez to sign it. Somehow, not being chided by her mum gave her the confidence to deal with them graciously, but take no nonsense if their comments got out of hand. They mostly meant well and were just thrilled that the wee barmaid they'd been kind to when she arrived off the bus from up north, was having her fifteen minutes of fame.

A few days on, things were calming down. She was pretty sure she'd had a wee chat with every regular about the photo and the match, the autographed papers had been taken home, and even better, all the rest were wrapping fish and chips now. It was a quiet shift, even Jim wasn't sitting in his usual spot yet. The corner door opened letting that familiar shaft of light and fresh air in, and Inez looked up, ready to say hello to a regular, since it was too early for anyone else.

A skinny vision in a floppy hat, definitely not a regular, stepped in and looked around. He caught Inez's eye and his face lit up. He walked to the bar, all eyes following this peculiar sight for Rab's Pub. This guy belonged at Annabel's or Tramp, not that Old Jim or any of the others would have heard of those. He sat at the bar, grinning and suave, but somehow also a little sheepish.

'Good afternoon, Sir, what can I get you?' Inez asked.

'Umm, wow, OK. I'll have a pint of lager please.'

Inez found the exclamation about being offered a drink in a pub strange, but fulfilled the order, and the bar went back to silent and Inez to stacking crisps. The guy looked around the bar nodding.

'Nice place. How long have you worked here?'

'A few months,' Inez replied.

'Right,' he smiled. 'You know I was so worried you wouldn't have a Scottish accent.'

'Right,' said Inez. 'Because I work in a Scottish pub? We're very authentic here don't you know.'

'No, I just really wanted you to have the accent too – I don't.'

'Right,' was all Inez could think to say, but she was thinking that he certainly did not have a Scottish accent, that was for sure, and wondered why he'd felt the need to mention it. He was a Londoner all the way. He seemed a bit odd. In a way, he looked like every other guy in their late twenties did right now, but that made him stand out in Rab's where the clientele was older, a lot of them former dock workers who wore a shirt, tie and jacket whenever they weren't in work overalls and that had stuck even though many of them were now retired or out of work. Not that this guy wasn't cutting quite a dash in his pastel striped blazer, leather trousers, heeled boots and floppy hat, with a trace of eye liner too. Inez smiled, wondering what Old Jim was going to make of him when he got here.

'How long have you been in the Big Smoke, love?' he enquired.

'I just came down earlier this year.'

'Bus from Glasgow?'

'How did you guess?' Inez smiled, warming to him. He was being very polite, had a nice smile and locked eyes when he was talking to her, even from under the flop of his hat, which somehow made her trust him rather than think he was a creep.

'I've been there and done that. Used to go up and down to Glasgow a lot. The bus was the cheapest way to go, but man, it could be rough. You still got family up there? You making enough money here to take the train in future?'

'I do have family, but hardly on the cash front. Not earning top dollar here and too many fun ways to spend it.'

'I hear you, it's not a cheap place to live.' He nodded, smiling at her kindly. 'Did you come here after college?'

'Nope, straight after school,' Inez laughed.

'Oh shit, you are young. Shit – *really* young,' he said eyes widening.

'Yup, I hear that a lot!'

The doors opened again, and Old Jim walked in. The mysterious customer turned around and watched him as he shuffled towards them. Jim's eyes were adjusting to the light in the dark bar compared to the sunshine outside, and his sole mission was to get to his bar stool. The man waited until Jim got seated, took his bunnet off and smoothed his hair, then said to him nonchalantly, 'Alright James? What you having? This one's on me.'

Jim looked surprised and delighted and exclaimed '******** ma boy! How're ye doin'? Great to see you!'

******** got up and walked over to Jim's chair, shaking his hand and giving him a half hug with his left arm.

'You look great Jim, you never change. Dad said he'd been talking to you. I'm glad you bumped into each other, it's one of the reasons I'm here.'

'Oh aye? Bet I can guess why,' Jim said knowingly.

'What can I say? I was besotted Jim, love at first sight. You know how I am.'

'Aye I do. Problem is it's every bloody time, and Inez here is out of your league. I should never have told your dad her story, ya randy wee bugger.'

'Don't worry, Jim, I've been the perfect gentleman, and now you're here to keep an eye on me. I'm hardly going to misbehave in front of you am I?'

Inez had no idea what they were talking about, but watched the familiar banter between the younger and older men, smiling because there seemed to be a very close relationship there. *Was this Jim's nephew, maybe?*

'I'll have the usual Inez hen, but add a half of your finest whisky please, since this here numpty is most definitely paying,' Jim said, flicking his thumb towards ******** who still had his left arm round him. 'And get off me, ya big Nancy.' He wriggled and mock flailed to get out of the younger man's grasp. ******** removed his arm and reached and dragged his own bar stool closer to Jim's, sitting down.

'Inez darling, do as the good man says, and I'll have the same expensive whisky to go with my pint too,' he said.

Jim put his head down and shook it sighing 'oh Jesus, here we go.'

'Yes, Dear Jim, I hadn't even asked this young lady's name but you gave it away the minute you sat down.' His cheeky demeanour was hard to resist and Inez was really enjoying watching this dynamic, because she'd never seen Jim so animated. Despite his protests he was obviously very fond of ********.

'Aye well, you can't have been here very long then, if I know you. What the hell you wearing there? Let me see the shoes? For God's sake man, that's an actual high heel like a lassie would wear. And what's with the hat? You're inside man, have some respect and get that thing aff yer heid.' Inez had been pouring their whiskeys and turned around right as the hat was being removed. She stopped in her tracks. ********, or *** *******, as she now realised he was, was laughing at Jim and turned to look at her approaching with the two drinks.

'Oh, so you really didn't recognise me? I wondered if you were just trying to keep me in my place,' he smiled.

'She'd be wise to, that's for sure,' Jim chimed in.

Inez put the glasses down and answered ***'s question. 'I suppose I just wouldn't expect to find you in Rab's.'

'I've been in here a good many times, but it's been a while. Unfortunately for me I haven't been in since you started working here.'

Jim muttered under his breath, 'Give me strength' as he lifted his glass. 'You going to take your eyes off her and cheers me, ya wee shite?'

'Cheers, Jim. And I know you love me really.' The men clinked glasses. *** turned back to Inez. 'You see, Inez, Jim here is my dad's best friend and let it slip the other day that the beautiful girl from *The Record*, works behind the bar at Rab's. I had to come and meet you.' He smiled and Inez couldn't help but swoon slightly. The whole thing was quite surreal, and she had no idea how to reply.

She managed, 'That's nice of you to say. Here I am. It's really me.'

'What a great picture that was of you sweetheart,' he said almost dreamily. 'It jumped off the page at me. The photographer really captured the joy of that day in your face, you know? I was there too, with my dad. Jim decided not to come with us, old curmudgeon that he is.' He shouted a bit as he mentioned Jim making it clear he was supposed to hear him. 'I got in trouble from my dad for going onto the pitch. But you just couldn't not go on, could you? It was just such an amazing atmosphere. Electric. What a vibe. The next day, hungover as...well, quite hungover, I called everyone I knew who'd want to talk about it. And some that didn't, too. I just wanted to keep reliving it. Even got a couple of the players to answer the phone...' he laughed and came back from his slight reverie and reconnected that swoony laser-beam eye contact again. 'Had you been to a Scotland match before, Inez?'

'Never,' she answered. 'My pal talked me into it. But I'm so glad I went.'

'For sure, and now you're the best-known Scotland fan in the world. Well, maybe apart from me, but I'm a reprobate, so everyone is gonna love you more.' He winked and Inez blushed.

'Now you're talking sense, wee man, reprobate's about right,' Jim chimed in.

The three of them talked easily as the two men continued to drink and rib each other. Inez could tell that her unexpected admirer really had been taken aback by how young she was, and he was nothing but respectful towards both her and Jim, even if he feigned impertinence sometimes to Jim.

The doors to the bar burst open, and Andy stood holding them open, a vision of a West End Diva, with his arms in a Y shape, legs crossed, head thrown back, backlit by the daylight. 'Yes, it's me. This sight before you is really me. Autographs anyone?' None of the regulars flinched. They were used to Andy's grand entrances when he was in a good mood.

'I'll take an autograph mate!' *** laughed and put his hand up over his head.

'Oh my, a fan, of course my darling,' Andy said letting the doors swing shut behind him, and shimmying towards the shadow who had called out, his eyes also taking a few seconds to adjust to the change in lighting. When he reached the outline of the customer with the cockney accent, he held out his hand and said, 'Enchanté my dear', chin up, aloof, channelling Liz Taylor.

*** took his hand, kissed it with a flourish, and said, 'The pleasure is all mine.'

Andy laughed, thrilled if a little mystified to have someone finally joining his antics. His hand was still cradled in the stranger's slightly calloused hand as his eyes adjusted and the features of this person with shaggy shoulder-length hair came into vision. Andy froze. 'Whit? Uh. Oh my God. Whit ? Just whit?'

'Nice to meet you, love. Yup it's me. Just been hanging out with Jim and Inez, patiently waiting for you to walk through that door into my arms.' He really was charmingly funny Inez thought. Or funnily charming. Maybe both. He held eye contact with Andy too, Inez noticed, and she looked at Andy to see him fall under the charismatic spell. *** ******* certainly did not disappoint.

In years to come, Inez had to give Andy credit – partly because he deserved it, mostly because he regularly demanded it – that his premonitions of two normal wee kids from Scotland rubbing shoulders with the *It Crowd*, indeed came to pass. Far from just rubbing shoulders, Andy and Inez quickly became parts of *** *******'s inner circle. *** was generous, not just with his money, but with his time, energy and experience. *** never did woo Inez, and Andy never managed to woo ***, but the three became close in a friendship that would last a lifetime against all the geographical and circumstantial odds that were against them after those few heady years of being attached at the hip in the late seventies London scene.

When they found Inez, *they* being the people who wanted to profit from the beautiful photograph of her gazing up at an anonymous policeman and wearing his hat, *** sprung into action with the full force of his management, PR and legal teams. The legal team secured Inez ownership, and therefore control, of the image. At first, she was just relieved that it seemed to her that it would fade into oblivion, but that was before the offers from poster companies started to pour in. They were hard to ignore. The poster business went hand-in-hand with the record industry, which was as yet still thriving. ***'s people's advice was very prescient – they told Inez that no-one could predict rights and ownership laws going forward, so they recommended she capitalised on things as they stood and grabbed her bird-in-the-hand with both hands. Her mum and Andy understood her hesitance, but the numbers being thrown around were life-changing - with sensible financial advice from ***'s people, there was a comfortable future secured for a wee girl who had moved to London straight from school.

The lawyers drove a hard bargain but as lucrative as the deal was for Inez, the poster company had no regrets. The image had an even wider appeal than they could have anticipated. Football fans bought the picture to revel in the memory of Scotland's glory that day and displayed small, framed postcard versions of it with their other souvenirs, which purported to be pieces of the goalposts or the famous slices of turf in Tupperware boxes. Students with high-brow tastes, but Blu-Tacked poster budgets, attributed lofty contexts and impacts of the piece over bongs in their bedsits. Apart from album covers and smouldering band shots, the other most famous art print poster of the time was of a female tennis player with no underpants walking away from the camera, hand on her bum. Mothers of teenage boys who forbade that purchase might concede instead to Inez's poster, which was much more tasteful, and if they squinted, they could choose to only notice the beaming smile, glossy hair and eyes full of joy, and not the glimpse of a nipple through a thin white tee-shirt.

The deal was also struck in time for the patriotic wave when Scotland headed off to no doubt win the World Cup in the summer of '78, and sales of Inez's picture had small resurgences every few years when the Scots dared to believe again. The inclusion of the photo in a beautiful anniversary coffee table book on Scottish football brought another nice little bump in earnings.

Inez's identity was strictly kept under wraps which added to the allure. Being in the days before internet sleuths, even on the odd occasion that she and Andy were caught in the background of tabloid pictures because the paps were trying to catch *** with his new woman of the moment, the pieces of the puzzle were too few for anyone to go searching. Andy used to laugh how different it would have been if he'd been the attention-hungry poster boy, but things had worked out well for Inez. A small moment in time brought her a new friend for life, allowed her other best friend a taste of the celeb life for the short era of his life when he craved it, and gave her the financial freedom to abandon London for a while and return to Mid-June to look after her mum and enjoy her final years with her after her diagnosis. Except that Inez fell in love – with the tranquil rhythm of life in Mid-June – and didn't look back.

42

After a stupefied moment that was long enough for Tom to know he had to talk to Inez, but not long enough to have worked out what he should say, he walked over and gently touched her elbow to lead her away from the others. They walked to the very edge of the clearing and turned to face each other, looking intently into each other's eyes in silence. Inez knew there was no need to question why they were here. There was no doubt in her mind it was because Tom had figured out that they had met before, in that exquisite moment when time had stood still and she had fallen in love with a stranger.

'No way,' Tom said quietly.

'No way,' she whispered back, with a gentle smile.

'How long have you known it was me?' he asked.

'Not from the start, but before you realised.'

'Why didn't you say anything?'

'What could I say? I've thought about that day a million times over the years, replayed those ten minutes, if it even was ten minutes, over and over. And when I ran out of replays, I'd wonder where your life had taken you. I invented lives where you had a house in the country with a wife and kids and labradors, or where you were an eternal happy bachelor, breaking hearts all over London. But wherever my mind took me I never imagined for a second that you'd think of our encounter as fondly as I did. I was just a wee girl you were looking out for in the chaos of a football match. You might not even have remembered me at all.'

'Oh, I remembered you,' Tom said.

'Well, I assumed you might if you saw that picture that was taken of us.'

'I did, but that's not why. It wasn't just that picture, no way. That short time we spent together, amid all that chaos, really was special to me,' he assured her. He wasn't sure where to start but wanted to be honest with Inez. 'I thought about it, about you, often, even though I shouldn't have.' He hesitated again, feeling that he was about to betray Ann by mentioning her name.

'Ann and I were making plans for the future. In that short time with you, you were warm, friendly and beaming, not to mention stunning. It was impossible not to be attracted to you. I told myself that we couldn't really have connected in that short space of time, and that I'd be able to put you to the back of my mind once the euphoria of that day had passed. And I mostly managed, but then a few months later that damn poster of you popped up – how did that happen?'

'The damn poster of us you mean, and it's a long story. An old friend – well, he was a new friend at the time – had my best interests at heart and helped me make the most of an unexpected situation.' Inez was searching Tom's eyes in the soft light of the late afternoon. 'Did you tell anyone it was you?'

'No. God no. In fact, do you want to know what happened the day that I saw it? I proposed to Ann. I was terrified she'd realise it was me, and even though it was just the back of my head, figure out that I was looking at you in the same way you were looking at me.'

'Do you think you were? Sometimes I remember it clearly, but other times I think I made the whole thing up. Except that there is photographic proof that we at least met.'

'I know I was. I was beguiled. It's those feelings I've had of being with you that have just floated past me all day as I tried to figure out how I knew you. They were transporting me back, but I wasn't sure to where, and although it's been maddening and confusing, I knew they were feelings that would be lovely and welcome if I could grasp them and place them.'

They were silent. Then Inez said, 'I don't know what to say.'

'Nor I. This is incredible, isn't it?'

'Literally – I can't believe it. What do we do now?'

'Can we exchange phone numbers and perhaps have dinner some time? Tell each other what's been going on since 1977? Well, I suppose we'll have to cover our lives pre-1977 since we knew nothing about each other in the first place.'

'I'd like that,' Inez nodded smiling. 'It's so lovely to meet you finally, Tom.'

Tom gave a small laugh. 'Right, I must warn you, that as I assured you he would, young Calum has placed you too. You gave yourself away when my hat ended up on your head. You really haven't changed a bit you know.' Tom instinctively reached a hand out as he said this, but didn't know what to do with it and it fell back by his side.

Inez pretended not to notice and said, 'Och that's just this golden hour light, is that what they call it? Can't see all the wrinkles.'

'I don't think that's it. It's like a day hasn't passed – in more ways than one. Shall we?' And this time, he offered an arm which seemed entirely appropriate to keep one of his wards safe on uneven ground with less daylight, and they started walking back to join the group.

'The question is – Calum now knows it's me in the picture – how long until he works out that it's you too?'

'God, I hadn't even thought of that,' Tom replied, and he squeezed Inez's arm and placed his hand on top of hers.

43

While Tom and Inez had been having their tete-a-tete, Calum had bounded up to the roof of the Y-station and plonked down beside Katie on the bench, just as she was saying goodbye on the phone. 'Oh sorry – I didn't mean to interrupt. Were you speaking to anyone important?'

'You could say very important. VIP even. Maybe I'll tell you later. What's up?' she asked in return.

'I have a bone to pick with you! I can't believe you didn't tell me who your aunt is.'

'You've figured it out, have you? Well done – I'd say you're in the minority – lots of people know that they know her from somewhere, but most don't end up figuring it out. Mind you, you've had all day with her and you're a super-sleuth, so what kept you?' Katie asked playfully. 'How did you finally work it out?'

'She had Tom's hat on her head. Then the penny dropped.'

'Well that's a gimme if ever there was one!'

'You know, maybe I've had other preoccupations today,' Calum said a little defensively.

'Fair enough. Tell me the truth – did you have her poster on your wall when you were younger?'

'I am extremely relieved to say that I did not. Imagine how weird that would be? I mean I'd seen it before, but it's also in a book my mum bought me one Christmas.'

'Yeah, I know the one, I have that too. And Inez. I know that Tom's in it too, by the way. I told Inez but didn't mention to anyone else – didn't think he'd want me to,' Katie said.

'He wouldn't, so that was a good call. So you figured that out before I worked out Inez – that's a bit humbling for my detective instincts right enough.'

'You got there eventually. The journalist part of my training kicked in I guess.'

'Do you know much about the story? Of how the picture came to be?' Calum asked. I've heard that it wasn't a set-up, that it really was candid moment, but it's such a perfect shot that seems hard to believe. And she looks like a model in it.'

'She does, doesn't she? Would you like me to tell you as much of the story as I know? With an extra special surprise ending? That comes back to who I was on the phone with?'

Katie relayed the story that had become family legend, and Calum took in every detail, and questioned any holes, as he was prone to doing. He was sworn to secrecy on the inside scoop about the well-known but mysterious picture – everyone knew the woman in the 1977 photograph, but no-one knew who she was. Calum did now, and it was a little thrill to be in on it, especially as it meant Katie trusted him enough to tell him. When she seemed to have finished, he reminded her she'd promised a surprise tie-in into her earlier phone call.

'Ah yes, brace yourself! You ready? It's very exciting!'

'Get on with it,' Calum chided.

'Drum roll...' and she rattled her hands on her lap.

'You're loving this aren't you?'

'Just a bit! OK seriously, if you cast your mind back to the main players, we had Inez and ...' she paused. 'Well?'

'Oh you're really asking me? OK, we had your Aunt Inez, her friend from Glasgow called Andy, and unbelievably, *** *******.'

'Full marks. Well, guess what? Andy and ***, affectionately known by me and only me, well maybe not only me, but me anyway, as Uncle Andy and Uncle ***...' she paused again, teasing Calum for even longer.

'Yup, got it, you get to call *** ******* your uncle - show off. And?'

'Uncle Andy and Uncle *** are on their way here now. They'll be here any minute. Let's go down and see Inez's reaction when she sees them. She's going to burst. Get ready for some emotional scenes!'

'HAVEN'T we had enough Take That?' Alec asked no one in particular.

'There's no such thing!' Ally replied, holding the phone up and swaying in time to *A Million Love Songs*.

He mock wrestled the phone from her, saying, 'c'mon, let's pick up the mood with a crowd-pleaser. I've got a song everyone knows.' Ally conceded quickly and stood nice and close - ostensibly to look at the phone to see what Alec was searching for.

'Anne Murray? A crowd-pleaser? I find that hard to believe,' she said.

Alec looked up to see Gemma looking over. He gave one tiny shake of his head with a smile and then winked.

Ravi yelled in exaggerated despair, 'No-oo - get the phone back from him Ally. You've no idea the rabbit-holes he'll take you down if you let him!' When he heard the instantly recognisable cheery notes begin, he groaned, 'of course – he wouldn't play the Monkees version would he? Oh well, could be worse.'

Alec was right of course, and the group formed a circle, arms linked or round each other's shoulders as if they were about to do the Hora and belted out Daydream Believer, laughing and smiling.

As the song faded Alec quickly shooshed everyone. 'Is that the sound of a car?'

'Oh good, that must be Inspector Beattie. We must have missed him radio-ing in all this din. I guess he'll be here soon enough though,' Tom replied turning with the rest of them to face the driveway. Katie put her arm through Calum's and squeezed his bicep in her excitement. His own heart was racing too – his mum was going to revel in this part of his account of today's events.

'That sounds like a big old engine on this car,' Alec mused. The car was yet to appear in sight, but he could tell even from a distance this was some large, probably SUV, car. 'Does Inspector Beattie drive something fancy?'

'No he doesn't, I was expecting just his regular squad car. But you're right – that's a roar coming up the hill,' Tom said.

They could tell the car was stationary for a few moments, and all knew that must mean it had stopped at the covered entrance to the driveway and one of its occupants would have to disembark and pull back the leafy gateway. But after a couple of minutes the engine cut, and there was silence. Then four slams of doors. Tom thought Beattie must have decided to make the last part of the journey on foot which made sense, but who had he brought with him that four doors slammed? He walked forward for a better view of more of the driveway, and Inez followed and stood by his side. They could hear voices, quite raucous ones. Then figures appeared, but the sun was so low in the sky now that the shrubbery flanking the driveway cast it into almost darkness. Tom thought he could see a figure with a hat on which must be Beattie, but then it looked a bit too tall. Then another figure appeared, also in a hat, with a gait and frame that Tom thought recognised as Beattie this time. *So who was the other person in a hat?* Five people in all were walking towards them, clearly doing the same as they were – letting their eyes adjust to the gloaming, watching and trying to work out what they could see up ahead.

A voice broke the silence, 'Hello? Anybody up there?' *Was that a cockney accent? Definitely not from around here anyway*, Tom was thinking when Inez's body beside him jolted and suddenly Katie had appeared at their side too. She had her hand on Inez's shoulder and was nodding frantically, grinning from ear to ear.

'Yes! It's who you think it is! And Andy too!'

'What? You're kidding? How the hell...' was all Inez could muster before Katie pulled Inez by the arm, and they both started running towards the shadowy figures, two of whom in turn increased their pace, the English voice shouting, 'There you are my darlin'! Fancy meeting you here,' and a Scottish one, 'Alright Gorgeous? Nice shoes! Interesting day you've had! We thought we'd come and hear all about it.' The aunt and niece just replied with laughter and screeches, and Tom felt a pang as he watched the embraces. Inez linked arms with the one of the shadows to walk back up to the Y-station, and the taller man wearing a hat put his arm around Katie. Beattie followed behind with what Tom could now see was Fraser Bam and his fiancée, who were also arm-in-arm. As the party came into view, he thought he must be losing his mind. He called Calum over.

'Have I gone absolutely mad or is that Sir Rod Stewart coming up the hill with Inez?'

44

The Gillie's Rest was absolutely jumping. Word of today's events had spread fast, albeit that the snippets passed around varied in detail and accuracy. All of them though, ended with the fact that Fraser Bam's Very Important Person was none other than Rod Stewart, who was now rumoured to be on his way to that very establishment.

The fiddle and accordion band was interspersing their set with some Rod Stewart covers, which were surprisingly good, and in their breaks to tune their instruments or whet their whistles, Rod's voice would strike up a song, courtesy of the jukebox. The mood was harmlessly rowdy, no-one quite able to believe the parts of the story they'd heard, and all sharing different theories as to the missing bits. Most people in the pub knew, or knew of, one of the group who had been stuck at the Glass Pass all day, so all were dying for them to arrive so they could fill in the gaps and make sense of this tall tale.

The arrival of the *hostages*, as they were being referred to by some, was anticipated a little too soon, and on the tenterhooks of excitement, a premature cheer went up when the pub doors opened, when in fact it was only another curious local joining.

The crowd enjoyed the surprise of the incomer and the collective amusement so much that from then on a similar ovation went up every time the door opened. The festivities and bonhomie rivalled their fondest memories of whatever Hogmanay at the Gillie's they happened to claim as the most legendary, which was different for everyone depending on their age and stage.

Again the door opened, and again the place erupted in hoots, whistles and applause, everyone cracking up at pranking another patron. Alec threw his long arms over his head and punched the air in appreciation, and when the crowd realised this was actually one of their awaited heroes, their volume turned to maximum, with chants of Alec's name from his friends. Ally and Jill, right behind him, quickly stepped to the side to let him have the spotlight as he hammed up his part in the happy mayhem. Enjoying the moment, he then mimed a *shhh* by putting his finger to his lips and made a downward motion with his arms, palms facing down, to command a hush. He cleared his throat dramatically before he announced, 'Ladies and gentlemen, I give you Mid-June's finest – Inspector Kenny Beattie, Sergeant Tom Armstrong and Constable Calum Kirkpatrick!' Ally couldn't tell how he managed to time it so impeccably, but the three men pushed the door open at exactly that moment, and *the crowd went wild*, as the saying goes.

Alec's friends and his two sisters pulled him into their midst, slapping him on the back and pushing pints of beer towards him. They'd hear about Ravi and Gemma in a quieter moment, though none of them would claim to not have suspected something was going on between the two of them. The rest of the horde swallowed up the three police officers in the same spirit: handshakes, pats on the shoulder and no shortage of drinks – tall or short, frosty or warming – they had their pick.

Ally had always enjoyed being tall – in her younger days

when she was in a pub, she was the one who could scan from her vantage point to establish which of their crushes were present and relay the names to her shorter friends. She stood on her tiptoes now to locate George, whom she had convinced to get a babysitter so he could join them as a surprise for Jill. She led Jill though to George, who promptly collapsed into his arms in tears and barely coherent babbling. Over her head, George widened his eyes at Ally questioningly.

She answered, 'Would it be trite to say *it's a long story* George? We had a wee tipple of champagne and Prosecco at the top of our hill up there, and when you hear all that happened to us, you won't be shocked that it went a little to her head.'

He leaned in to try to not yell his response above the rammy, though he still had to speak loudly. 'I feel terrible for Jill that she didn't get to go the concert. She was really looking forward to it. I know I was grumbling about managing without her, but that's only because she does so much I didn't know how I'd cope. I really did want you two to have a night away and a magic time.'

'I know George, I gotcha, it's all good. Just give her a wee cuddle – you both need it.'

Turning to see where Alec had ended up in the commotion, she again stood tall to look around. Towering over the knot of revellers that stood between them, he was looking straight at her already. He smiled, and she smiled back and nodded a 'there you are'. Holding up both hands which somehow were holding two pints and a whisky glass, he looked from one to the other quizzically, asking which one she'd like. She pointed to the pint glass, and he gestured her over with a bob of his head.

The doors flew open with such force that it got most people's attention even above the voices – most chattering and laughing, some singing along to *You Wear It Well* which the jukebox was playing. Andy, still prone to a diva-like entrance, threw his hand up in the air, and looked dramatically at the crowd, chin high, head aloft. He held their attention for a glorious split second before Sir Rod pushed him aside from behind and saying, 'Oh give it rest, you silly old queen. What do you know – they're playing my song.' With a sweep of his arm, he turned and bowed to Inez directly behind him and then took her arm and twirled her into the pub right as the song hit the titular lyrics. Partly because of a hair and make-up primp by Katie on the journey here, mostly because she was glowing with happiness at being with three of the people she loved most in the world, Inez was radiant. *Wow*, Ally thought. The timing of Alec's build up for our boys in blue had been impressive, but as she caught Tom Armstrong gazing at the twirling Inez, Sir Rod had nailed his dear friend's beautiful entrance.

It was one of those nights that to look back on seemed like several nights in one. No one reminiscing in the future could believe it only lasted for just the several hours it did – it felt like a large number of the residents of Mid-June had gone away for a long weekend together. There was an occasional respite from the wall of noise when the band took a break, and maybe there was a psychic group agreement to forget to replace the music with the juke box. During those moments the *hostages* were sought out as the jigsaw pieces of their experience were being gathered, compared and pieced together. They, in turn, found solace in landing with each other, by accident or on purpose.

Tacitly, Ally and Alec were clear and unabashed that they were actively trying to find time with each other, but they were having little success. All evening, they gravitated towards each other, their paths would converge, and they'd resume a chat, then only manage to share slivers of themselves before one or other would get pulled into another conversation. Sir Rod was one interruption, approaching Alec to ask if his music featured in any of Alec's lectures and giving him a hard time when the answer was no. 'You've got to be kidding me. Nothing about how deftly I've spanned genres and pivoted to change with the times? Shit, *The Killing of Georgie* could be a class in itself – all the issues and themes I covered in that one. Are you his girlfriend?' he turned to Ally and asked, clearly hoping to find a fellow advocate to lobby the Laird.

'No, but I may have some negotiating power,' she answered looking mischievously at Alec, who wondered where she could be going with this. 'I work on events at Glenberry Castle – a stretch target of mine and Alec's mum has been to put on a concert in the grounds. That may be the perfect chance for Alec to spend time with you, learning more about your career. You'd have been top of our list if we'd only known your connection to Mid-June through Inez.'

'Oh you're good!' Sir Rod laughed. 'You should hang on to her up there at the castle Alec – she obviously doesn't miss a trick. Well, *never say never*, so they say. I'll have my manager get in touch.' And he was pulled away to join in singing one of his own songs.

Just as Alec was nodding at Ally 'well-played,' Fraser and Oona found them next. They had deliberately snuck in unnoticed when the rest of their party was in the thick of being lauded. Oona had made it through her day-drinking hangover, but it hadn't taken much of a top up to have her squiffy (her word of course) all over again. 'Guys, have I told you how incredible Fraser was today? Can you believe he's uncovered all that crooked business with Wyllie and that rotter Les Mitchell? And all those old constituents that thought the sun shone out of his bum! Ha! You've shown them darling.'

Unlike Oona, Fraser couldn't relax and think of this as over. He knew there could be a long scandalous road ahead. 'Oona, let's not throw accusations around just yet,' he said putting his arm around her and turning to Alec and Ally, 'I'd appreciate your discretion. We really shouldn't be naming names at this early point.'

'You got it, our lips are sealed,' Alec said with a knowing wink in Oona's direction.

Oona caught the wink and surprised him by being more with-it than he thought with an equally knowing wink back at him, but aiming her nod of the head in Ally's direction.

'Oona!' Fraser chided, catching the not-at-all-subtle gesture.

'It's OK, Fraser, don't worry,' Alec said. 'Oona – you're actually doing me a favour. If you don't mind, I'm going to steal your lovely friend Ally away to those two seats I've seen just open up in the corner and try to hide her away to myself.'

Ally didn't know if she blushed, but her insides flipped at his frankness and then again as he took her by the hand and led her on a determined pathway through the throng. To their utter dismay, they were stopped by one of Alec's friends who had an arm around Rod Stewart. 'Mate…' Alec tried to protest.

'Just quickly, promise – real quick,' was the slurred response, 'we wanna get a picture with Rod here. C'mon, you can both join in.' There was some semblance of a group ready with someone tee-ed up to take the picture, so Alec conceded. He gently pulled Ally into the crooked line of tipsy pals and put his arm around her shoulder to pose for the photographer. Right as the picture was being taken, he couldn't resist turning his head to sneak a peak at this woman that his mother happened to also think was perfect for him. Ally also risked a quick look at Alec and though it was just a split second, it was the same split second as the picture was snapped, and it caught them smiling at each other. A few months later, that photo was not just Alec's screen saver, but was also printed and framed on his bedside table.

As they left to claim their quiet seats one of Alec's friends asked, 'Rod, how do you look so good?'

'All the shaggin' mate!' was the response and an uproarious

laugh went up and the band struck up a what sounded like the ceilidh version of *Do Ya Think I'm Sexy*.

AT THE BAR, Katie, her red-wine-rosy-cheeks back for a second evening in a row was with Andy and Calum. Andy was giving a blow-by-blow account of the events of 4th June 1977, and unfortunately for her Calum was hanging on his every word. However, his earnest interest only added to his appeal. She was used to men who liked to talk instead of listen, so it was refreshing to see him rapt and asking Andy interested questions. When the detail reached such a level that she could tell this could go on all night, she subtly – or maybe not, she couldn't be sure, but she was tipsy enough not to care – nudged Andy's calf with her foot from her position on a barstool. 'Where's the gorgeous Inez got to anyway?' Andy asked a little too quickly. 'Maybe I'll go and find her and I'll catch you guys a bit later,' he said as he wondered off.

'So he's not your real uncle either? Just like Sir Rod?' Calum asked.

'Correct. Isn't he fun? I love seeing Inez with Andy and Rod. She comes alive. It's so easy to see that young woman from the poster when she's around them.' And now Calum was all ears for her and her stories of Inez's life after 'The Poster'. Gemma's erstwhile bartending colleague, wondered from his spot behind the bar, if the straight-laced and sober Calum realised how much this vivacious, chatty woman was flirting with him.

TWO OTHERS who were circling each other were Tom and Inez. They were enjoying and joining in the laughter and singalongs, it was all good for the soul, but both were aware of where the other was at all times. Neither was sure what they'd talk about – there was just a draw that was impossible to ignore, an invisible string pulling them together.

Eventually, the age of their knees and hips compared to many others' in the pub, prompted Andy to seek out a table for Inez, Rod and himself, and he was lucky enough to find one in a corner where conversation was just possible. As he was beckoning to Rod and Inez, Tom was nearby, and he gestured to him to join them too.

'Well Tom, apparently, you're on the brink of retirement. Are you sure after tonight – all these plaudits must feel good, no?' Rod asked, adding, 'I can't ever imagine retiring – I love the attention too much.'

'Oh I think I'm inclined to think of today as one hell of a swan song. Out with a bang – pardon the tasteless pun – it was unintentional I assure you,' he said rolling his eyes. 'I've got to say though, when I tell this story ad infinitum as I probably will, one of the hardest parts to believe will be that I was rescued by Rod Stewart!'

'We didn't rescue you mate, I just couldn't resist being in on the action and insisted to your gaffer and Fraser Bam that I surprise Inez. As I say – I'm an attention seeker.'

'How did you three come to be friends anyway?' Tom asked no one in particular.

Andy took a breath to reply, but Inez touched his arm to tell him she was going to take the lead. 'Well, talk about hard to believe – try this for size! It comes back to that notorious picture of me, and until now, an anonymous young policeman,' she paused and gestured to Rod that he was allowed a turn.

'OK, so – I saw a picture of a gorgeous Scottish fan, quite an alluring one at that – don't worry Inez, I won't mention the nipple. Oops, sorry, just slipped out!' Inez swatted him for his cheekiness. 'Anyway, you understand, Tom – I had to meet her. I should be ashamed to admit that I hunted her down, but after all these years I wouldn't change a thing. I found her – and this guy – ,' he thumbed towards Andy, 'working in a pub, and instead of the fling I was angling for (she was much younger than I thought Tom), I got two friends for life.' Rod put an arm around each of his friends and pulled them in.

Andy rested his head on Rod's shoulder with an exaggerated 'aww,' and reached round and stroked his hair. Rod took the cue and stroked him back, looking at him with puppy dog eyes, until they both pulled away with *eew, get off me*'s, making Tom laugh and Inez shake her head – she'd witnessed their schtick for nearly forty years.

They regaled Tom with a few of their favourite and oft-told anecdotes, making each other laugh more than him, as there were plenty of inside jokes and *you had to be there* moments. That didn't matter though – Tom was happy to be caught up in them revelling in each others' company and in watching Inez laugh and react to Rod and Andy's side of things, which he gathered by her expressions and cries of mock dissent, tended to err on exaggeration.

'Anyway, I'm sure Tom's heard enough of your tales from days of yore. Enough, you two!' Inez scolded.

'I know sorry, Tom,' Andy said, 'we tend to get carried away – we don't see each other nearly often enough, so we get a bit silly when we do. How about this new memory, though, to add to all the legends?' He paused in amazement. 'Tom, all these years I've teased Inez about how much her life changed for the better because I talked her into coming to that Scotland-England match with me. She became an icon because of that picture, it led us to meeting Rod, and thanks to him she got to remain an anonymous icon. But I never in a million years would have dreamed that one day I'd be sitting down drinking a pint with the policeman she was smiling up at in the picture! I propose a toast. To us! A new gang of four. Founded in 1977 – though we wouldn't know about it for nearly forty years.' He raised a glass, prompting the others to do the same.

Tom felt like a bit of an imposter, but Inez caught his eye as she said, 'to us,' and if a man in his late fifties can, he got butterflies.

The band announced a *Dashing White Sergeant*, which should be impossible in such a packed place, but the patrons of the Gillie's Rest were always up for figuring it out. They struck up a warm-up reel while people formed their groups of three. Rod got a tap on the shoulder which he was about to decline, until he turned round to see Alec's two sisters, and quickly found his dancing feet.

'I'm out of here in case I get nabbed,' Andy announced. 'Ceilidh dancing is not my thing. I'll go and get the drinks. Same again?'

'Actually no, I think I've had plenty thanks. I should be going soon,' Tom said, having to stop Andy in his tracks, as the question had been rhetorical.

Inez moved her hand to the middle of the table where Tom's was, so that their fingertips were so very nearly touching. 'Don't go,' she said. 'Do you really have to?'

Tom hesitated before he answered, 'Well I suppose I don't really *have* to, but I don't know if I can have another pint.'

Andy, pretending to be oblivious to the chaste intimacy in front of him, said, 'Tom, what you should know is, Inez and I have lots of names for one last drink. And one last drink is obligatory. So would you care for a final-final, a cleanser or a tipper-over? Because you're having one of those.'

'Tell you what,' Inez said still smiling at Tom. 'Tom and I will share a pint of final-final.'

'Just a half each?' Andy asked.

'No, just bring us one pint, and we'll share it,' Inez clarified.

Andy shrugged and turned to the bar. Tom looked at Inez quizzically. 'Is that one of the *one last drink* traditions too? To share a pint?'

'No. I don't know what made me say that. I guess so that

those two idiots won't be able to bully you if you'd rather not have much more, because they won't be able to tell that I drank most of it. So I suppose I was trying to save you from their high spirits,' she paused thoughtfully. 'Actually, I don't know – it just felt like a nice thing to do tonight. The matriarch and patriarch sharing a drink – literally – at the end of a long day,' she said with a small smile. 'Do you mind? Does that sound weird?'

'I don't mind at all, I think that sounds lovely. I'd be honoured.'

Tom moved from their fingers-almost-touching position on the table and took Inez's hand properly. They stayed still for a moment, locked in a gaze, each conveying to the other the signal *this is OK with me, this is good.* Inez gave the smallest of nods then turned in the direction of the dancers to see Sir Rod being reminded how to do the *Dashing White Sergeant*. Tom kept looking at her long enough to see her eyes wrinkle in amusement and affection before he turned to enjoy the spectacle too, still holding her hand.

The End

ACKNOWLEDGMENTS

This novel has been a long time coming. I had many stops and starts along the way, because I was busy running a family and a business, or I was dealing with loss and grief, or just because I kind of forgot about it for a while. I am so grateful to my friends and loved ones who were there for all of those things, and for their enthusiasm when I announced that I'd written a novel. Every time you asked me an interested question about how the book was coming along, it spurred me on to make it happen.

The Glass Pass is about fateful chance encounters and one of my own was meeting Kate Fridriks, author of *Real Gone Kid*, when we were walking the West Highland Way. Kate has been so generous and encouraging — I'm confident we're both in this author-thing for the long-haul! Kate also introduced me to Sarra Cannon's self-publishing course, which was invaluable. Thanks to my beta readers, to my tenacious proof-reader Kelly Ferguson, and to Robin Jovanovich for allowing me to hone my writing muscle at *The Rye Record*. I was absolutely blown away when Rory Kennedy, an artist whose work I already loved, agreed to create my cover. It's stunning, thank you Rory!

The dedication was to my parents, who passed during the writing of *The Glass Pass*, and would have loved this chance to brag about me. I am honoured to have the rest of the Carey Buggars still cheering for me — my brothers Campbell and

David, and their gorgeous families: Tanya, Elspeth and Marni, and Helen, Emma and Iona.

Of course, the biggest shout-out goes to Graeme, Gregor, Anna and Kirsty. Thank you for your unwavering support and belief in me, in everything I do. Making you proud will always be my highest ambition and proudest achievement.

THE GLENBERRY WIVES
AUTUMN 2025

Curious about what happened to your favourite characters from The Glass Pass? Join Ally a couple of years later — now married to Alec, pregnant with twins, and living at Glenberry Castle. When a letter from the past casts doubt on the entire lineage of the Douglas-Lauder family, Ally is drawn into a mystery that stretches back generations.

Through discovered journals and papers, she becomes immersed in the life of Mimi, Alec's American grandmother, who arrived at the Castle in 1959 — thirty years after women had won the right to vote, but true equality and independence were still far from reach.

A story of friendship and family told across two timelines — of secrets kept, quiet battles fought, and the futures women dared to shape for themselves and generations to come.

Stay updated on the release of **The Glenberry Wives** and other upcoming works by visiting www.leecareyauthor.com or following me on Instagram @leecarey_author.

ABOUT THE AUTHOR

Lee hails from Glasgow and now splits her time between there and Rye, New York. Her published works to-date include the front end of the Annual Report for Scottish Power plc, in her first career as a Chartered Accountant, and the Health and Fitness column for her local newspaper, an adjunct to running her own outdoor fitness business.

Above all, Lee loves time with family. She also likes outdoor workouts, champagne with friends, and the beach. She has amateur interests in Shakespeare, ornithology, and architecture, but seems unable to retain any relevant knowledge about them, so don't use her as your phone-a-friend.

Lee hates mashed potatoes.